Totally Bound Publishing books by L.A. Kennedy

Single Books
A Touch of Frost
Pocket Full of Posies

The Genesys Project
Immortal Amour
Dark Amour
Wicked Amour
Poisonous Amour

The Cursed
Witchful Thinking

I0598122

The Cursed

WITCHFUL THINKING

L.A. KENNEDY

Witchful Thinking
ISBN # 978-1-80250-744-7
©Copyright L.A. Kennedy 2024
Cover Art by Kelly Martin ©Copyright August 2024
Interior text design by Claire Siemaszkiewicz
Totally Bound Publishing

WITCHFUL
THINKING

Dedication

For Cyn. I'll see you there.

Lasciate ogne speranza, voi ch'intrate:
Abandon all hope, ye who enter here.
—Dante Alighieri

Chapter One

Covered in blood and hair was not how I liked to end the night. To be fair, I didn't want to start my day like that, either. Neither the blood nor the hair belonged to me, but it was still gross. Not only was it not my blood but it was animal. The beast in question was a goat, a really scared goat who'd had his throat nicked instead of cut. Blood went everywhere. I helped hold it down after it lost what looked like a gallon or two down the front of my shirt. I didn't like seeing an animal suffer and was painted red because of it. People, on the other hand, I probably wouldn't have helped hold them down. I am not a people person, to say the least. I'm barely a person—or so say the zealots of today. Being the only legal and licensed full-blooded witch practitioner in the country, let alone in today's society, is better than the days of the witch trials, but not by much. Sure, I haven't been hanged or burned at the stake, but I wasn't going to discount it as a potential ending. Three hundred years and some change wasn't that long ago for some of us. The scent of bonfires still hung in the air, and we were just as flammable as our ancestors had been.

The pitiful goat was crusted under my nails and turned the tips of my hair into small, red dreadlocks. But it was better than what had coated me last weekend...human blood. The group had collected an ounce of blood from each family member — or so they claimed. They had hoped human blood would be more powerful than that of an animal, that it would give the spell the kind of kick it would need to work. The blood was old and smelled of sweet death. They had a two-liter bottle filled with human blood that they had collected from sixty-seven people...again, as they claimed. I doubted they had almost seventy family members kicking around to open a vein and fill the bottle. No one had that many relatives that gave a shit about them.

My gut told me one of two things had unfolded. One, someone gave more than they should have, and I didn't take part in feeding the gods — human sacrifice. Or, the other option, they had stolen the blood from a blood bank, which has happened more times than I could count. The latter, which I suspected, might as well be a jug of water. It would have been old as the sin that got them to this point and filtered to all hell. Blood donations are spun in centrifuges to separate it into transfusable components. Red cells, platelets and plasma were separated. Spun blood was worthless to me unless I needed a transfusion, which had also happened more times than I could count. *We live in dangerous times, my friends*. Rather than argue where the liquid gold came from, I took them at their paper-thin word but still had to explain to the family that their blood loss wasn't significant enough. It would not be a sacrifice if they were still standing. It wouldn't be worth a lick in hell if someone didn't suffer for it. Truthfully, if they had slaughtered a busload of people, I would have found some other lie to tell them. I didn't serve up dishes fit for gods for any reason. The moment a witch started messing with the gates of hell, they found themselves on the other side of them. *No. Fucking. Thanks.* Been there, done that, and the only thing I brought back from hell was a T-shirt and Trauma, with a capital T.

Contrary to popular belief, I didn't dabble in the dark arts. I wouldn't use human blood to stave off a demon, even if it did work. That was asking for more trouble than it was worth—my soul, however tattered it may be. The family had expected me to perform a summoning and make a deal with a devil for them. Nope. I wasn't selling my ass on the corner of hell because the head of their family had made a devil's pact years ago. They offered me more money, and I declined, pointing out the obvious. The money wasn't doing them any good. Why would it help me? Money didn't spend in hell…only souls did. I wore that blood on my way out of their front door, tossed in my face as a parting gift. The last I heard of them, they had traded a firstborn for more time from the ultimate debt collector. That they had exchanged a child for money and headed to the Caribbean told me I had made the right decision. I'm sure a week on the beach would help them overcome that devastation. It's easy to ignore the horror of what we've done while sitting in a cabana with a piña colada in our hand. People are, by far, the scariest of all the monsters I've ever faced.

And I'm asked why I'm not a people person?

Because most people suck.

I pulled into my driveway as dawn pressed down over the hills. The sky was a billion pure eyes of fading light. The grass was green, even in the hush of the approaching sun. It was as if the night and dawn had become one beautiful moment, untouched by the pending chaos of the day. I stood at the foot of my stairs and watched the sunrise as a canopy of gold. Dawn had come, and I had welcomed it. I felt it sink into my bones and chase away the midnight scares.

The sky changed from tinges of charcoal to a vibrancy that felt safe. The sun always meant shelter from the boogeymen for people in my line of work. Monsters bumped in the night. They scraped at the moon and howled each time the sun rose, hence the sacrifice I had watched. It was another desperate attempt to stave off the darkness. In all my years, it had never worked. The dark came as quickly as the sun, and with the night came the unnatural beings and beasts we feared. To be fair to the creatures that plagued my nightmares, I had been attacked more times while sitting under the blistering sun than at night. The sun was merely a false sense of security, but I'd take any kind of safety, even the fake stuff. With a witchy target on my back the size of a small car, sometimes pretending everything was going to be just fine was the only way I could get out of bed in the morning.

It was January, but it felt like March. Winter in Vancouver was usually chilly and rainy, with a hint of spring tempting us into leaving our jackets at home. The only thing dependable about Vancity weather was that you couldn't own too many umbrellas, and the long-term forecast always included rain and clouds. If it didn't, the weatherman was probably new to the scene. You could start your day in a thin layer of clothes and end it in boots and a raincoat. This year was no exception. The weather report called for snow in the next week or two. Looking at my flower beds, blooms poking out of the ground, I found myself irritated more than usual. They were the only thing the cold hadn't killed, my spirit included. After too many months of doom and gloom, my tired, rained-out soul was ready for my coming holidays. Literal blood, sweat and tears earned me two weeks in Mexico. *Lord have mercy on my pasty Irish skin.*

Outside of a goat blood bath, it had been a typical day for me. My first lecture of the year had gone well, aside from the regular religious crazies that inevitably made their way into one of my classes. They say my soul is damned because I taught demonology and the occult. I say it was damned long before today, but no one really asked my opinion. My soul was spoken for and has been for ten years. When I was sixteen, I got into a vehicle with a drunk driver. He totaled the car. All of us died. I was dead for almost two minutes.

Since I willingly got into the vehicle and knew the driver was drunk, the devils see that as suicide. Suicides go to hell. Do not pass go, don't even think of collecting two hundred dollars. Straight to jail — or so I was promptly informed when I woke up on the other side of the gates in a cage exactly my size. If you think the lineups for Black Friday sales are bad, try waking up in Hell, with a capital 'H,' on a Sunday morning, once the afterparties cleared out. Sobering up in hell was a hangover that no hair on the dog would ever rid you of. Processing souls looked like a bitch, but they ran a tighter ship than most big-box stores.

Two minutes in hell is a lifetime, then some. Time moves differently in the below, and one hundred and twenty seconds went by like years. How did I walk out, you might be wondering? A loophole — he only one to have ever existed…twins. When my mom was pregnant, she was pregnant with two. My body absorbed my twin, along with the soul. When I went to hell, I went with both souls. They couldn't have both, or that would be cheating. If there's one thing hell is good at, it's following the rules to the letter. Sure, they bent the rules as much as they could, but they never outright broke them. To do anything different would bring on their end. Breaking the rules brought winged heat from above that none of us would survive. No devil or demon would dare allow this. I was released, but not before they stamped me with a return address on my back for when I die. The next time I go down, there is no loophole, no typo and no way out. I've been marked as property of the tarpits. My soul, whether tethered to another, has been counted. There is no way around it. I was alive and well and given another chance but marked 'return to sender'. I didn't fret. Most witches ended up down there, anyway.

The crisp morning air nipped at my blood-crusted hands and forced me up my front steps. Another protection spell for a cursed child had come and gone. I didn't have the heart to tell the family that a little goat's blood and prayer wouldn't keep the demon from collecting his dues. The mother had sold her firstborn to a hellspawn twenty years prior for reasons that made sense at the time until it was time to pay the debt. There isn't a way to renege on a devil's pact. It wasn't Wal-Mart. There were no returns, and no manager the mother could demand to speak to or blast on social media. And if there was, I bet she wouldn't have liked what that manager had to say. The mother got her riches and now had to give up her child. If she didn't, the entire family would be dead by the end of the week, after the devil toyed with them until it grew bored. In the end, the beast of burden would have the child and would take the family as compensation for wasting his time. It was in the fine print.

I hated nights like these, but they paid my bills and kept my skills sharp as a demon claw. The family had paid for my consultation and had asked my opinion. I told them the truth but softened it as much as I could. But there was no way to ease them into this reality. I watched the local witch coven perform the protection spell but stressed to the mother that she was wasting her time and money. The demon would come. It was her choice to go as a family or to give it what it wanted. I'm sure I'd be reading about their deaths in the paper by this weekend. Sadly, I wasn't a popular guest at that party. It didn't matter. There wouldn't be anyone left to give me a bad review. Not that I cared. At twenty-six, I already felt like I was ready to retire. A few bad Yelps and I'd be that much closer. My kind burned out pretty fast. It wasn't our own personal anguish that aged us. It was the grief of others that wore us down and charred off our souls.

I could hear my answering machine click on as I put my house key in the lock. I had turned off my ringer before I had left. I knew it would be a late night and didn't want to risk being woken by the shrill of a phone once I finally got to sleep. The door and lock were original to the house, and although my key always stuck, I couldn't bring myself to replace either of them. The door was painted bright red, faded in places, but still held the original protection spells from days long past. Who was I to complain about the creaky jamb or barely working lock when the darn thing kept out the boogeyman?

A phone call this close to the witching hour meant two things—either someone was dead, and I was on their list of regrettable contacts, or someone needed something I wouldn't want to give. Neither sounded fun at almost six in the morning. I closed the door, locked it and reset my alarm system. The door may have kept out the creatures in the shadows, but it did little to keep out the bad guys with a soul and a pulse. I owned a gun and have home security for those types of monsters.

"Ailis...err, Dr. Kyteler, it's Miguel." The recording started on my machine.

My heart plummeted, crashing into the new butterflies in my stomach, and I instantly wanted to vomit. I paused and decided whether I would pick up the phone. Miguel, my long-ago friend, mentor and lover, among other things, was either going to tell me someone was dead or he needed a favor. At the crack of dawn, I wagered the latter. I had missed two text messages from him already. Neither said someone was dead. Both I had ignored. When I cut someone out of my life, I did my best to follow through and sever all ties. But hearing him say my name, one of the few who had ever pronounced it correctly, had made my breath catch in my throat and dig up long-buried emotions. Most people called me 'Alias' or 'Ail-is.' They butchered my last name as well. My name, for the record, is 'Ay-lish,' an Irish name. My last name, Kyteler, pronounced 'Kettler', had an even longer history than my first.

"Miguel, I'm here," I answered.

I didn't bother hiding the suspicion in my voice or my deeply rooted contempt for the man. It was either bad news or worse news. Either way, him being the one to deliver it bothered me more than if it were someone else on the phone. Grudges are capricious creatures. One this strong could only be explained away by the other emotions I felt for him. A person can't hate this profoundly without there being love.

"What do you want, Miguel?" I asked, trying hard to keep the bitterness from my voice. I wouldn't give him the satisfaction of knowing his voice still hurt today as much as it had the last time I had heard it.

"I need a favor." Four simple words that were as complicated as the secret to life. In case you're wondering, there is no secret to life. We all die in the end — some earlier than most, if we're lucky.

"The last time I did you a favor, I ended up in a Mexican prison," I replied. I would have preferred the news that someone was dead over this.

"To be fair, Ailis, you killed two dozen people," he answered with a hint of laughter in his voice. I could almost picture the grin on his face. The urge to want to slap that smile off made my hand squeeze into a fist, cracking the dried blood around my knuckles.

"How was I supposed to know he was the head of a vampire line?" I felt defensive. I was young, scared and stab happy with the monsters at the time. To be honest, I was still pretty stabby when it came to monsters. Stab first, and ask questions later. Anything short of that, and I was the one with the headstone. "He attacked me. I had no other choice."

What Miguel had said was true. I did kill just over twenty, but they weren't really people, per se. The dead man in question, a vampire, had attacked two people in the lounge of my hotel. I staked him, and he lit up like the Fourth of July. Subsequently, his demise caused the death of his weaker ilk. His freshly made clutch had gone up in ashes. They weren't strong enough to survive his death. Vampires have short lifespans for a reason, especially the freshly dead. They weren't meant to be here. They were a curse from hell — a joke, if you will, cast by demons. And the stupid ones never made it far in their new undead life. They dropped like flies in honey.

I like to call it karma. If you want to be a monster, you get to die like one. I didn't mourn those deaths, but I did have a lot of questions to answer when the badges showed up. I had been arrested and spent two days in prison on a slab of cold concrete, being called a devil worshiper. The name-calling didn't bother me. They weren't very creative. I tried to explain the difference between believing in the devils and worshiping them. It fell on deaf ears. Keep in mind, this was during a time when the world had just started to wake up to what had really been lurking in the shadows for as long as time existed. Devils have been walking the earth and have been living in the houses next to us for as long as we started living indoors. To be fair, vampires had been a myth to the general public up until I roasted one of them in plain sight. Mankind couldn't ignore it once it hit social media—flames, screaming and all that crispy jazz. I could understand why they thought I was a murderer, but common sense should have told them that people weren't generally combustible or turned to fine ash within seconds. It takes hours to burn a human body to ash, and even then, there were chunks of bone and teeth still found in the dust.

But that was the way mankind kept sane. Ignore it until it blocks your view of your television, then lean around it. Most of mankind didn't have the capacity to really appreciate who they shared this world with. Those who chose not to believe or tried to turn a blind eye to hell were usually the first to go down when the demons came up. You can't hold up a cross to a vampire and expect it to work when you have no faith in the power behind it. Without true conviction, you might as well say goodbye now. That's like not believing in winter and being confused when you slide down your driveway on a patch of ice. Not believing in it didn't make the snow stop falling any more than it kept the demons from crawling out from under your bed.

"A little birdy told me you would be in my area soon to give a lecture. I need your help," Miguel said. I could hear the panic in his voice. He was trying to hide it, but fear wasn't something you couldn't cover up with a smile and a cheerful voice. Miguel wasn't the type to be quick to sound the alarms. If I could hear it, it was worse than I thought. My stomach turned at the possibilities.

"And I'm sure that little birdy didn't struggle too much." I already knew it had been my assistant, Philip, who'd squealed. He couldn't stand up to a fly. Worse, he had really liked Miguel and cried when he heard Miguel wouldn't be around anymore. I think poor Philip took the breakup harder than I did. "I'm going on vacation, Miguel. My lecture is three hours long, then I'm off the clock for two weeks. Call someone else."

I was firm but knew if he were put in a position to need my help, it was because there was no one else he could call. There just aren't that many experts in my line of work. No one ever walks out of hell with the inside scoop, and demons weren't in the business of giving interviews to the curious, not without taking your soul as payment. A few years ago, a reporter interviewed a lower-level demon. The found recording was nothing more than a screaming, splattered reporter and the kind of laughter that made your skin want to crawl off to the nearest church.

"I know about the lecture. I'm the one who gave them your name," Miguel said. "The consult is for my team."

"I didn't see your name on the list of attendees." The little warning hairs on the back of my neck were up. *Suspicious? Who, me?* "Why do they need me when they already have you? You know more about demons and devils than I do."

"Yes, but I don't know hell like you do," he answered rather quickly, like he had practiced this conversation a million times before he had dialed my number. The words stung a little. I didn't toss that fact around like an award. No one who goes to hell is proud of it.

"The answer is no. I won't help you, and I won't be coming at all. I don't like to be lied to, Miguel. When I asked them who referred me, they said it came from an acquaintance. You, Miguel, are not my colleague or friend. When I don't show up, you can explain to them why they've gotten their money back instead of me."

"Please, Ailis. You owe me. I'm calling in that chit now." There, he said it. The words that had been hanging over my head for a decade. It landed like a bomb waiting to go off.

I fell silent. My pulse raced in my ears. I did owe him a favor...a big one. Once upon a time, Miguel almost died saving me after hell had to return me, begrudgingly. Sure, I came back, but I didn't come back whole. My soul was torn to shreds. My aura was a watered-down mess of taint and hell. It resembled soggy toilet paper. My sanity was as broken as my will to live, which hung on by threads. Miguel, once a priest, almost lost his own soul to save mine, several times over. He fought off every demon who came my way, and they came in hordes. Hell was resentful and took it out on me every chance they got. I couldn't defend myself, so Miguel had done it for me, shielding me with his soul. Miguel lost a lot of his friends and a chunk of his soul for me. So, yeah, I owed him. That token had sat on the back shelf for years, gathering dust. I had been waiting for the day when he'd call in that favor.

Like a slow-moving clock in the back of my mind, it counted down until I heard from him for this very reason. Like it or lump it, that's just how the world worked — quid pro quo, tit for tat, yin and yang, peace and torture, heaven and hell. Balance was everywhere, even in the places I hated. This call would be one of those places I wasn't a fan of. I didn't want to owe anyone, not even the holier-than-thou, 'I-only-kill-when-I-have-to-and-I-decide-when-I-have-to' Miguel. Yeah, I held grudges the same way hell did — for eternity. *What of it?* A gal needs a hobby, and mine just so happened to be resentment.

Miguel wasn't a priest anymore. He was a detective of sorts. He was attached to his local police force, the last I heard. It wasn't that he lost his faith. On the contrary, he had more faith than anyone I knew, including myself. He lost his will to serve the church when it started to feel like he wasn't giving himself to his God or the people, but rather, he was making the church richer by the day. He was protecting the sinners and the greedy, those who condemned man and created war and famine while dining on caviar and lobster. When Miguel left, he was excommunicated and didn't look back. Now, he was what I would call the judge and jury for the nasty little monsters who stepped out of line. Miguel specialized in demons in a country where eighty percent of people were Roman Catholic. He killed the monsters told to little kids to scare them into doing what they're told. Silly parents… The boogeyman was coming, no matter what. There were two certainties in life, death and taxes. Demons were somewhere in the middle, cashing in on both.

Miguel taught me everything he knew. In turn, I gave Miguel a play-by-play of hell in all its horrific glory. It's not a vacation a person soon forgets. I signed hell's guest book and would be back for another stay. There were only two of us, demon experts, on this continent. In the world, there were a dozen of us, but Miguel and I were the only two that I knew of who specialized in the cursed and damned, with firsthand knowledge — Miguel, a man of faith, someone who had touched hell enough times that I could smell it on him like a cheap perfume after a night in a brothel...me, a witch who had been dragged down the halls of hell and stunk of brimstone and matchsticks. How I managed to stay away from him for two years still boggled my mind. Sheer stubbornness and not a lack of demons, in my opinion, is what kept us apart. That, and a smashed heart I didn't entirely trust yet. *This favor was going to fucking hurt.*

We weren't as close anymore, not once he left the church and began down a dark path that had no U-turns. Not because I had some moral high ground when it came to the church. No, I agreed with him wholeheartedly. I had distanced myself because his ethics became more clouded than my own. That said a lot, since my scruples were questionable most days. I was scared of him, or at least what he was capable of doing and becoming. I watched him kill someone who was possessed. He had tried to save her and failed. He couldn't let her loose, he had said. She'd have killed dozens of innocents, he claimed. But to watch the man you love kill an innocent? Well, it took the wind from the sails of our love boat, to say the least. It polluted my view of his righteousness. I wasn't exactly in a position to judge him, but I didn't agree with what he had done. Truthfully, I think what made me most uncomfortable was that I could almost understand why he did it. I saw a lot of my future self in him, and that is what I feared the most — seeing who I would become if I stayed with him.

Perhaps I disliked the parts of him that were more like me than I cared to admit out loud. But the hardest part of walking away was not what I saw when I looked into his eyes but that I had loved him almost enough to turn a blind eye. I had loved him almost enough to want to ignore what he had done. The thought that I could pretend had been what shut the door between us. Once you overlook or make excuses for the bad parts, you lose a part of yourself to their madness. Damn him for opening the wound again. Damn him for reminding me of every reason I still missed him. And damn him for the tears threatening to fall the moment I heard his voice again.

"Ailis, did you hear me?" His voice cut through my stroll down memory lane.

I groaned. "Yes. I heard you. I'm thinking."

Miguel chuckled. "You don't sound all that happy to hear from me."

"I'm not," I answered honestly. "If you're calling in your favor after years of us not exchanging so much as a Christmas card, it has me wondering how soon I'm going to die and go back to hell. I mean, should I cancel my subscriptions and drop my cat off at the neighbors?"

"You don't have a cat. Cats don't like you." He tried to make it sound like a joke, but it was a little too close to the truth. "You make a sorry witch, Ailis."

"That's not true. I have a trash goblin, a crabby stray — not that it's any of your business," I replied. I felt defensive all over again. "Did you call about my cat or to insult me?"

Cats didn't like me because they were always in between this world and the next. They didn't like that we had that in common—or so that's what I told myself. Some say cats can see spirits, while others say that cats *are* the spirits. Either way, they usually freaked out around me. It was unusual for a witch like myself to not have a bond with cats or other animals. But I didn't have a bond with much, not after my parents were killed when I was eleven, by monsters, and my only living grandmother died when I was eighteen. I left for university, and she died three days later. Part of me thinks she held on until she knew I made it. The other part of me was angry that I couldn't have anything pretty in life. Having Miguel had eased the sting of losing the last connection to my line. Then he had to go and fuck that up.

I should have known better. All good things come to an end. Every morning I wake up alone is a reminder of how much can be taken away, and that no matter how many promises a person makes, they still leave in the end. The harshness of the world, in all its painful truth, tends to scrub away a person's willingness for future companionship. Since Miguel, I hadn't bothered to try again. Why have a person to love if it was only going to end horribly? In the words of Sylvia Plath, 'It is so much safer not to feel, not to let the world in.' I'm sure she didn't mean for me to isolate myself, but I'd take it however I wished. Miguel had been the only person I had let in, and I had done everything in my power to push him out at the end. I had my reasons. He just didn't like them. But he didn't have to.

"I called because I need you," he finally answered. "Please."

"Why me? Why now? Why the secrecy up until now?" I asked. "I don't like being a puppet in your show. Why the cloak and dagger crap to get me there?"

"Would you have come if I had asked?" Miguel asked.

"No, but you could have called in your chit then and saved us both the time and energy," I answered. "I wouldn't have prepared a lecture if I was only coming there for your benefit."

"I didn't want to need you, but now I do. I need your expertise. I need it more now than ever. There was a ritual killing last night," he answered. "Up until now, there were a few missing and some questionable markings found at tourist sites. At first, I thought it was a localized incident. When the powers above started asking questions about the markings, I sent them to you. The local police do not understand hell or the markings of the pits like you do. But now, with someone turning up dead, I'm glad I sent them your way."

"Very convenient to have a token witch in your back pocket. What expertise do you need from me that you don't already have, Miguel? I can't kill better than you, and I can't condemn an innocent, either. I'd be in the way more than I'd be of any help." I made sure he could hear how angry with him I still was. His situation didn't change anything. His needing me didn't remove the stains he had made. "This isn't your first dead body, Miguel. From what I recall, you're well-versed in death."

For him to need me meant the proverbial crap had hit the fan and splattered the bystanders. Miguel was an expert all on his own and in areas I wouldn't even touch. He believed in any means to an end. We didn't share that belief. To want my knowledge above his own told me demons or devils or something that went bump in the night for the first time. It meant something big and bad was happening, and he didn't know what it was. That sent a shiver up my spine and into my skull. I knew them well, hell, that is, the upper and lower crust of the damned. Intimately. But he had been hunting them for almost two decades. I haven't. I gave talks and lectures. I lent my assistance to law enforcement when things got weird. I only hunted when I had to, when I got caught in the crossfire. I could count how many demons I had sent back, and none of them had been easy for me. Each hellion I sent packing had carried a price for using my inner energy, the abilities that made me a witch. And when you touched hell, the cost was immense. Everything around you slowly withered away, along with your soul. I wasn't in the habit of selling off chunks of myself for anyone but myself.

"The favor is owed. I'll brief you when you land, Ailis. I'll meet you at your resort," he finally said. His voice sounded like he knew the price of his demand from me. I wasn't a demon, but I'd still make him pay through his nose like one would. He'd probably wish I'd take his soul and let him die when I was done. I was a spiteful woman when it came to my grudges. But it wouldn't be a grudge if it didn't come with a painful reminder.

"Why can't you tell me now?" I asked. Miguel holding out made me nervous. Secrets until the bitter end were never a good sign. It usually meant the information would keep me from coming. Then again, anything to do with the underworld was a good enough reason to unpack my bags and not get on the plane. Secrets or not, I didn't want anything to do with the real deal. Lectures and consultations were one thing. Poking at the pits with my bare hands was entirely different.

"Words have weight, Ailis. You know that. I'm tired and don't want to call in the darkness." His voice hushed like the dark could hear the very mention of its name and would come to collect once the night settled back in.

"Good enough reason." I wouldn't have asked if I wasn't standing in front of a sun-kissed window. He was three hours ahead of me and was probably standing under the blistering sun. After the caress of hell, your soul craves the light and pushes you to seek it out. "Can you give me a hint as to what I am walking into? I'm not coming into this blind, Miguel. I need to prepare differently for this now-crappy vacation. I hadn't planned on needing to stay alive more than usual."

"Bring everything, Ailis. Bring whatever you can get onto a plane and out of the country. Whatever you can't bring, I'll have it here. Ah hell, Ailis, something has ravaged a woman in the dead of night. A young woman—rather, pieces of her have been found cut-up bad in Tulum. There are several women missing from the area, and now a body on the ground. It's supernatural and religious, given the way she was killed. She died in a circle. I think a circle of protection, but I don't know. This isn't my area of expertise. I'm not a witch. I don't think we're dealing with your run-of-the-mill sociopath or a lower-level devil. It's something else...something I'm unfamiliar with. It's a combination of what you know and what I know, but so much worse than either of us has seen. Nothing has been touched at the site. They're waiting on you."

"Why haven't they moved the body?" I asked. "It's rare for me to see the victim on the ground."

"The locals have collected what they can, but I didn't want to disturb the scene any more than I had to. If this isn't an isolated incident, the more you're able to piece together now, the better our chances will be of stopping this from happening again. Once you see what I've seen, you'll understand why we're waiting on you."

I let out a breath I didn't realize I was holding and unclenched my jaw. He was right to have called me. I wouldn't say it out loud, though. I didn't like him enough for that. I thought of what I'd need for a mixture of my skills and his, and he nailed it. *Bring everything.* Thankfully I could get a lot onto a plane, given my line of work. I was a consultant for the FBI, most federal and provincial government branches in Canada and a scattered few in the US. There just aren't that many demon experts in the world and none like me. I wasn't exactly in demand, but it did afford me some leeway with the authorities. I'd have to make a few calls and precheck my luggage through security, but it was doable. I had learned some hard lessons along the way, and now I packed like my life depended on it...because it usually did.

I once was called to a crime scene in Belize, to one of the islands off the coast. Two planes and a water taxi later, I felt nothing but regret. I hadn't taken everything I had and should have packed heavier for that trip. It was a large-scale infestation. One lower demon ran amuck, infecting four citizens with rage. They went on a killing spree. They targeted the elementary school first. The local witch doctor was killed trying to stop the demon and his horde. I didn't know this until I had arrived and was already knee-deep in bodies. I never would have gone had I known not even black magic could stop it. I almost died. Not to mention I was eaten alive by sandflies and came home with a stomach parasite. Now, I go nowhere until I've read the file, packed accordingly and at least looked up travel advisories. I didn't need the consultation money bad enough to risk another eternity in hell or those bloody fly bites. Hell should invest in some of those flies. It was torture. The demon had set me on fire, but the only scars I came back with were from the bugs. The only silver lining of that trip was the five days it took for me to be well enough to fly home. Five days on the beach weren't too shabby of a way to end the trip, and it was better than the casket I thought I'd fly home in.

"Answer me this one question." I could feel a rock in the back of my throat. *Nervous? Scared? Who, me?* "The blood forming the circle, is it animal or human?"

"They were feeding the gods, Ailis." His answer carried the weight of the world.

My back hit the wall. My legs felt like liquid. It was human blood at the scene. The only time Miguel or I had used the term 'feeding the gods' was for human sacrifice. Many moons and civilizations ago, when human sacrifice was still a thing to do on a Sunday night, the priests would use the blood and organs of a sacrifice to feed their gods. The people thought it nourished their gods, and without it, the sun wouldn't rise, and the world would end. "I land at Cancun International just before supper, around four your time, tomorrow. The flight is six hours, nonstop. I have a car picking me up. I'll meet you in the lobby at eight. I'm sure Philip gave you my itinerary."

"Yes, he did. Can you get an earlier flight? It's messy, Ailis," he asked. It was not like him to be so rushed. He had the patience of a saint. And like every other saint in history, bodies seemed to fall when he was near. Only with Miguel, it wasn't biblical.

"I haven't slept yet, Miguel. I've been up for twenty-four hours. Even if I could, I need to wash up. I'm covered in animal blood. I also need to pack, send out notes on a few cases I'm consulting on and get some sleep. Hell, precheck is going to take a couple of hours. It always does when I'm trying to get my gear on a plane." I looked down at my crusted nails and frowned. I had planned on an entire day at the spa. Didn't look like I would be getting a manicure any time soon. Thankfully, blood red was in style. Well, maybe not blood-crusted red.

"Okay. Just don't miss your flight. I need you here on the ground. I'll see what I can do about holding the scene. I have the site taped off, but each hour washes away the kind of evidence a demon expert would need. The body isn't in a dry cavern. It's a closed cenote and water-filled."

"Wait...a cenote?" I asked. What I would ask next would mean life or death, demon or psychopath. "Sacred or natural?"

"Sacred," he answered, the weight of that word not lost on either of us.

The history of the Maya was riddled with offerings to the gods, with ceremonial offerings of precious objects, and later shifting to human sacrifice. Bones of warriors, children, and maidens have been found littering the floor of cenotes, dating back over thirteen thousand years. These were places of great power, good and bad, depending on who went knocking and why they were knocking in the first place. Each cenote had a use, and finding a fresh kill in a sacred pit made my stomach flop. It could be a coincidence, or it could very well mean someone was ringing hell's doorbell. Given that Miguel had called me, my money was on the doorbell.

"A place of death doesn't sound like a place I want to go into, with or without a fresh body." I didn't like small spaces, let alone one used solely for sacrifice. I didn't like the idea of going into a cavern, either. Being closed off from the world was a little too close to hell for me. The deeper down you went, the harder it is to get away from the bad guys. "I'll be there. While you're waiting, ask around, and see if any of the local historians or professors know why this site in particular was chosen for a sacrifice. Was it specific to a god or demon? When was the last time it was used for such things? Maybe there's an old boogey hiding in the hills, who hunts every hundred years or worse, is waiting on someone stupid enough to release them."

"Will do. Text me when you land. I have to go." He hung up without saying goodbye. His manners were usually better than this. He was scared, and it took a lot to spook someone who played with monsters every day. *So much for a bloody vacation – no pun intended.*

Mexico had a small demon population, smaller than most places. The rituals once performed there had warded the lands from mass infestations. But, as the ruins crumbled, so did the wards. The Maya population wasn't big enough to maintain the hexes of protection anymore. And as each stone fell, the wards become weaker, allowing more demons to move in. Up until five years ago, the only things that bothered people in Mexico were Aluxes – fairy-like spirits. They were irritating, but nothing like a demon could and would become. The generations following the original Maya people did not have access to the writings of their ancestors. The Maya books were burned, save four, by the Spanish in 1562. The Spanish had thought they were severing the link between the Maya and their 'satanic' beliefs. All the Spanish did was burn the tools used to keep the land free from the nastiest of the underworld. It bit them in the ass as they kicked the bucket from diseases most believed were unleashed from hell.

I counted myself lucky. Vancouver didn't have a big demon problem. They weren't fans of the weather. Too wet. I don't suppose they get too much rain down in hell. I don't blame them. Most of us didn't like the rain, either. As for me, I get what I paid for. I live in a temperate rainforest with just under two hundred days of rain a year if the weather is in our favor. They didn't call it 'Raincouver' for nothing. I expect to get wet. Now vampires, on the other hand, were a nuisance around here. The perpetual rain and clouds for half the year made for perfect living conditions for those highly allergic to the sun. They weren't a big enough problem for the city to have its own active hunter. She was in retirement, bored stiff. Nevertheless, when it came to monsters, give them time. They always become a problem if they haven't been kept in check. But right now, the bigger problem on my mind was seeing Miguel. This would hurt more than any run-in with the damned. I'd sooner take my chances with hellspawn. At least I wouldn't want to sleep with them. Sex was great, but good sex? Now that was addictive and worth a little pain. Here's hoping my sobriety would hold. When it came to Miguel, I felt like a recovering heroin addict who was stepping into a drug den. *Let's see how long it'll take before I heat up a spoon.*

Chapter Two

With sandpaper eyelids, packed and ready, I researched Mexico. Outside of an unusual number of missing persons and shallow graves, I didn't find anything that made me unpack. It didn't matter where a person went. Every city has skeletons. So, to Mexico I traveled, with half a hope I'd come home with most of my soul intact. I wasn't foolish enough to think I'd get to walk away with all of it but enough to keep the demons at bay would be ducky. Here's to praying my next boyfriend didn't drag me through demons and devils and a dozen regrets.

I ended up with two hours of sleep before I got on the plane. It was more sleep than I thought I'd get. The nightmares were worse than usual — and that was saying something. That should teach me for looking up folklore right before I shut my eyes. Mind you, it did add a much-needed change in flavor from my usual tortured night ritual, where I dreamed that I was trapped in a cage in hell, being torn limb from limb by demons with no faces. The problem wasn't the nightmares. The issue was that they had been a play-by-play of the truth, like someone had filmed it and played it back for me every night so I wouldn't forget. I had spent lifetimes in that cage, seven seconds shy of two very long minutes, to be exact. I wouldn't soon forget, with or without the dreams throat punching me in the sanity every night. Each morning I'd wake up with the taste of sulfur in my mouth and the smell of brimstone on my pillowcase. The research may have given me nightmares, but I still filled my backpack with books and photos, all related to the folklore and ritual magic of Mexico. It would be a pleasant diversion from the white-knuckled flight. I wasn't a fan of airplanes, thanks to my aversion to small spaces and heights and death traps. I didn't trust airplanes as much as I trusted my ability to drive.

Checking through security was a nightmare. It always was, no matter if you're smuggling contraband or being a good little tourist. I didn't bother bringing weapons. I wouldn't have made it past security and would likely be under arrest for trying without law enforcement approval, which I didn't have for favors called in from ex-boyfriends. I didn't worry. I knew Miguel would have what I needed on the other side. That was one of the limited perks of knowing a murderer/'I had no other choice.' I left my Book of Shadows at home this time. It had always tempted security into a strip search, even though I was as innocent-looking as they came. Frizzy, long red hair, blue eyes, a splatter of tiny freckles, and I stood five foot eight inches. I wasn't physically threatening by any stretch of the word. I worked out, but I wasn't solid muscle. I looked like every other soccer mom in line, minus the kids and inherent need for an afternoon martini. I'm not judging. I'd be a raging alcoholic if I had a bunch of crumb-crunchers hanging off my hips. Once I started carrying around a book to damn people or a weapon, all of a sudden, I wasn't harmless anymore. They didn't trust me any more than I trusted them. To be fair, I wasn't harmless. I just wouldn't win any arm wrestles.

The airplane was a tin can with wings, only heavier and would fall out of the sky with more fiery speed. Perhaps years ago, it was the cutting edge of engineering, but now it looked more like an abused steel coffin waiting to throw you into the drink or a mountainside. It was one of those planes that didn't have first class. It had 'economy-flex', which meant you were in the front of the plane, the first people to be killed should the plane go down. If I could stand up and see the rear of the aircraft, the plane was too damn small. When the attendants did their song and dance on safety, I tuned it out. Realistically, the life vest part was of no importance to me. If we crashed, we were dead. The vest wasn't going to keep me alive if we slammed into a mountain, and they didn't deploy a miracle as it inflated. If we landed in the ocean, I'd be nothing more than an apple for sharks to bob for. If we went down, I didn't want to float around waiting to be eaten or freeze to death. I'd rather drown right away and get it over with. Now, had there been instructions on a parachute strapped under my seat, I'd have paid more attention. Alas, there were no chutes on commercial planes. Between the cost, weight and likelihood that you'd die trying to use one at over thirty thousand feet, they currently weren't an option. I'd argue that slamming into the tail of the plane or dying due to lack of oxygen was a much better end than chumming the water. But those kinds of comments didn't help you board any faster than having a weapon or a book of curses.

I preoccupied myself with literature and stories that made *Slaughterhouse-Five* look like a slumber party rather than focusing on plane crash statistics. I had my favorite books...my go-to for creature identification. The internet, to be honest, had more readily available information than my books, but I wasn't about to pay another dime to hurl my way to Mexico. I turned down the drink offers, although I knew a few drinks would have calmed my nerves. Unfortunately, I needed a clear head when I landed. The food, I turned down as well. Flights didn't have good vegetarian food. My choice to not consume meat had nothing to do with my moral compass and everything to do with it smelling like hell, like people being burned and tortured. The taste of meat, no matter how much sauce and how many seasonings were added, tasted like my own skin. The thought of it made me sick. Thankfully, the woman beside me was too busy drinking, toasting the end of a brutal divorce, she said, and didn't want to 'harsh her buzz with food.' I bought her another round as a thank you.

Mexico in January is as beautiful as it is in July for those who don't live there...green and lush and blooming. Residents argued it was cold as a witch's tit—or so someone two rows back from me had commented. The tunnel leading from the plane to the airport was stuffy. The cooled air wasn't enough to hide the heat pressing from outside. The moment I stepped off the plane, I orientated myself to where I was. Even inside a tunnel, I knew precisely where True North was. What kind of witch would I be if I wasn't a walking compass? The stroll through the airport and into the covered area outside was uncomfortable. The heat hit me like opening an oven with your face just inches away. It dripped down my back and stung my eyes with salt. The air was sweltering, making it difficult to breathe at first. Each breath felt hotter than the last. My light cotton pants and shirt clung to me like a second skin. I had dressed for the heat but not for the inevitable sweat. I was as Irish as they came, from my red hair to my pasty skin — the same pale skin that would burn to a crisp in the Mexican sun. I had a dash of Italian from so long ago that it didn't help the foreseeable sunburns.

Here you woke sweaty, went to bed sweaty, and even after a shower, you'd be sweaty. It was an ever-present warmth that lasted around the clock, day in and day out. Why I chose Mexico, knowing it would be a temperature that would make me feel sick, was a regret I now sucked into my lungs. I always picked a place where the sun beat down at an intensity that made the bad guys not want to chase me. One of the locals outside the airport had told me I'd get used to it when he saw me chugging down my water bottle. But at that moment, I didn't want to get used to it. I wanted to get back on the plane and head home. It may have been winter in Vancouver, rain and all, but it felt like summer in Mexico — and not their cold season. It would take me the entire two weeks of being here to get used to it. Unless I lived here, I'd never truly grow accustomed to the insistent force of it, not in the way the fully clothed locals were. Just seeing them in pants and long-sleeved shirts made me even hotter.

The air was heavy, but not just from the sun. No. The air was filled with static power. Not enough for the average person to notice, but enough for me to shiver, even though my body was retaliating from the temperature. I would bet any money that those who were sensitive to magic and supernatural elements were feeling uneasy. Uneasy… That word didn't really cover what was going on in the pit of my stomach. It felt like I had passed through an icy shower or briefly touched arctic air that left my skin tingly. The anxious thrum down my spine made me want to leave the airport.

"Do you know where your soul is going when you die?" A man approached me, holding a Bible. He was as clean-cut as every other Bible thumper I'd seen. His dark hair was parted on the side, his suit was black and crisp, and his manicured nails and soft-skinned fingers held his little black and gold book of holy roller rhetoric firmly in his hands. He didn't look like he had spent a single day in his life doing manual labor.

"Indeed, I do. Do you?" I asked.

"Into the arms of my Father, our Lord," he answered.

I should have walked away, but my dislike for the church was the same as Miguel's. The rich grew fatter while the poor died of starvation and disease. Devils and demons tapped on the doors of those who would sell their souls to feed their families, while the church turned a blind eye to why a man could be so easily possessed. It isn't always a matter of how strong their faith was. Often, it had everything to do with a soul so unselfish they'd rather rot in the pits than see their children suffer. Sometimes, a God-fearing man could be convinced to sell his soul for a loaf of bread, and a mother could be easily swayed by a demon for medication for her dying child.

"Ahh, shucks, lucky you." I snapped my fingers and smirked. "I have a one-way ticket straight to hell, into the eternal fire prepared for the devil and his angels, where I will be ripped apart over and over, only to be put back together for the torturous journey to begin anew," I replied. "Eternal damnation, checking in at the abode of the damned, yada, yada. Thanks for asking, though."

His eyes widened, and it took him a few moments to recover. "It's not too late. Repent now and save your soul."

"If only it were that simple," I answered. "That's not how things work down there. If it were, hell would be empty."

"All the devils are here," he replied.

"Ain't that the truth," I answered and stepped away, leaving him clutching his book of promises and well-worn-out lies.

I scanned the covered area for my name and my driver. There were dozens of people coming and going, loading into shuttles and taxis, juggling luggage and children. The nice thing about staying at an all-inclusive resort were the perks, like getting picked up in an air-conditioned car and not having to lug your own luggage around. My vacation may have been hijacked by monsters, but I'd still get the buffet and, eventually, the spa. I was looking forward to both. The rest? Well, welcome to my life, the life of the damned. I've never gone straight from point A to point B. It's always been a zigzag of unfortunate events and unexpected happenings. I have almost grown used to it. After all, things worked out in the end, and the paychecks were nice. But it didn't stop me from complaining about it every time.

I didn't see my driver on the first glance around and missed Miguel the first time, as well. But there he stood, not but thirty feet in front of me. He was trying to get my attention with a two-armed wave. There was no mistaking Miguel once I noticed him. Everything about him was burned into my memory. He was wearing the same hat he had on the last time I saw him. The last time was when I watched him kill an innocent woman. If I hadn't owed him a favor, I'd have hung up on him, having never had to see him in that old-as-sin hat again. But I always paid my debts, even when I didn't want to. You never know who may try to buy them, and you never wanted to run the risk of owing a bad guy in the end. I wondered if Miguel was a bad guy now. He certainly fit the bill. Little by little, like any bad guy I've met, he did what he had to do to complete a job. Only this time, he had a witness. Did I have room to throw stones? Not really. But would that stop me? I was currently holding a rock, ready to chuck it. Hypocrisy was alive and well in my world.

Miguel took off his hat and walked toward me. I was frozen in place. He always had that initial effect on me. He was a handsome Spanish man, with dark wavy hair, eyes of orange-brown and skin that looked like it had been kissed by Huitzilopochtli himself, the god of the sun. He also happened to be the god of war. It was probably not a coincidence that the name came to mind. When our eyes met, my breath hitched in my throat, as it always had. The only other place I had seen eyes the same shade as Miguel's had been on a cat. Alas, Miguel was pure human. No trace of a cat was to be found. His hurried walk brought me from my memories of my long-ago crush and the wedding songs I had picked out on our first date. Once, many moons ago, he had made me swoon, the kind of weakening of the knees you only read about in pocketbooks. Watching a man slaughter an innocent sure makes a gal readjust her standards and firm up her knees. My feelings for him died with that girl and her plans for the future. Deep down, I wish I hadn't seen it. Ignorance is bliss, and bliss was something my life could do with a little more of.

Miguel smiled at me once I took a step forward. The worry lines faded from his face. His eyes held warmth, like we were two old souls meeting once again. I'd agree on the old-soul part. Mine was well into retirement for the second time. His? Well, killing people must age the soul incredibly fast. One way or another, when the red man himself dragged him down, his soul would feel the slap of a thousand years. That was my only solace in life. If the bad guys weren't punished up here for their crimes, they'd face it in hell. That thought alone helped me get over a lot of shit in my days.

Although Miguel offered friendship with his glance, I wouldn't call us friends any longer. The heave in my stomach had told me so much. It wasn't nerves. It was anger. It was sadness. More than that, it was pity. I mourned who he had been and who he had to become to win an unseen war. My heart hurt for him, knowing where he would end up. Having spent time in the cages of hell myself, I was scared for him. Killing a demon buys you no time in the slammer. Not even hell cared if you butchered your way through their ranks. They saw it as a favor. Kill the weak so they didn't have to deal with the fallout. But taking a human life, an innocent soul, was murder, pure and simple. At least, it was to mine and his God. And the devils, regardless of who your god was, chained you up for the taking of life, no matter if your reason was 'I had no other choice.' A dead soul was a dead soul. A balance restored was ordered.

Miguel was genuinely happy to see me. I would almost call it relief. It wasn't reassuring. If anything, it made me question my decision to come. Having him sell my favor to the highest bidder would probably turn out better than the situation I had just walked into. Seeing his face, unshaven by two or three days, thaw into something softer wasn't endearing. It was uncomfortable. He looked disheveled, as if he had slept in the same outfit since his last shower, which looked like days ago. I hadn't seen him like this before. He was always clean, hair parted and wind-swept, pants holding a crisp ironed line and shoes buffed. Miguel always presented himself in the way his Abbi, his grandmother, had taught him—ready for court or church at the drop of a Bible. Today, he looked like me after I had been released from prison, not but an hour's drive from the airport. I could feel the beginnings of fear taking root in my stomach and moving to my ribcage.

"Ailis," he said. "Are you done tormenting the local Bible beaters?"

"Miguel," I replied. "He came up to me willingly."

"I doubt he'll make that mistake again." His smile faded to something flat and cautious. "You don't seem happy to see me. I thought you'd appreciate me picking you up rather than someone unknown. I know you're not a fan of strangers."

"You *are* a stranger. I don't know you anymore, Miguel." My answer was sharp. "But my discomfort comes with seeing your relief at my arrival. Anyone who is relieved when they see a witch makes me uncertain, afraid even."

"Could I not just be happy to see you?"

I raised my eyebrows and gave him a questioning look. "We didn't exactly leave things between us pleasant or friendly. And now I'm here for whatever reason you were too scared to say over the phone. Shall we cut the crap?"

I watched the warmth drain from his face. He now looked as I remembered him. To the core, Miguel was a hunter, a warrior, a killer and a questionable

Christian. I had heard him once referred to as a Holy Warrior incarnate, fighting the good fight. Little did they know the blood on his hands hadn't been all from righteous kills. I didn't want to think of how many more kills he had made in the name of a god that never asked for this level of devotion. The eyes now staring at me were the eyes of someone who had crossed one too many lines, and there was no way back. I wondered if he knew what he had given up for the cause. Like any good sacrifice, it was always something you want, something you hold dearest, a part of your soul you need the most, that you must give up. Anything less wouldn't really be a sacrifice, would it? I don't think the man upstairs was taking inconveniences in exchange for what you couldn't part with, or I wouldn't have a cage reserved in my name. I'd have cleared that debt and some.

"It's not just relief. I *am* happy to see you," he replied, but his voice betrayed him like a scorned lover.

"Let's not start with lies, Miguel. We know too many secrets to begin with a lie." My voice was louder than I had wanted it to be. I blame the airport, planes landing and taking off. But I knew I sounded brassy for one reason alone...anger. It was a fine wine that I sipped daily. I had a lot to be angry about. Life, in general, was enough. The world, as a whole, gave more reasons for rage than I could count, and I should have been a rage-drunk wino by now.

He nodded one sharp nod. An acknowledgment. "Truth between us."

"Why are you here? And not my driver?" I asked again.

"I thought we could go straight to the crime scene in whatever daylight we have left. I know you don't like the dark," he replied.

I hesitantly dipped my head in agreement. It made more sense than I wanted it to. I wouldn't have enjoyed going at night. I was only called in when the bad guys were monsters. I do everything in my power to stay the hell off their turf when I can—their turf being the twilight shadows. I didn't like the night. It was good for two things, lurking and for those who couldn't be out in the sunlight. Darkness had this way of kissing up to you, tempting you to stay out later. The shadows are flattering and glib. It'll be your favorite thing until it blocks off all your exits, and you're trapped with nowhere to hide. When I was a child, I was afraid of the dark. As an adult, afraid isn't the word I'd use. Cautious, uncertain, terrified? Yes. But truth be told, what could find me in the dark, could snag me in my bed at home at dawn. It didn't hurt to have a little healthy fear, though. It's kept me alive, save that one particular time. As my grandmother always said, nothing good ever comes after midnight.

Miguel's stare was hotter than the Mexican sun. "Why do you seem so uncomfortable with me being the one to drive you?"

I groaned. *Damn.* I demanded the truth from him but didn't want to give it back. "I'm not ready to see you, Miguel. My body craves you the way it did years ago, but my heart still wants its pound of flesh and gallon of tears. It makes for an interesting and very confusing combination. It's difficult to navigate, and I guess I wasn't ready for it."

He smiled and lifted his arms in a shrug. "The body never lies. It wants what it wants."

I rolled my eyes. "Get over yourself. Where are we going?" I immediately changed the subject to something less embarrassing.

"The location is two hours away — in Tulum, at one of the cenotes."

"Had I known we would be in Tulum, I would have changed hotels."

He turned and shook his head. "Would you have? Knowing a woman has been chopped up in that area?"

"It doesn't really matter where I stay, Miguel. If it's my time to go, where I am won't matter." I said matter-of-factly.

"Why tempt fate?"

I shrugged. "My fate will roll out as it chooses, whether I seduce it or not."

He didn't like that answer. Miguel grabbed onto one of my rolling suitcases and turned. He walked ahead of me, and I followed, lugging my other suitcase with a duffel bag of gear hooked on top of it. I stayed behind him. I needed time to recover from the surprise. I knew I'd see him at some point this evening. I just hadn't mentally prepared myself for seeing him now. I knew it would hurt, but I thought the old wounds had scarred over by now. Turns out they were merely scabbed, and I was picking at them. I should have known better. Maybe if I were lucky, a demon would swallow me whole before I had to feel just how deep the cuts were.

Miguel had looked back twice. Both times he had pain in his eyes. Up until five minutes ago, I had questioned if he knew what he had given up with me. The look on his face now told me he knew damn well what he had lost. That look made me reach for the locket around my neck — a locket given to me by Miguel. It held no pictures or inscriptions. No, it was much more precious than that. It was filled with lightning-struck wood, a powerful protection against all harm. The locket, being made of pure silver, with a cross on the front and an arcane symbol on the back, added another layer of protection. But it would do nothing to protect me from heartache. Unfortunately, there wasn't a talisman for that. I'd already looked.

I was still hurting, and that pissed me off. I didn't know what strummed my heartstrings more, that I was the one who left or that he didn't try to stop me. I tried to push the hurt back down and reach for my anger instead. I did anger better than sadness. I welcomed it. It was something I could feed or starve at my whim, something I could control. But today, I was scared, which silenced my temper. I feared what I could feel in the air. I was afraid of what had slaughtered a woman. My stomach turned with the unknown. What's easier to work through, fear or hurt? I picked hurt because I was getting into a vehicle with it for two hours. I had to blink a few times to keep the tears where they belonged. I wouldn't cry in front of him. He wouldn't get another one of those precious salty gems from me. Each deep breath drew me out of the past as if it were a physical effort on my part. I hadn't made peace with my broken heart. I don't think I ever would. And I wouldn't if I came each time he called. In his defense, this was, in fact, the first time he had called. But once was enough. And once would be the only time. I wouldn't become a bitter cat lady, pining over a lost love. Or a dog lady, since cats hated me.

I'd get over being around him, eventually. The initial shock would fade, and I'd go back to my hate for him. Hate was a warm blanket on a winter's day. It was easier than anything else I could feel right now.

Chapter Three

The first half of the drive was spent in silence. Quiet, I could do. I was never the type of person who needed to fill every moment with noise or idle chit-chat. The silence was comfortable and spoke for itself. It was peaceful, in a way, where you felt at home, no matter where you were. It was familiar. The hush of the vehicle gave me time to think, time to recover and time to consider my initial plan to verbally attack him the moment he was within my reach. I had rehearsed a grand speech, over and over in my head, during my flight. I would tear into Miguel and give him hell. I would give him back the pain he not so delicately wrapped as a parting gift for me.

But those words sat on my tongue like poison. The same void created years ago still sat between us, intentional or not. Words weren't going to give me closure or repair it. But, to tell the truth, I didn't really want to. We could never go back. Did I even want to try? My toxic words wouldn't make a lot of difference. When it came to me and him, I was at a loss for meaningful things to say. So, I grounded myself and focused on the task at hand, one foot in front of the other. Stay alive. Keep my hands out of hell. Keep my clothes on. Keep Miguel out of my bed. I'd survive this if I just stuck to the plan. I'd have to. The alternative would be another regret to add to the list—and I had enough of those for a lifetime.

Truth is, I wanted to throw myself at him. In the back of my mind, no matter how hard I tried to silence my lust for him, my body still reacted to Miguel as if no time had ever passed. I was hooked from the first time he touched me. The parts he had once favored with his mouth and teeth twitched with promise that I'd give in. The thought of his hands on my skin once again made my pulse speed up. My body had grown addicted to his. I was a card-carrying alcoholic when it came to him, and I had gone cold turkey. I squeezed my hands into fists and reminded myself why I'd left. I told myself it was worth it. I couldn't have stayed. But my libido wasn't a force I could reason with. It simply didn't give a damn what my reasons were. She was a greedy bitch and only had eyes for him. *Double damn.* This was a mistake.

"Deep breathing exercises?" Miguel turned off the faint radio.

I nodded and breathed out. I focused on five things I could see, smell, touch, taste and hear. It helped when I felt anxious. The problem was, he was what I could see. His skin was all I smelled. His body was there to touch. I could taste him on my tongue, and his voice reminded me of Sunday mornings in bed with him.

I lied about why I needed to ground myself. "Keeps me from ripping you a new one."

Miguel veered off the main road. He took the turn sharp and fast. The tires skipped on the loose gravel and dirt. When he came to a stop, he slammed his Jeep into park and gripped the wheel until the leather cried a protest. "By all means, Ailis. If it'll help, go ahead. Get it out now. Do this here, because this isn't happening at the scene. Once we're there, we're on *her* time, not ours."

"No. I'm not here for that, Miguel. We have a truce until I'm done paying my debt." I turned in my seat to face him. I didn't feel trapped, but the air between us felt like two years' worth of unspoken words and needs I wouldn't feed.

"A truce? I didn't know we needed one," he replied. He glanced from me to the road. He could feel the pressure in the car. He, like me, squirmed in his seat.

"I don't trust myself around you, Miguel. That makes it hard for me, because I don't want to give in to it. It makes me angry to know you still have that kind of control over my body." I looked over at him. He was staring at the road, but I knew he could see me.

"It wasn't all bad," he replied. "You can't say it was."

"You're right. It wasn't. But I don't trust you, either. You scare me. The day I start trusting a monster is the day I die." I positioned myself back in my seat, facing forward, a little taller than I was moments ago. That's the thing about hard conversations. They either built you up or tore you down. And I wasn't particularly short at the moment. Miguel, on the other hand, looked like a few inches had been shaved off the top. Did I apologize for that? I didn't feel sorry in the least. The words needed to be said. If I didn't say them now, hope would be allowed to grow.

"And I'm one of the monsters you don't trust?" He didn't hide the sadness in his voice.

"You know damn well what you are, Miguel, even if you can't say it out loud." I knew I should leave it alone. The scab didn't need to be picked any more than it had been. Neither of us needed to bleed any more than we already had. But we picked anyway. People will do what they've always done, poke at things they shouldn't touch. Hell, that very reason was why I was employed.

"Are you going to cut me up the entire time you're here?" He asked.

"I brought a lot of baggage with me, Miguel. And one of those bags is filled with knives," I answered. "If you didn't want to open up old wounds, you shouldn't have called me."

"You haven't lost your charm," he replied.

"Just tell me about the murder, Miguel. We can make each other bleed later." I could have cut deeper, but I didn't get on a plane to be dragged through the emotional gutter. That's not why I agreed to see him. Debts brought me here, and I wanted to clear it up and get on with my life.

He took it as the hint I intended it to be and let me change the subject. He pulled a yellow file from beside his seat and handed it over. In that split second, when his hand touched mine, every fiber in my body electrified. My nerves fired, and my breath hitched in my throat. The anticipation, the chance of being together again, was too much for me to handle, and I pulled my hand away. I tried to be casual about it and hoped if he noticed, he wouldn't say anything. He put the Jeep in gear and pulled back to the main road.

He cleared his throat twice before finally speaking. I'm pretty sure he noticed my reaction. So much for my tough-girl persona. "It's everything we've got on the murder."

"What sort of crime scene is it?" I asked as I opened the file. "What are your first impressions?"

"It's nothing like I've seen before, Ailis. It's not simply a murder, more like a slaughter." His voice grew quieter. "The victim, she was…gutted, butchered. It was ritualistic, tied down and brutally ended. They took out her organs. The markings you were originally called here to speak on were found carved into the stones of the cenote."

"Why haven't I heard about this on the news? I looked online and found nothing."

"We've kept the ritual part out of the reports. One more dead body doesn't make headlines around here. People go missing all the time in Mexico. Kidnapping is a booming business in many parts of the world. Mexico isn't immune any more than Vancouver is."

"Has anyone reported her missing yet?" I asked. He nodded, eyes not moving from the road. I don't think he was simply paying attention to the road. He didn't want me to see the look in his eyes. But I could feel it. Sadness. Under all that sadness, secrets. "What about the others, Miguel? And there's been more than a few. I hate feeling like I'm not only being lied to but I'm also being played. You wouldn't have handed over my name to the locals, almost two weeks ago, if there weren't more people missing and suspected dead. That there is a fresh body on the ground is merely a fluke."

"There are other women missing, but I can't say for sure if they are connected to this scene or if they've fallen victim to other crimes," he answered.

"I looked it up this morning," I replied. "Hundreds of missing persons happen here yearly. The statistics are pretty alarming. I ran a few searches for missing persons in the area. Your vic is the only one reported missing from Tulum over the last two weeks. She went missing along with a dozen other people from the surrounding areas. I linked five of them through their social media."

"Linked them? What do you mean?" he asked.

"There are photos of them together. They've checked into the same locations together. They're friends on all their social media platforms. They didn't just know each other. They vacationed together. They were friends in the truest sense of the word. There's no way I was the only one to discover this. A few clicks and I had enough information to know a cluster of friends were gone. Finding the last body, it's a pretty damn good indication there are other bodies...or will be," I glanced over at him. His focus was the road, but his posture said so much more. I knew his tells better than he thought I did. He was hiding something. I'd figure it out sooner or later, but I would be pissed off if I had to do it the hard way. "You can cut the crap now and stop lying to me—or we can play the song and dance until the bitter end, and more people will die. *Your* people, not mine. It's your choice, Miguel. This isn't my community. These aren't my friends and neighbors. I'll sleep fine while you lead your sheep to the slaughter. If you want to play your cards close to your chest, great, but be careful you don't find the other players in your game putting down their hands and walking away."

"I'll look into it." His answer was clipped. "I don't want more bodies on the ground, Ailis, believe that. We checked out the victim's social media. Her friends knew nothing."

"Her closest friends are probably dead," I muttered. "Her nearest and dearest, do they have an alibi?" In most cases, you're killed by someone you know and trust to keep you safe.

He gave me a look that said I thought he didn't know how to do his job. "It's the first thing the local cops checked out. They weren't involved."

I smirked. "You mean, they weren't there. But don't rule out involvement until all the pieces are on the table, Miguel. Your enemies can be on the other side of the world and still be the reason you're being toe tagged."

The first few pages were nothing more than scene notes. What I really wanted to see were the pictures. Police notes on ritualistic killings were vague, at best. They simply didn't know how to describe the scene in the detail I needed. Most tried. Others simply said there was a body in a painted circle. I had given a few lectures on crime-scene detail, what to look for, what to document and what to stay clear of and call a priest for. Over the last two years, I had noticed an improvement, not in the written work, but in the photographs. When they were at a loss for words, they took more pictures. That, on its own, was the icing on the cake. Those photos were what helped me identify the boogeyman for law enforcement, more times than not.

The body was positioned spread-eagled. Her wrists and ankles were tied with blood-soaked rope, the kind you'd find on any of the boats in the local marina. The knots were fixed to metal spikes that had been pounded into the stone. Around her was a perfect circle of white powder, likely salt, for protection. The body was positioned over a symbol in the middle of the ring. An ankh. It looked like a cross, but the top was a loop. It was painted in what I could only assume was blood. Blood was a powerful source of magic. Whoever did this had every intention of succeeding and using whatever means necessary to accomplish the job. The ankh is the ancient Egyptian symbol of eternal life.

Written within the Egyptian Book of Living and Dying, the ankh is the key to life. The loop at the top represented the rising sun. The horizontal bars are for feminine and masculine energy. Together, they formed a symbol of fertility and power. But that was just one theory behind it.

"Odd for them to be using an Egyptian symbol in a sacred Maya site," I muttered, more to myself. "There are dozens of local symbols to choose from."

"I thought the same thing," Miguel replied. "Do you know why they'd use a symbol like that here?"

"I don't know. Regardless of what the symbol means to the person using it or why they're using it, it is seen by all users of magic as a mark of everlasting life and protection. It is used in high-level spells for protection from the big nasties and to ward off danger. They could have simply used a familiar and powerful symbol rather than research the ones used by the originals of the land and risk gambling on an unknown."

Miguel nodded, and I shrugged. I flicked through the rest of the photos. The victim's body lay like a broken doll, her head at an awkward angle and held in such a way that I knew she wasn't sleeping. I pushed away the thought that she had once been a person, full of life and a future. If I looked at her as a person, I'd lose myself in the grief of what I was seeing. Cruel as it may be, once she gave her final shuddering breath and the light burned out in her eyes, she was nothing more than an empty husk to bury. Her soul was long gone, along with her organs and sanity, through a gaping wound. I knew they had done this while she still had a beating heart, or what would the point be? It's not a sacrifice if you're not losing something important, like your life. Her life fed the circle. Depending on what was being raised in the circle, her fear would have been a nice wine to wash down her organs with.

"Why would they take her eyes?" I whispered, swallowing the threat of vomit. "There aren't many spells calling for eyes, ears, brain, tongue, lips. I mean, if she were being cursed, then perhaps."

"Depends on which flavor of evil did this. The original sacrifices, not too far from the cenote we're going to, the priests removed the eyes, tongue, ears and heart, all for religious reasons — either to keep them from telling lies, forcing them to hear the truth, feeding the gods, or simply as a punishment."

"Does anything in her history suggest she should be punished?" I asked.

"We all have reasons for punishment, Ailis." Miguel laughed bitterly, the truth being too close for his comfort. "Nothing stands out, though. She was described as a good God-fearing woman. Whoever did this didn't do it as a punishment. It has sacrifice written all over it."

I nodded as I took in the information. I was so used to looking for monsters at scenes like this that sometimes I forget how monstrous human beings could be. I pondered the likelihood of a person being responsible for the carnage but couldn't picture a person with enough strength to tear her to pieces. People just weren't that strong, nor were they born with the right equipment...like claws.

"Is there anything significant about the location?" I asked. "I mean, I'm looking at a map here, and it's not near any churches or demon crossroads. Why here?"

"The ruins of Tulum are close by. The wood used as part of her binding is from the Ceiba tree. The Ceiba tree is sacred to the Maya people. The tree was a connection to all three worlds — the underworld, earth and heaven. They believed that the souls of the dead ascended to the top of the trees, a direct route to heaven. It's why you find them in cemeteries, at all ruins, religious ceremonies, churches, and even growing randomly in the streets. To this day, people still believe."

"Strong resemblance between Maya beliefs and many religions of today, with the Tree of Life in the Garden of Eden," I added.

Miguel nodded and grinned as if I were preaching to the choir. He knew the big book better than I did. "These trees also mean life. They grow near water. Their root systems can break through stone to get to a water source. If you see one, you know water is close by."

"That's all well and good, but why pick the cenote? It's not closed off from the public. It's easy to get to, neither out of sight nor out of mind. Unless they wanted it to be found?"

"The cenote feeds the trees with fresh water. It is a place where souls would go to please the gods. Five years ago, I was called in on a dive into a new cenote. They found skeletons of long-ago sacrifices. The cenotes are a place of worship and power."

"A sacrifice in a place of great power. If you knew this, you didn't need me. You already have the answers to the questions I would have." There was nothing in this carnage that stood out as unusual. Well, more unusual than anything else Miguel has dealt with in all his years.

"When you get there, you'll understand. It's a feeling I have in the pit of my stomach," he answered. "This is bigger than me. This is bigger than you."

"Do I thank you now or later, if I'm alive, for hauling me into something bigger than the both of us?" I was back to being angry. I'd take it. A few minutes ago, I wanted to take my clothes off and see if Jeep sex was as good as bedroom sex. Anger may hurt one of us, but it didn't embarrass me like my desire did.

I stayed silent for the remainder of the drive, read the rest of the reports and studied the photographs. Dread pressed down on my shoulders like an invisible hand. I could feel the sun inching down with each minute. I didn't know if Miguel and my libido were the problem or knowing we only had a couple hours of daylight left that was itching at my patience. Both of us shuddered when we saw the sun's last attempts to hold the sky and begin to set. The road soon degraded into dirt and rocks and dips, covered in a blanket of dusk. It was manmade and shook me like a margarita that I'd give a small appendage to be drinking poolside at this moment.

I unrolled my window. The tension between us was thick enough to eat. The hottest it had gotten between us were hurt words, but the air held a faint smell of sex. The open window did nothing to help. Waves of muggy air billowed in and pasted the scent of my craving to my skin like cheap body spray. Beyond the slight draft, which felt like the wind off a fire, there was nothing. It was silent, but the kind of quiet that was loud and unexpected. You noticed it, like ears ringing or the silent scream of a broken heart. Even with the noise of the vehicle, we should have heard birds or insects and animals. But the closer we got to the cenotes, the quieter it got. There was a stillness in the air that made me anxious. No life. No nothing. Not even a breeze. It was as if time had forgotten about this place and left it as it was the moment the clock stopped. I glanced at Miguel, who had a knowing look on his face. He could feel it, too.

"It isn't always this quiet, is it?" I asked, and he shook his head. "You could hear a pin drop out there."

"It was like this when the body was found. Usually, it's brimming with life, especially around fresh water," he answered. "We should be hearing birds, critters and creatures that hold out from the sun in their dens, nocturnal animals getting ready to hunt by moonlight. It's as lively in the evening as it is during the day."

The road opened up on either side of Miguel's four-door Jeep. The charm on my necklace vibrated, and we both looked at each other. A large meadow with sunburned weeds waist-high on either side cast premature shadows on the makeshift road. It made my skin prickle with goosebumps. We turned into a manmade parking lot that was filled with police vehicles and what I assumed was a coroner's SUV. Flashes of red and blue strobed over the long grass and dust-covered vehicles. Most of the vehicles still had their motors running. It had been a long time since I had seen this many cars and trucks with their engines running. Vancouverites frowned on it, along with straws, plastic bags and to-go containers that didn't leak. I didn't mind. I recycled everything and never had leftovers long enough for them to soak through my cardboard container.

The only vehicle in the lot not running was the ambulance. They didn't hang around scenes when they weren't needed. That they were still around and not running hot made my stomach flop. I caught the eye of the paramedic in the passenger seat. Her eyes carried every haunted story ever told. There was a weight to what she had seen that she carried on her shoulders. I knew that look, that pressure that shaved inches off her height. Every time I am called out, it is always the newest worst thing I've seen. My shoulders have been in a perpetual knot for six years. It was probably the worst she had seen, which was saying a lot, given her line of work. She looked away, probably seeing the same in me. Tonight was not the kind of night for looking into a mirror, so I wasn't insulted.

Beyond the cars was the law. They were just sort of humming around, fidgeting, waiting. I wondered what they were waiting for. Usually, by the time I got there, everything was done. The scene was ready to be closed down. The body would be removed, and that was that. What I was seeing didn't match what I was used to. Then again, I didn't exactly know how things were done in Mexico. The only time I had consulted here, in person, I hadn't seen it through to the end, given I was a guest at the local jail. This evening, something was up. There were too many cops hanging around, doing nothing. Aside from the person responsible for the crime and loved ones, no one willingly hung out at a murder scene if they weren't needed.

"Strange," I whispered, more to myself.

"It gets stranger," Miguel replied.

"Why are there so many people still here?" I asked.

"To keep the scene intact until you got here," he answered.

Miguel pulled his Jeep in next to a dark blue or black truck. It was hard to tell with the setting sun and flashing lights. It was a crew cab with a roll bar attached to the box. Bold white letters on the side — *Policia*. The movement to my right showed dozens of police in full uniform holding Heckler & Koch MP5 submachine guns. That was some serious firepower for a crime scene in the middle of nowhere. But the police were seriously outmanned and outgunned in Mexico. The cartel was more than what I would call an issue. They ran the streets and killed anyone who tried to stop them. The drug trafficking syndicates made our local dealers in Vancouver look like a mild inconvenience. The last I heard, there were a dozen or so cartels active in Mexico. I felt as safe as a virgin on her wedding night, machine guns or not. Coming to Mexico to help solve a crime was a flip of the coin for how I was going to die. I crossed my fingers and hoped I'd be shot over cocaine rather than hauled into a cavern and staked to the ground to feed the gods.

Once my feet touched dirt, I knew why the officers were milling around and was surprised any of them were still there. I understood why the location was selected. It wouldn't have mattered if it had been done in the middle of a mall, on the side of the road or at the current resting place. The energy in the air would have stopped most people in their tracks and sent them in the other direction, freeing up the place to do dark and dirty deeds. Dread coated the air like a broken bottle of intense perfume. My necklace felt like it was a few degrees from causing blisters on my chest. I would have moved it, but I wouldn't risk losing it. I leaned on the Jeep, my head hanging between my arms, until the wave of nausea passed. I felt sick — food poisoning, gut-wrenching sick. My skin was clammy, as if I had been fighting a fever, and it finally broke. Whatever was called into the circle below was still lingering in the air. It reminded me of how I felt after intense pain, utter and immeasurable anguish and exhaustion. It felt like the dread that hung over me for a year after hell had spat me back out.

Primal fear pushed against me, tempting me to reverse my steps back into the Jeep. It knotted my stomach. Thankfully, I wouldn't be sick. Nothing was getting out of my stomach, with a knot that size blocking the way and a throat as dry as ash. My jaw locked my teeth together. Unless the fear could keep the sun up so that I could do this in the afternoon, the fear wasn't going to make me listen to it or cave in to it. But it did make me pause and take several moments to come to terms with what I was feeling. Nothing short of pure, unadulterated fear, the kind that told our ancestors to clench their assholes when they were scared, could make me pause and process emotions. This was not good. This was so beyond not good that I glanced up at Miguel and glared. I was pretty sure this wouldn't be the last glare he'd receive from me during this trip.

"Now, do you see why I called you?" Miguel asked. He had a death grip on the push bumper of the Jeep. His feet shuffled on the ground, fighting the same urge I had to turn around and head back to where the very air didn't make me want to vomit. "I've never run into something that had this kind of emotional sway over others while not even being here to do it. Those who can don't come out of hell for less than an entire city of souls."

I didn't talk. I only nodded. I didn't trust my voice yet. The dread crept over me and numbed my brain. My only thought was that this was it. Today was the day I was going to die. There was no turning back. I am nothing more than a cow being led to slaughter. Only, a cow has no idea it is about to die. I knew damn well this could be my last day. Miguel moved around the Jeep and stood at my side, joining my deep breathing. It was a tool he taught me from a time when panic used to take me over every time I smelled something burning. The scent of meat or a match blown out were the two biggest triggers. How I've put myself back together into a functioning person, I had to lend thanks to the man I was currently hating.

"Dear God, what the hell is that?" I finally whispered. I ran my hands down my arms in an attempt to clean off the sticky anticipation held in the air, as if the air itself eagerly waited for my reaction to the show below.

"It'll go away. Just give it a minute. It was the same for us all."

"How did you get any of them to stay? If I didn't know we were walking into a hellhole, I would have left. I'm practiced, you're practiced, they aren't." I pointed at the police.

Miguel shrugged. "It's the firefighter effect. They run into a burning building, knowing they may not make it back out. They're scared, but they're trained and focused."

"You can't possibly believe they are trained for this, Miguel."

"Not for *this*." With nothing specific to point at, Miguel waved his hand around the scene. "But I *do* believe they are trained to go into hell for innocent people. You can't be in law enforcement, in these parts, without being willing to go toe-to-toe with evil, once or twice."

The initial sensation subsided. It left behind a powerful desire to leave. My fear was replaced with focus. Like a firefighter, I grabbed my gear and headed into my own form of a burning building, passing officers who glared the moment they saw me. I wonder what little ghost stories Miguel had told them about me. It didn't matter. We all would share the same brand of nightmare tonight, witches and humans alike. And tomorrow, when I still came back, with new lines around my eyes, they'd hate me a little less. Cops were weird like that. They only seemed to warm up to me once they saw proof I had a soul and suffered just like everyone else. If they only knew how much I suffered by just being here, with my greatest pain, not but a foot to my left, maybe they'd cut me some slack.

Chapter Four

The cenote was a deep cavern, completely enclosed outside of one small opening in the ground. The wooden stairs that drew you to the bottom were slick and steep and threatened a broken back with one misstep. They led to a small wooden platform, covered in a black rubber mat, above crystal-clear water. Down the levels of wooden and neck-breaking steps, I was in the sinkhole. It felt like a casket. And it was, just not for me. *Not yet, anyway.*

I didn't see the body at first. I had never been inside a cenote before. It was a lot to take in. The formations alone were worth taking a second look at. I wouldn't have admitted it out loud, right at that moment, but it was breathtaking. The stalagmites hung from the ceiling like icicles, growing down from the rock ceiling to meet the water. They grew up from the floor of the cave to meet in the middle. They looked like elephant trunks. Small underwater lights somehow made it seem magical, beautiful, almost a religious experience. But at the center of the beauty was the reason I had come…death. The limestone slab beyond the wooden platform held our victim, the sacrifice, the reason the walls started to feel like they were closing in on me. Once revered as sacred by ancient Maya people, it was now a crime scene, and there was nothing holy about what happened here.

The combination of odors confused my mind. The sickening smell of pennies coated my tongue. It was the taste of fresh blood. The natural heat generated from the cavern gave the smells a heaviness, like breathing in soup. Rotten flesh blanketed the air in a choking aroma. It smelled like butchering day at the farm, halfway done, and the farmer left for a two-week summer holiday. I should have been used to this by now. I had been to enough crime scenes and seen more dead bodies than I bothered counting. You'd think I'd have thicker skin. But the strings these scenes pulled in my heart hit me like an emotional sucker punch. Fear and sadness clutched my stomach and squeezed with all their might and made me thankful I hadn't eaten on the plane. It didn't help that a light breeze flowed down into the cenote, echoing through the cavern. It made me think of old horror movies of haunted houses and hiding in the attic, waiting to be killed.

Messy, Miguel had called it. I would hate to see what he thought horrendous looked like. There was blood everywhere, splattered on every surface, like someone had taken a spray bottle and made sure each surface held a piece of her. The lack of light didn't dull the blood. Instead, it somehow looked worse…dark and shiny. I knew it was bright red, almost fire engine. It was too glossy to be old enough to be the truly dark stuff I was used to.

I swallowed hard. I didn't want to vomit on the evidence. I coughed down my urge to laugh. I didn't want to make a mess, yet there wasn't a thing I could do to make the scene worse unless I killed someone else. I eyeballed Miguel. If I were going to kill someone, he was at the top of my list. I'd strangle him with my bare hands.

"You're not looking too good, Ailis." Miguel leaned into my ear. "Do you want to go up for some fresh air?"

I shook my head. "A little air now isn't going to take the sting out of this. And for the record, this isn't just *messy*, Miguel. This is downright horrific. Let's get this done and over with so I can go to my room and scrub my skin until the smell goes away."

"It never does," he replied softly. He had seen one too many scenes if he still smelled them.

I swallowed again and tried to breathe around the stench, but it was the kind of smell that got into every pore and held on until the soap came out to wash it away. I blinked rapidly as the cavern tilted to the right. Finally, I closed my eyes and fought the vertigo. I counted to ten, and when ten didn't work, I upped it to twenty. I told myself not to run up the stairs in fear, for no other reason than not to be laughed at by the men with the guns. They didn't look like an understanding bunch.

I stood at the edge against the rock and took in as much detail as my shocked brain could. The light was poor. Little lanterns had been set up along the walls for tourists, but they did little for crime-scene analysis. My eyes roamed the floor, looking at the smeared blood and tracks. Somewhere in all this mess were clues, possible prints from the murderer. But unless they had foot impressions that weren't human, I didn't think the tracks would be helpful. The scene had been screwed over six ways from Sunday. I didn't say it out loud. There was a body down. Whoever found her wasn't thinking of evidence collection. Those with souls always went into savior mode before they put on their detective hat. But every track, good guy or bad, led to one thing—the body or what was left of it.

The photos didn't do the scene justice. It was much worse in person, as most things you could have gone without seeing usually were. But it was the smell that no amount of detailed notes could have described. It hung in the warm air like rot. The Mexico heat and enclosed cavern had turned it into a garbage pale of meat in the sun. This wasn't a fair start to my vacation, looking at a mutilated body. I'd be sending Miguel my vacation package bill, with as many trips to the spa as I could fit in. I may have owed him a favor, but this was well beyond cashing in a marker. This would stain me for the rest of my life, and Miguel could cover some of those costs. When I got home, I'd be sending him my therapy bill as well.

I took a deep, shaky breath and focused, but no matter how hard I tried, I couldn't get enough air. I had thought it was hot above. Down here, it was worse. I could taste the body. The heat had made it worse, like she had already started to decay in the oven that was the cenote. The brilliant red of the blood told me the body was fresh. The taste in the air hinted at something different. She smelled like a week had passed. In some cases, a spell would speed up the timeline from death to nothing more than bones and worms. And in others, feeding the gods would age a body like a week in the sun.

Under the smell of death was Angelica, used for protection. I wondered who was in need of protection.

It certainly wasn't the splayed victim. I crouched to see the finer details, unnoticeable to the naked eye. The circle around the body was salt, as I had suspected. The symbol beneath her was painted with blood — whose blood I didn't know and wouldn't until the lab reports came back. But it was a safe guess that it belonged to the victim. Placed at the four corners were crystals…agate and microcrystalline quartz. Both were used in spells for protection from danger. I stood and took a few steps back, gaining a different perspective. Small bells were placed at various places leading up to the body, every foot or so. I pointed out the bells to Miguel. He stood casually, several feet to my right. He had seen the show before and didn't look like he had any desire to see it again. I didn't blame him. I could have gone a lifetime without seeing this.

"Why did they use bells?" he asked.

"Bells are often used for banishment. A bell is rung to settle a bad atmosphere. It's why you find them hanging over the doors when you go into shops. Old habits die hard. Whatever they summoned into that circle — or tried to summon — they were terrified of it. There are layers upon layers of protection, charms and objects. Whatever they were doing, they thought they'd need more defenses than usual. A simple chalk and salt circle would keep in most demons. This, all of this, is overkill." I pointed back to the stairs and frowned. "There are five hex bags hanging on the stairs. They were making sure nothing came down, and nothing went up."

"So, this couldn't be a demon doing this?" Miguel asked.

"No. First, why would a demon draw a circle of protection? They don't have a soul to hold the circle, and they can't protect themselves against their kind. Plus, if a demon wanted to butcher her, he simply would. He wouldn't go to all this trouble. Second, I've never heard of a full card-carrying demon able to spin a circle, soul or not. It's not a skill many have, including witches. To get a circle this big and maintain it long enough to do this to the victim, there's got to be more than one witch at work here. This would take a hell of a lot of juice, and one witch just isn't enough to funnel this kind of power, over what likely took hours to do."

"What the hell were they so scared of?" Miguel thought the question out loud, for no one in particular. I was wondering the same thing.

I glanced at two police who were crossing the line to collect the remaining evidence off the body. I held out my hand, as if I could will my words into action. "Don't step on the line!"

I was too late. An officer on evidence collection duty stepped across the circle and hit the salt with his shoe. He cut a clean line in and broke the circle. He disrupted whatever spell was used to maintain the magic. I felt the protection go down like a curtain at the end of a show. My ears popped. Energy filled the cavern and slammed into me. I had felt thousands of circles break but had never felt one like this before. My skin cooked. I watched a soul leave the circle and pass through me as it tore out of the sinkhole. I screamed until my throat was raw and had no sound left to make. My legs buckled, and I landed on my knees, the stone jarring my body. I covered my ears as the pressure built into something similar to ice picks shoved into my eardrums. Power filled the air until I couldn't breathe. I couldn't feel anything outside of pain and the misfiring of nerves. I didn't know if I was lying down on my back or side or front. I was simply there, trying to scream and breathe and think, none of which felt possible. If ever I wanted to know what lying on the bottom of the ocean felt like, I was certain this moment was it.

Even the passage of time and light slowed, and the sounds became dull. It was as though I was hearing voices from underwater. Aside from the thump of my heart, no muscle would move. That pounding inside my chest beat to a rhythm that no doubt was the speed of the chant used to execute the woman. I could almost hear it in the back of my mind. Her mutilated body and soul were left to the judge and jury from hell. The slashes that dragged down the front of her, as if she were nothing, just meat, blood and bones, were done when she was alive. There was too much blood for her to have been dead. The screams that echoed for only me to hear told me she had been just that—alive and fighting to remain that way.

The force of her leaving soul had propelled me backward. Her soul grazed mine in that fraction of a second as she left her tomb. But in that blink of time, I felt hell…evil, with a capital 'E.' It was the only word I had to describe the wash of black energy and pain coating her life force. Behind her soul came the flow of hate. It was pure evil on the heels of a broken soul. She had fed gods, but not all of her was choked down. Her soul hadn't given up and held on until the bitter end, feeling it all. But even in the worst of the pain and terror, staring hell right in the eyes, she held on and endured. I couldn't help but to both pity her and feel proud. I sent up a prayer for her soul. For that reason alone, I'd endure to catch those responsible.

"Ailis!" Miguel's words came through like a verbal slap. He was screaming my name over and over, shaking my shoulders.

I opened my eyes wide and clawed my way up his arm until I stood without the risk of blacking out. "Get me the hell out of here, Miguel. Now. Get me *out*! I want out, *now*!"

He led me on shaky legs, up the stairs and into the open. The air felt cold, unlike the furnace we had just stood in. The sun had set while I had stared at evil in a hole in the ground, and my usual anxiety from the night was nothing compared to the cenote. Nothing outside, in the dark, would scare me as much as what I had found below. Hell could open up, and I'd welcome the diversion. I had never felt a trapped and butchered soul before. I had felt souls move onto the next life, but they weren't tormented and half consumed. This soul had been barred in the circle, held there by her own death. And whatever the witches had summoned was eating the victim while we stood there. She suffered twice, once in life and once in death. While we poked around, she fought tooth and nail for her soul.

The rage was starting in the pit of my stomach, clearing away the fear. I paced, unable to put two words together while the anger rode me like I was its bitch. The stench of blood and sulfur clung to me. There wouldn't be enough showers or spa days in the world to wash the smell from deep within. Miguel had been right. The smell would never leave. My mind kept wandering back to the blood on the walls, the stones, the floor. I knew, without a doubt, this was not the first kill and wouldn't be the last. As horrendous as it was, for what was done to the poor woman, the scene was far too neat for it to be the first time. And with the soul now gone, they would try again. I didn't know if I was happy the soul was released or regretful that we would cause another sacrifice for having let it go. Had we put another soul on the chopping block in place of hers?

I stopped a few times in front of Miguel, only to shake my head and pace again. Every day I am reminded that hell isn't nearly as bad as what walked the earth. *Certifiable crazies.* Hell was creative and horrific, but you expected it. You counted on it. No one ever wakes up in hell, outraged at what was being done to them. No. You wake up knowing full well what it was all about. But here, with people who still had souls, no one thinks they could be the bigger monster. People, by far, out-demoned the demons. Mankind could teach the monsters a few things.

"Do you know what could have done this?" Miguel asked after I threw up twice, cleaned my mouth and shook my head at his question, showing I was coming back to myself.

"I don't know who could have trapped a soul like this. It looks like the workings of witches, but the kind of power needed for this? I've never heard of Mexico hosting witches of that caliber. The Coven would never allow powers like this to go unchecked. Witches of this black of magic would have been hunted down and burned by our council. I would have heard about dark arts witches in Mexico long before I got off that plane, and I wouldn't have come. I'd have waited it out and allowed the Coven to solve this for you." I squeezed my eyes closed and tried to will away the memory of what I had seen.

"If not witches, who?" he asked.

"I don't know, Miguel. Not even hell has that kind of power, and upstairs doesn't do this crap. Not even a rogue would attempt this. Whatever it is, we're looking for someone damn powerful," I replied. "We're in the market for something that can bind a soul, allowing it to be eaten like a buffet...slow and steady. No demon can do that, not without a pre-existing deal. Even then, they'd just take the soul. There's no point to what we saw, not for the usual suspects."

"What or who can bind a soul?" he asked. "Could a demon find a witch to make the circle for them?"

"Sure. Then what? Even if a witch made the circle, demons don't hold souls in them. They drag them to hell. Poof. Game over. But to hold or trap one for hours? The only thing that comes to mind, who could do this, is a hellhound. They have the ability to hold a soul for as long as they want, but this?" I motioned to the cenote and shook my head. "There's nothing in the literature that says a hellhound would do something like this, torturing a soul on this side of hell. They simply don't care for such things."

"So, we're looking for a hellhound?" The look he gave me told me I was thinking a little too far outside the box. This would be the first time in recorded history a hellhound did the bidding of another. They are as neutral as it gets in hell. Their main purpose is to guard the entrance to hell and bring damned souls to their fate. They weren't known for dabbling in dark arts or hanging out in tourist traps.

"I don't think so. I didn't see any signs of hellfire or burned tissue. I didn't feel one, either. I'm merely saying that hellhounds are the only ones that I know of...yet," I answered. "Having said that, the attack on her body, if I didn't know any better, I'd say it was a hellhound that clawed her up. It isn't clean like a knife would be. But it looks like an animal attack, only neater.

I've only seen this a handful of times in my entire life. And each time, the person had sold their soul to the devil. A devil doesn't collect his property personally. Hell-bound souls are collected by hellhounds. But a witch can't summon one. No one can. Not even a devil can. They come to collect because it's their job to fetch. Nothing short of another hellhound can call on another. But it's something like it."

"Do you think there's a rogue hellhound or similar loosed in Mexico?" Miguel asked.

I shook my head. "Have you felt one? I haven't. They wouldn't go unnoticed by those of us who sense powers like that. I was scared going down into the cenote, but it was a mixture of dread, small spaces and not wanting to see a butchered woman. But I wasn't hellhound-level terrified. When I was vacationing in hell, I felt them. I heard them. I think we'd notice — at least I would — if one was near. A few years ago, when I consulted on a crime scene, it had been a hellhound collecting. The scene was a week old and up in the mountains. The residual energy made me sick. Hell, it made those who didn't even have abilities sick. We couldn't get dogs to track a damn thing. They were scared nearly to death. These are dogs that'll track a demon, and they wouldn't get out of the truck. And that body was in worse condition, torn to bits. Claw marks ripped down his front and back. But this, the body down there, was methodical. The cuts were for a purpose."

"Good point. If it's not heaven or hell, what else could have done this, then?" Miguel asked.

With that one question, I felt the pressure starting to build of needing to solve this, but I didn't have the answers he had hoped I'd show up with. I don't know what he had expected? For me to waltz in and know instantly? I wish it were that easy. But nothing on this side of the gates was that simple, especially when it came to demons and devils. It once took me three weeks to identify a fairy as being the culprit in a crime, and that crime was cut and dry. What had happened below was far from that.

"I don't know, Miguel. That's the truth. I'm not a detective or a cop. I don't look at this stuff the same way as you. This isn't my area. I'm a bookworm." I sighed and rubbed my eyes. Dried-up tears made each blink feel like dust under my lids. "I'm too young to be stained with this many memories that I didn't create."

"I didn't call you because you thought like a cop. I called you because you don't. You're here because you know hell, and this"—he pointed toward to the cavern—"is pure evil."

"Yeah, evil... That's exactly what I was thinking. There's a lot of lore I'd have to pick through to come up with a stab in the dark for you. But that's all it will be...a wild guess. This just isn't in any textbooks I've read. This doesn't happen. Demons are summoned for a reason, however big or small that reason. But whatever they were summoning didn't come. We'd have known if hellspawn had touched those walls. But they're feeding whatever it is, power—broken souls. When it finally makes its appearance, a lot of people are going to die. Whoever is doing this will never contain it. I know that much. I can feel the building power. I can feel the threat. It feels like the moment the sun finally loses its fight with the night."

"Could you contain it?" Miguel asked with a thread of hope in his voice.

"Usually, it would depend on what it is that needed to be contained, but I wouldn't count on it this time. I simply don't know enough about the demon being fed or who is tempting the fates with dark arts. To be honest, I wouldn't even try. Whatever is trying to get out of hell feels far more powerful than even I would attempt to control. I'd run, just like everyone else," I replied, dashing his thread of hope.

"Have you ever summoned something this powerful?"

The question surprised me. "Just because I'm a witch doesn't mean I poke around where my nose doesn't belong. You should know better than anyone. I don't screw around with hell. I don't summon things, Miguel. I've never tried. I don't need the damage to my aura and don't need any more taint on my soul. Summoning comes with the highest cost. It stains your soul. Enough stain on the soul, and it dies. And there you have it, a witch without a soul. You can't walk around without a soul and not be one of the monsters. It's a painful death that I wouldn't wish on anyone. The soul literally shrivels up and dies. You end up with a demon walking on this side of the crust."

"So, we'll be dealing with not only a loose monster but a once-human sociopathic demon?"

"All demons were once human beings with souls. You know that. But yeah, that pretty much sums it up. I don't know who will have the higher body count — the monster being called or the brand-spanking new demon without a devil to reel it in. Demons are lower-level and answer to the devils, the real horrors of hell. Without a leash, it would be hell on earth until it was banished to the pits," I glanced around the parking lot. The unease made it hard to remain in one place. The power in the earth gnawed at my bones and turned my stomach. It felt like I was waiting for something big to happen. The anticipation coated my skin with a clammy sweat. "Miguel, there's too much power here for one body, one soul."

He nodded. "I don't have your abilities, but I can feel it, like the panic of being late or needing to do something. Standing around makes it worse. It feels like we're walking over a grave."

I paused at his comment and wondered if Miguel were sensitive to spirits. In all the years I had known him, he hadn't ever mentioned it, so I let it go. If he wanted me to know, I would. "That's a good analogy. When the Spanish conquered, they brought smallpox, measles and influenza. Together with what the demons unleashed on them, typhus and yellow fever, the death toll was massive. The Aztecs or Maya people were using the cenote to send their loved ones to heaven, making this a mass grave. There's power in death, even old death. The fresh body only added to it."

"From the way you're looking into the trees, that's not what you're thinking this is, is it?" Miguel asked.

I shook my head. "This wasn't the first body to hit the ground here, Miguel. It's just the first one you've found."

"The cenote was closed over the holidays for two weeks," Miguel replied. "Do you really think this isn't the first one?"

"That's exactly what I think. I'd bet the lab will come back with multiple samples, and they'll match the others who are missing or those not yet reported." I rubbed my temples. Between lack of sleep, anxiety and whatever power rolled through the air, my head was pounding. "Whatever it is, the demon who fed, it's still hungry. I can feel it in my gut. This isn't over."

"I don't believe in demons," came from the peanut gallery. A police officer of maybe thirty stepped forward. His name tag said 'Martínez'.

I glanced at the cross around his neck and fought to call him a hypocrite. You can't believe in one and not the other. That's like saying you believe in the sun but not the moon, even though it popped up every night. "You don't need to, Martínez. They believe enough for you both."

"You're saying that some fallen angel did this?" Martínez asked.

"No, not exactly. A fallen or higher devil wouldn't bother with trivial games like this. They would simply kill everyone. The games they play end in new diseases, plagues starting in the fields of an elementary school and movements like anti-vaccinations and science deniers. Who do you think rekindled the flat-earth movement? Devils kill in masses, not in singles. But a demon? Oh yes, they revel in chaos, big and small."

Martínez paused. He looked confused. I wouldn't needle him. All his learnings were from a time when no one truly believed in demons and devils. The church was great at making threats but never telling the truth. "What's the difference between a demon and devil, higher and lower?"

"In some religions and cultures, a devil started as an angel who lost his grace, falling from heaven and God. They became devils once they were tossed out of heaven. Some religions say three angels fell, some say two hundred, and some say three-quarters of angels were thrown from heaven. The main difference is that a demon started as a human being and not an angel.

They were people once—humans, for better or worse. After years, decades, centuries in hell, their humanity has been shaved away, leaving nothing but hell wrapped up in a meat suit made of man. They have forgotten what it means to be human. It's like any other bad situation. You become what you need to become to survive the hell you're in."

"You don't know what you're talking about. Hell can't turn someone bad. You have to decide to be bad. Hell doesn't take innocent or good people." Martínez didn't bother holding back his contempt for me with a glare that said I was beneath him.

"Don't bet the farm on that one. Sometimes good people do bad things, but it doesn't make them bad. And sometimes, good people just get the shitty end of the stick when it comes to judgment day. Suicides go to hell. Are you saying that people who are so broken by society that they end their suffering in the only ways left deserve to rot in hell? It is a sin to fornicate, to be gay, profanity, idolatry, a man wearing a dress. The list is endless and just as goddamned ridiculous. Do they deserve to be dragged into hell?" I asked, and he didn't answer. No one ever had an answer. "No, I didn't think so. Not all who walk the road to hell deserve to be cast into the pits. Now imagine what hundreds of years of torture does to a soul, especially one that was never evil. Don't think for one minute that a person wouldn't give anything to make it stop. Sure, a human can decide to be bad and eventually become evil. But in hell, they don't give a shit what you want to be or the choices you want to make. Hell is simply hell, and it doesn't care what you want. It takes everything you were and eats it away. Once you're down there, it changes you. Not every demon decided to be the way they are."

"It sounds like you're defending demons. Is that why you're here? To protect demons?" Martínez asked.

I could feel myself getting angry. I was tired of having to explain myself. I was tired of fighting with those who cared not to learn the truth. "No. I'm stating the facts. As much as we want to believe differently, humanity isn't infinite. There isn't an endless supply of strength for them to draw on in hell. There is no sense of community or love or compassion. There's just more pain, more hate, more evil, more horror. Eventually, it carves away everything, quite literally, and every single person will break under those conditions. Spend enough time in hell, and you do what you need to do to survive, even if it means you become a monster yourself. They always do. For some, it just takes time, but there's nothing but time there, and time means nothing there. But the soul feels every tick of the clock like lifetimes lived. Seconds feel like decades. The soul can only take so much. Eventually, it burns away."

Everyone breaks. I broke. Each time they put me back together, I'd split in half again. It didn't take long. I pretty much walked in there a broken soul to begin with. I didn't like to admit it out loud, but I'd begged all the way there. I cried for so long that I had no tears left, just the shaking hiccups of fear. I kept thinking that they'd let me go. After what felt like years to the damned, mere seconds to the living, I gave up. Hell is nothing like what a sane mind can imagine. Then again, people generally do not feel pain like that and live to tell others. My grandmother had taught me everything I knew up until that point and did her best to tell me the truth about hell. But her words would never come close to the reality of it. Nothing on this side of the gate could possibly come close to an ounce of what hell can deliver.

The truth was, hell is everything you think it isn't and more than what you think it is. Heaven and hell have the same gift, a perfect view into your soul, every action, good or bad, every tear shed and wish cast. Only, in hell, you live the horrible parts over and over. When I was told I could leave, I didn't believe them. They had to yank me out of my cell, kicking and screaming. They dragged me all the way to the gates and tossed me out, locking the door behind them. I tried getting back in if you could imagine. I tried climbing over and squeezing between the bars. I thought it was a test, a new torture, something other than what it was. Then I woke up with doctors working on restarting my heart. I lived lifetimes in under two minutes, and I stayed broken for years. To be honest, I'm still broken. Those two minutes made cracks in my soul that would never heal.

"Assuming you're right..." Martínez started and stopped when he saw me shaking my head.

"I wish I were wrong, Martínez, but I *am* right. That's not my ego talking. That's knowledge, experience and everything they've ever shown me." He looked like I'd just told him Santa wasn't real. I had no desire to soften the blow. That wasn't why I was called in. I came because of what I knew. "As I was saying, hell has a hierarchy, just like everything else does. For example, in the mortal undead world, Nosferatu, vampires, are at the top of the food chain. Below them are their servants, zombies and animated corpses. They each toe the line, just like demons do."

"I thought vampires were demons?" he asked. He looked from me to Miguel.

Miguel shrugged. "What I believed is not the same as what is true. I said they were as bad as demons, not that they were."

"They are just as bad," I agreed. "But they're not all demons. Some believe that vampires were cast out of heaven and banished to earth, cursed with bloodlust. Others say it's a curse. To tell you the truth, I've never asked one. They terrify me. They're one of the few creatures who don't follow the same rules as heaven and hell. Vampires are like devils in that they both share the same broken moral compass. I can see why there's confusion about what they actually are. The growing theory is that they are a curse from hell, and that curse spreads with their bite. But I'm not about to go ask one if it's true."

Martínez shook his head. "For someone who claims to be nothing more than a solitary witch, you sure know a lot about them."

"It's my job. I'd give anything not to know what I know. I pray you never need the kind of help I bring, that your life never depends on what I know. If ever you do, you're in deep and sinking," I replied.

He lifted his cross and kissed it. "I doubt I'll need someone like you."

"You're feeling unease. We all are. You think I'm an easy target to take it out on. I'm not. Go find a different dog to kick." My words were heated. It wasn't Martínez's fault, not entirely. Ignorance is bliss, and he was pretty damn blissful. I turned from him and started back to the Jeep. Miguel fell in beside me. "I need to speak to a guardian."

A guardian was someone who died in place of another—a sacrifice, such as saving the life of a child at the cost of their own. They are given a choice, upon death, to be a guardian, a caretaker of man, or they're given the option to ascend and suffer not another day. It's rare, but at times some guardians grow tired of all this shit and give up their positions as guardians to live and die as a human once again. It is considered a reward for their service and dedication, to be given life once more, a second chance around the block, but they often do not see it that way. It's a curse, more times than not, to be forced to do life all over again, after everything they have seen as a guardian. They go right back to the grind, aging, working, eating, sleeping, and for the most part, drinking themselves into an early grave with memories pouring them drink after drink. Their only solace is that they finally get to die. The only one I knew owned a bookstore on Main Street back home, a family friend. On the side, he fed me bits of information I needed when consulting or writing a lecture. During his hundreds of years as a guardian, he had either seen the monster firsthand, killed it or was there when the damned thing came to life. He was better than any book on the subject. There were things he wouldn't talk about or tell me. Nine times out of ten, when that happened, I didn't want anything to do with the monster in question. As I said, silence speaks volumes.

Chapter Five

Miguel and I drove to my hotel in absolute silence. There were no words of comfort. Nothing could be said to take away the disgust of what we had seen and felt. I got out of the Jeep and didn't look back. I didn't trust what Miguel would see in my eyes if I looked at him. I wanted closeness to chase away the horror and hell of the night, but my choices were limited to a man I didn't want to bind myself closer to, and I walked to my room alone. Miguel was also the only man I ever thought was worth the pain. Sometimes physical touch was worth the agony it caused when it was over. Yet, I walked into the hotel and checked in alone, dragging my luggage and emotional baggage behind me.

I didn't dare ask Miguel to come up to my room. I wasn't that brave anymore, not after today. I'd skinned my bravery off at the crime scene. I had once loved to touch him, not always in a sexual way but in a knowing way. I remembered every curve of his body, the way his muscles moved under my fingertips. How he'd sigh when I touched the right spots or groan when my hand left them. The problem was I couldn't just stop at running my hands through his hair. I would melt into his body like ice cream on a hot summer day, like my body belonged against his. I shook the idea from my head. Once the case was solved and we parted, I'd either crave him all over again or seeing him would be enough to get him out of my system. I had no faith in the ladder. I wasn't foolish enough to think I'd go home without a few new scars, physically and emotionally, but touching him would only make things all the more difficult in the end. It wasn't a coin toss. I knew seeing Miguel again would hurt. It didn't matter what side the coin landed on. Either side involved pain.

There weren't many things that were certain in life outside of it ending. Life could really hurt, no matter how hard you tried to protect yourself. Of that, I'm absolutely convinced. Everything that had once touched your soul always burned you in the end, until it ate up your heart, and you felt nothing again. Heartache doesn't go away, not entirely. A broken heart doesn't heal when there's still love inside it. It's worse when you tried to stuff it down, and I'm a stuffer. Ignore it enough, and it goes away. *Uh-huh. And all love is blissful, and monsters are just misunderstood.* As children, we're never taught the truth of growing up. We were too busy learning the recorder. That has come in really handy in adult life. I've lost count of the times I've resolved a difficult situation with a quick blast of *Three Blind Mice*.

I left Miguel to his thoughts and wrapped my arms around my own silent whispers, lugging them into the hotel with me. The resort staff carried my luggage and helped me check in. The hotel's beauty was tainted by my mood. The only thing I remembered from the lobby was the red poinsettias, the color of blood. Once in my room, the first thing I did was hang a witch's ladder on the door and one on the sliders to my balcony. It was nothing more than a humble piece of string, tied into knots woven with my hair and blood, before a full moon. Each knot held a powerful spell of protection. It was sealed with a drop of life, my blood. Sure, it wasn't going to do anything for my bad dreams or a higher-level hellspawn, but those weren't my main concerns. The lower-level demons were the ones who tormented me when given a chance. The higher-level would just kill me and toy with me in hell. I could hang a witch's ladder made of rope, dripping in blood from twenty virgins, and they'd use that rope to drag me into hell with.

"Ailis," Miguel called from my door, and three sharp knocks followed. I opened the door, prepared for another showdown. It's what we did…beat a dead horse until we got it out of our system. I stepped to the side and let him in. He looked through his lashes, and my heart jumped into my throat.

"Miguel." It was the only word I could get out. My throat felt tight and dry.

He didn't rage, but there was heat. He towered over me, an inch between our bodies. He hadn't touched me, but I felt him on every inch of my skin. "Tell me to leave, and I'll go."

I froze like a deer in the headlights and said nothing. He closed his eyes and nodded. When he reached for the door, I grabbed his hand and pulled it away. "Don't go."

That was all it took. His movements were sudden. He grabbed my waist and pulled me against him. His lips were rough and soft at once, starved yet gentle. I grabbed his hair and pulled his mouth tight against mine. My body melted into his as it had so many times before. The soul never forgets, and it felt like not a day had passed between us. He pushed me into the wall, holding both my arms over my head with one hand. With my head to the side, he kissed my neck while he pushed my shirt up to expose my stomach and breasts with his other hand. He kneaded my breasts until my silence finally broke and I moaned. When my legs felt like they couldn't keep me upright, he held me against the wall with his body. The heat between us had always been there, and not even the passage of time dulled the fire. When my legs felt like they couldn't keep me upright, he held me against the wall with his body.

"Tell me to stop." Miguel's words were hot against my neck. "One word, and I'll stop."

"Don't stop," I answered.

He lifted me onto his hips and wrapped my legs around him. I locked my ankles and pulled at his shirt. He yanked his shirt from his jeans and over his head. I mirrored his movements and pulled my top off. My skin, clammy from the heat, burned under his touch. He slid his fingers under my bra to the back, and it fell to the floor at our feet. Miguel led us to the bed with my pulse hammering in my ears. I held on to his shoulders and kissed him as if tonight was my last night on this earth. He inched down the bed, pulled at my pants until they landed on the floor and crawled up my naked body. My breath caught in my throat when his mouth grazed my thighs. My back arched. My nerve ends were on fire. This moment, trapped under him, washed away the horror in my mind.

"Please," I moaned and propped myself up on my elbows to watch him. "I need to feel anything other than horror."

I caught a reflection of us in the mirror on the wall, at the foot of the bed. I watched him struggle out of his pants. Before I could offer help, he closed his mouth around my core. My elbows gave out and I fell to my back, squirming under the pleasure and excitement of it all. I gripped his hair and held on. It felt like I was about to fall off the world. He rolled his eyes up to meet mine. There were no words to describe his hunger, his need. The uncertainty I had seen in his eyes earlier today was gone. This was more than sex. It was as it always was with him.

Miguel was the type who took his time, drawing out every sensation. Tonight, though, his mouth was almost frantic as he pressed his lips into every inch of me, sucking me into his mouth. He pressed my thighs wide and ate down my begging need for release. Lost to immediate pleasure, my back hit the mattress, he pushed his fingers inside me, and my moan filled the room. Miguel drank down my orgasm as it broke free in squirming delight. My body came alive, filled with burning, twitching pleasure, and I moaned his name in one long shuttered breath.

He climbed his tanned, muscled body up my front until I felt him press against my still-pulsing entrance. He perched himself up over my body. His body flexed, posed and ready. He was always ready for love or war. With us, it could have been either or both. But the feel of his fingers along my skin made me willing to call a ceasefire for now. I reached for him and wrapped my hands around his hard sex. I squeezed him until he shuddered against me. I could feel his pulse in my grasp. His elbows threatened to unlock and send him onto me.

"Do you have protection?" I asked.

He shook his head. "This isn't about me, tonight. We don't need any."

He let himself fall, only stopping once his chest touched mine. His hardness pressed against my stomach, and I writhed for more. His mouth lingered on mine, while he danced his hand down the front of my body. Miguel kissed my neck and shoulders, grazing his fingers ever so slightly down my side. The tickle sent my hips into his and his readiness. He nipped and licked my neck as I squirmed against him. He slid his hand slowly over my hip, to my thighs, teasing strokes until his hand met my open legs. He held me with his arm around my shoulders and pulled me tight to his body. My core burned for his touch. I closed my eyes and arched the places he touched. The feel of his fingers along my skin made my body tighten. When he finally found my most sensitive places, my toes curled, and I sighed a muddled plea. I pressed my hips against his hand, a silent demand for the release.

I moaned my response, half wordless and half nonsensical. The sensation built until it was all-consuming. I moved my hips faster, willing him to bring me closer to that edge of pleasure that would shatter the night. I dug my nails into his back and dragged them down his flesh. I groaned into his mouth as I came undone. My climax tore through me like a storm, and I bucked against him.

Miguel dragged his pants to the bed and pulled a condom out. He grinned. "I know, presumptuous."

"I thought this night was about me?" I teased.

"Fuck it," he answered and pulled me onto his hips with me above him.

I straddled his hips. He felt larger in this position. Although, in any position he was a fairly large man.

Miguel rolled my nipples between his fingers, just enough to be on the good side of pain. I felt full, and it was exactly what I wanted, what my body needed, him under me, grinding against me. I moved in slow, deliberate circles. He grabbed onto my hips and moved against me. Just as I began to pick up my pace, he spun us in one fluid motion, me on my back and him above.

He kept himself up with his arms and watched my body beneath him. He pushed himself so incredibly deep that wave after wave of desire rocked us both. My groans edged on desperation, and I gripped his skin with my nails, pleading for more. Miguel pushed and pulled himself from my body, gripping my hip until all I could hear were the sounds of our flesh joining. I moved against him, begging him to push deeper, harder. He lifted my thighs around his waist and claimed me—hard, fast, unyielding. I locked my legs around him as he pushed deeper and deeper until I could hardly breathe. No thoughts beyond this moment could break through.

He pulled out just enough for me to feel empty and thrust himself back in, slowly, deliberately, teasingly. He positioned himself to watch my face. He had always loved to see my expression when I was lost to an orgasm. I shuddered when our eyes met. He pushed and pulled until he found the rhythm and spot within that made my heartbeat catch in my throat. With each stroke, I felt the distance between us close, and I held on to him as tightly as I could, if only for the night. I moved my body in time with his as we drew out the pleasure in each other.

Every inch of me burned for him as he moved harder and faster to my call of his name. As my pleasure built, he knelt and lifted my legs higher to deepen his plunge.

I watched as he lost himself in the moment, letting the darkness of what we had seen seep out of him. Miguel pulled my body to meet his with each thrust until I felt nothing but ecstasy.

"Together," Miguel commanded from above me.

My pleasure burst from within me and mixed with his. He roared my name, pushing himself as deep as he could go. The bed shook under the force of us both. Yet, he didn't stop. He whispered my name and kissed away the parts of me that were still tainted from the night. As the orgasm built, he pulled me against him and worked me until I was nothing but pleasure. His body tightened. Between the sounds of skin on skin and my name on his lips, the world fell silent around us. I opened my eyes, and for the briefest of moments, I saw the Miguel I remembered, the man I loved and I had to look away. He collapsed on top of me, his heart pounding against my chest like a scared rabbit.

With my toes curled, I waved the white flag. The world went silent around us. He tucked himself behind me, and his heart thumped against my back in tune with my own. My pulse hammered but for different reasons. I knew what was coming next. Regret. I just didn't know who would have more of it...him or me.

Miguel inched to the foot of the bed and, without a lingering thought, grabbed his clothes and dressed. "This doesn't change anything, does it?" He didn't stop dressing. He knew the answer.

"No, Miguel, it doesn't," I told him. "There are too many things still left unsaid."

"I didn't think it would. But now you'll be able to focus on the case and not jumping my bones." He tried to make it sound like friendly banter, but his voice was empty of emotion, and his words fell flat. He could have been talking about the weather.

"Do I say thank you or kick you out?" I asked.

He smiled. "Neither. I'm leaving."

"Rest easy. I'm sure we'll go back to cutting each other up tomorrow." I sat up and grabbed my housecoat. I didn't feel comfortable heading for an argument while I was nude. There was something vulnerable about being naked.

"We chased away the monsters for tonight, thank you." He pulled on his shoes and headed for the door. "Until we bleed again, good night."

I threw a pillow at his back as he walked out. "Bastard."

Miguel left me alone with my thoughts, my emotional baggage and knives, and a head full of crime-scene memories. They were better than thinking about him and his body against mine. Should I be angry about what just happened or relieved that I wouldn't be consumed by the thought of it? I didn't know the answer to that. Miguel was a diversion. A good one, but it complicated things. I couldn't jump on his lap every time I got overwhelmed while I was here, or I'd never get out of bed. It was time to face the music. I was here for only one reason—murder, not sex.

Room service came and went with me plunked like a rock on the edge of my bed. I stared at nothing. I was numb. I was angry. I was scared of what would come next. All three emotions cycled. I ran my hand back and forth over my brow, feeling the screws that held a titanium plate in place. The only physical scar on my body from the car accident that landed me in Hotel Fire and Brimstone. I wasn't wearing my seatbelt and was thrown into the dash and window. My face was a mess, and I'd shattered my skull. I was told we'd been doing fifty over the limit and had wrapped ourselves around a telephone pole, narrowly missing a father and son driving to the pharmacy for cold medication. After I was stabilized in the hospital, neurology and a plastic surgeon reconstructed my forehead. Whenever I'm thinking too hard, I touch the little screws just under the skin. It wasn't often that I noticed it until I had been doing it long enough for it to hurt.

I finally picked up my cell and called Samuel, a retired guardian back home. He would either calm me down or scare me into getting onto a plane and going home. I was hoping for the plane. Being at the resort didn't feel good anymore. The idea of being away from home made me feel out of place, out of sorts. Home was my sanctuary, my place of refuge. Here, in a strange room, an unfamiliar city, I felt exposed and defenseless. At least if I were at home, I wouldn't be screwing my once-enemy.

Samuel answered on the second ring. He always did. "Ailis, someone either died or you're about to, at this hour."

I smiled. "Sorry, Samuel. I wouldn't call you this late if it weren't important." I knew he'd be awake. The man rarely slept. If I thought my dreams were bad, one stroll through his graveyard of horror would have left me unwilling to sleep myself.

"I know. Don't you worry about me. I was still awake. What's gone wrong?" he asked. His voice was soft and comforting. It always had been. It felt like the hug I needed. I told him everything and spared no details, not even the embarrassing part when I puked twice or how hurt I still was with Miguel. "Well, you've got me stumped, and that's rare. More bodies will fall before you have your answers — of that, I'm sure. If you think the wounds are from an animal, it probably was...or at least is involved somehow. Whatever you're hunting, it is tied to the ability to control a soul, tie it to a circle and feed it to hell. Ailis, you should not be involved with this. Your soul is already damaged. You cannot risk an attack on your soul from a power this great."

"What the hell can do this?" I pushed for more answers.

"You've answered your own questions, Ailis. Hell can do this. Whether we believe a demon can hold a circle or not, demons learn new skills every day. But demons being schooled on new talents is not the concerning part. Whatever mankind knows, you best bet hell knows — or is soon to find out. What concerns me most is that souls are being bound after death, and no demon can do that, no matter what new trickery they learn," he answered. "You need to learn to trust your gut. You have a sixth sense. Trust it. In my experience, if it feels evil, it is. If you feel witch work, they're involved. If you can feel hell, they've touched ground."

"Why bother with the song and dance? I mean, it's a waste of time for hell to toy with souls like this."

"Have you thought that this may not be hell doing this but someone trying to bring hell out? Drawing them out with a slow-burn soul?" Samuel asked. "Most demons and devils down there can't come out on their own. They must be summoned — and at great cost."

"Who are they trying to bust out? Lucifer himself?" I asked.

Samuel chuckled. "It would take the will of God himself to break him out."

"Any god or just Him?" I asked.

"Him. But I think you're on the right path," Samuel answered. "It would be someone mighty powerful if they're butchering countless innocents to feed it. And something of this power would need an awful lot of souls if one or two hasn't done the trick."

I pursed my lips in thought. "Who the hell are they trying to break out? Who would need this many souls for a day pass?"

"Of that, I'm not certain, but whichever demon it is, it's not worth sticking around to find out," he replied. "Those you're hunting are dabbling in arts far darker than midnight. You're dealing with powers that have been lost for hundreds of years, Ailis."

"Lost for hundreds of years? What was it?" I asked.

"These are secrets that are not mine to tell, for the safety of both you and I." Samuel's voice grew quieter as if he were willing the darkness away from his voice.

"Bullshit, Samuel. That's crap, and you know it. Why are you scared to talk to me about this?"

"Because I want us both to live until the end of our naturally given days, Ailis. It is not crap. It is common sense. There is knowledge out there, young child, that not even I wish to have. Not everything is worth knowing."

"Speak for yourself," I countered.

"I am, which is why I know you will do as you usually do, jump in, head first, without looking or asking how deep it is and smash your head on every rock on your way down." His words came out in a long sigh.

"I always swim back to shore on my own," I said as a tease.

"One day, you will not have any bloody arms left to swim with." He raised his voice just enough to get his concern across.

I smiled, even though he couldn't see it. That was Samuel. We had a lot in common. You couldn't push us to do anything we didn't want to do or keep us from that which we definitely shouldn't be doing. Stubborn to a fault. "If you hear of anything else, let me know?"

"There will be more bodies, if not already," he replied. "Check other holy sites. I doubt this is the first body, and it won't be the last. There aren't many outcomes when you play with hellfire. They'll either succeed and raise the demon, they'll be killed by whatever comes out or they'll be stopped before then. Either way, a lot more people are going to die. If they're using souls to feed a beast from hell, it's going to take a lot of souls to accomplish what they've set out to do."

"Thanks, Samuel." I am always thankful for his help, even if the lack of information irritated me like a swimmer's itch. "Are you feeding my cat?"

He sighed and let me change the subject. After the horror, I craved a conversation that didn't further stain my sanity. "Of course. Have I ever *not* fed your cat?"

"No. Sorry. I just don't like leaving the little monster for so long. I've never seen it catch a mouse or even a fly. I don't want it to starve because I'm away."

"It's a cat. It's not going to starve." He laughed. "You know, you should really name your familiar. It's rude to not show it more respect, like a name."

"It's *not* my familiar." I prepared for another argument about all witches needing to have a familiar. It was a pressure point between Samuel and me—me being the one who fought against it. "That thing hates me, Samuel. I think it only sticks around because I feed it."

"A familiar will match with a witch of similar character. You and your cat are the same in disposition and attitude. You both are hateful little creatures." Samuel made a good point.

"Its name, if you need to know, is Cat," I replied.

"You still don't know if it's a boy or girl?" Samuel laughed again.

"No. It won't let me look. Why? Is it important?" I asked.

I didn't need to see his face to know he was smiling. "No. I suppose not."

"Well then, the name is 'Cat', and it's *not* my familiar."

"I beg to differ. You fight against the truth. Having a familiar doesn't make you a dark witch. Having a tighter bond will strengthen your damaged aura," he responded. I had once argued that only the dark witches needed a familiar to weld their spells. He hadn't let me get in another word. He knew I'd only argue. I always did. "When I went over yesterday to feed it, it was already inside, sleeping on the couch. When I went back today, Cat was sitting on the top of your bookshelves, watching me."

"I didn't know it came inside when I wasn't there," I mumbled. "How the hell is it getting inside?"

"I don't know. When I left yesterday, I put it outside. I thought, maybe, you had accidentally left it inside. But today, it was back inside. So, I tested a theory."

"Don't you dare touch my damn cat, Samuel!" I snapped. I didn't know where the instant anger came from. It may not be *my* cat, but it was my cat. It was independent and owned by no one. Just like me. It doesn't have to make sense for it to be the truth.

"You see, you're bonded with the little spitfire."

"What did you do, Samuel?" I asked. If I could have, I'd have strangled him through the phone. Well, if I was willing to take the stain on my soul, I could have. I wasn't. Not yet. Not until I knew what he did to Cat.

"I didn't touch it. When I went in today, I went near your picture window. Cat was just suddenly there, hissing at me. The closer I got to the window, the angrier Cat became. I backed off and tried for your bedroom. The damn thing attacked me." His voice was on the edge of laughter. "The window, I get. Cat was abused there when you had a break-and-enter a while back. It could just be a sore spot for the little beast. But your bedroom? The only place in your home where you feel safest. It is where you keep your altar. It is the only room that is untouched by the outside world."

A few years back, religious nuts had broken in and spray-painted my living room. They had painted slurs on my picture window. Every time I looked at it, I felt violated all over again. Cat had played victim that night. They'd tied it up and tried to burn it alive with gasoline. The intruders should have died for it, but I couldn't make myself kill them. I was pretty damn close to it, though. They were ignorant but hadn't done anything to deserve death. Now, had they killed my cat, I'd be talking to Samuel from prison.

"Once I stopped testing Cat, it darted away. But each time I tried to open the wrong cabinet in your kitchen, I'd hear it hiss from the other room. You may not want to call it a familiar. That's just fine by me. But it showed up when you sent out a call for help after you left Miguel. A cat, exactly like you, showed up the night your heart broke, and it calmed your raging spirit. You don't see the importance of this?" Samuel sighed a long breath when I didn't answer. "Bond with Cat. It'll guide you. It's why it came. If you don't, it will never be what it was meant to be. You will extinguish the light within it."

"Some good it did when my home was burglarized. Aren't they supposed to protect my home when I'm gone? Isn't that what they do?" I asked.

"It's not a guard dog, Ailis. It protects you, not your property. Get a damn dog if you're so worried about your house. The cat is a young soul. It's learning, just like you are. Give it a chance, and it will come when you need him most. Trust in that."

"Aren't familiars supposed to be old souls sent to guide me? What kind of guidance could it give me if it's a fresh one off the line?" I asked. I had purposely stayed away from learning more about familiars. It had made me feel too weird, not normal—a reminder that I wasn't like everyone else. I didn't admit it out loud, but being an outcast, being hated for being a witch, had taken a toll on me. I didn't want to be any witchier than I already was.

"It kept the intruders contained. They didn't make it out of your living room, did they? If they could have harmed you, Cat would have fought to the end, just like you would have. It would have given all his life force to protect you. Do you really want your cat to die to keep some paint off your walls?"

"Well, no, I guess not."

"If it could have, would you have wanted Cat to kill them all to protect your precious window, when not even you were able to bring yourself to do it?" Samuel didn't wait for me to answer. We both knew I didn't want that. "It knew you would come and would save it."

The night of the break-in, I had felt anxious. I couldn't sit still. I left work, near tears and drove straight home. Although I had planned on grocery shopping before coming home, I didn't make a single stop and went straight there. When I got there, I could hear my cat howling mad. I didn't stop to think of why or what could cause such anger. I was in motion and through my front door before I had a second thought. I saw red the moment my eyes landed on my cat. The paint pissed me off. My home being violated angered me. But seeing my cat tied up and covered in gasoline with a lit match, I was boiling with rage.

"Just as you know, Ailis, deep down, it would save you. How many times have you woken to the sound of its hiss? A warning of passing demons. How many times have you curled in your bed crying, only to hear a faint purr? It is doing the best it can with a person who still chooses to deny all she is. If you will not bond with it and teach it how to become a stronger familiar, I offer my services. I will train your familiar since you are so determined not to."

I felt a stab of pain in my heart. The hint of losing my cat twisted my stomach. "I'll hurt you if you touch my cat, Samuel." The words were out of my mouth before I could close my lips. I winced at how rude I had been. I knew he wouldn't harm my cat. "I'm sorry, Samuel. I'm on edge. I didn't mean it."

"Yes, you did. I take no insult. I would expect nothing less. A bond with a familiar is stronger than the love of a partner. It is why we don't touch the familiars of others. To do so would be instant death. No threats. No warning. And no stain on the soul for the bringer of that death. It is not vengeance. It is expected and known. I would carry that stain for you since I'd be seen as causing my own death. Anyone who touches a familiar and dies for it goes to hell. It's seen as a suicide."

"Huh, that's news to me," I replied.

"Wars have been started for a lot less, Ailis." He was right. People killed each other over an inch of land and rocks. Why not for something that's actually important? "A cat, especially, is not to be trifled with. A cat is valuable, Ailis, over all other familiars. It visits places we cannot. It sees things we cannot. A cat can detect wavelengths of light that we're incapable of seeing. They can not only sense the energy, but they can also see spirits, elementals and so much more. A dog will guard you in the physical world, but you can guard yourself. A cat, though, will follow you into the very pits of hell and guard your very soul to the death of their own. A witch with a cat familiar has it pretty easy in the pits. Even hellhounds respect that bond until it is gone. It is why cats are so highly regarded as sacred, going all the way back to ancient Egypt."

"Thanks for the history lesson on cats, Samuel. Is there a reason for it?" I asked.

"Knowledge is power, Ailis. Some is worth having, while some is not worth the pain to obtain. Remember that, as you dig for information you should not have. Now it is late, and I'm out of lessons. I can't convince you to come home?" he asked, hopeful.

"No, I'm in this until the end. But I appreciate your concern," I replied.

"If you're not coming home, I'm glad Miguel is with you," he answered. "Like it or not, I trust he would go into hell for you or make them pay for taking you. A love like his doesn't ever die. It is in his nature to tie himself to only one, and it'll take death for those bonds to break."

I rolled my eyes but eventually smiled. "I know. That's what makes this so bloody hard. He and I are too much alike in that department. I feel like there never will be a day where I don't think about him."

"Take love when and where you can, Ailis. The world is too dark not to reach for the light at every chance. Trust me, stubborn witch. At the end of the day, it is love that keeps us from doing the unthinkable, to keep us from not waking up for another tomorrow." His sigh was long. This was a conversation he had tried to beat into my head for years. Love meant forgiveness and kindness and understanding. It kept you alive and *blah-blah-blah.* "But that is a conversation best left for days you don't feel wounded. I am here if you need to find a little light in the dark."

"Thank you, Samuel, for the talk and your love. You settle my soul," I replied.

"And you cause me heartburn," he answered with a chuckle. "Much love and peace to you tonight. Call me when you find another body—and you will. Perhaps the next scene will provide us with the clues needed."

"I will. Good night," I answered and hung up before he could push me about Miguel the same way I had tried with him, about the secrets I should not know. We'd go around in circles until the sun came up, which wasn't that bad of an idea, come to think of it. It would keep me too busy to fear the pressing night. He had done as he always did, calmed me before I closed my eyes. I knew Cat was a slight diversion from the horror of my day. I loved Samuel for that very reason. He knew my heart was hurting and offered his voice as a hug. Sometimes, when things are awful, a hug makes all the difference. Other times, a gun works just as good.

I left Miguel a voicemail telling him to start looking at holy sites for more bodies. They're either still there or about to be. I turned on all the lights, double-checked the doors and went to bed. My soul begged for the sun to rise, and I prayed I would live to see it. I cried myself to sleep, as I did every night. This time, I cried for the soul that had been skinned alive because I remembered the rawness of my own soul after less than two minutes. I hated remembering. I wouldn't admit that some of my tears were because of Miguel. Lies were only beautiful if you kept believing them. And I couldn't tell myself that I hated Miguel, not anymore. I merely wanted to because it would have been easier than admitting that I missed him as you would a limb.

Faintly, through the sound of the air conditioner and waves on the beach, I could hear the purrs of my cat. If I had been at home, Cat would be kneading my chest right now with purrs that would vibrate through my broken heart. I knew the dream coming would be brutal. I always heard the purring before the sleepless storm in my head. Knowledge wasn't just power. It was survival.

Chapter Six

I knew I was dreaming. I always did. I could feel the blankets over my body, even as I dreamed.

I stood in the living room of Miguel's house, back home in East Van. I could hear him call my name from bed. I closed my laptop and research. I always stayed up too late with my work unless I was reminded that I was a mere mortal and needed more sleep than the demons. I was of the mind that one more cup of coffee would do the trick, whereas Miguel knew sleep was the only solution for being tired.

Miguel was sprawled on the bed. No matter the time of year, his skin was tanned, and his body was a furnace. His all-white bedding made him look darker than he was. The end of the day, just before sleep took us, was my favorite time of day with him. He reached for me, and I froze. The memory was real. The excitement in my stomach matched the dream. We did make love that night. It was the last time our bodies had touched. I didn't know it then, but I would pack my things the next night while he was in the field, his hands covered in the blood of an innocent, and I would never return.

"I'm dreaming," I whispered. My smile was gone, replaced with a solemn frown. "I don't want this dream. I don't want to remember this."

Miguel dropped his hands and sat up. "I love you."

"I loved you more," I answered.

"Please, help us..." Miguel's words faded to nothing more than a whisper. "We need your help."

I nodded and turned from the bed. I moved away from Miguel and stepped through his doorway, only to stand in the cenotes. I would have no choice but allow my dream to play out. It went from a hurtful dream to an even worse memory. If I tried to fight it, the more horrible it would get. I stood there and let it cut me up, a technique I had learned from Samuel was to let the nightmare run its course. I let go of my desperation to wake up, to scream, to run and claw my way up the stairs. It didn't matter where I ran. I'd always end up where I was intended to be. I would see what I was meant to see. Even the scariest of dreams had some value — or so said Samuel. I allowed the horror show to take shape and play to the end, as he'd taught me. It was the only way to end them, to keep them from growing into a night terror. Losing the little bit of control I did have in a dream was worse than enduring it tenfold.

I focused on my surroundings and matched them up with what I knew to be true. I stood in the cenote. It didn't perfectly match what I had seen in real life. The light here was a little brighter than it had been in real life. It was colder than it should have been underground. The stone under my bare feet was bloodier. But it was the bare feet that told me I was still in the dream. I didn't go anywhere barefoot. More specifically, I wouldn't have arrived at a crime scene with naked toes.

A watery film coated my eyes. When I blinked away the tears, the dream changed. I was standing with my back against the stone, overlooking the scene. I was watching the *murder unravel. The victim had already been tied down. She was screaming, trashing in vain. I could feel her fear. To my right, she appeared. She grabbed onto my hand and watched with me. Her hand was cold, but I didn't pull away. Through her touch, I felt her pain and suffering. Around the circle stood seven witches, nude, save shoulder-to-toe red cloches. Seven, a powerful number. Seven virtues, seven sins, the seven sisters... I couldn't see their faces, no matter how hard I strained. I tried to step forward but couldn't move. At the foot of the circle sat a wolf. It stood, her body lengthening into a woman. When she stepped into the circle, her body changed again into something monstrous. She extended her arm, exposing claws and ripped them down the front of the soon-to-be dead woman. I screamed, echoing the victim in the circle. The dead woman holding my hand echoed me.*

The dream popped when she let go of my hand. I woke before I could see what happened next. That knowledge could have helped. Even awake, I could feel the presence of her in my hand. The chill still rested in my fingertips. I could hear my heavy breathing and pounding pulse in my ears. The sweat on my forehead was enough to fill a water bottle. The air conditioning was cranked, yet I was blistering hot. It was only a dream, but I could smell the cenote, the blood and the decay in the air. I'd never forget the mangled body or the smell of her rotting flesh — one more memory I shouldn't have, one more to add to the ever-growing list of reasons I'll end up in the looney bin before long. Yeah, we witches burn out quick for a reason.

My cell phone vibrated on the wooden nightstand, and I jumped. "Hello?"

"Ailis, we found another body." It was Miguel.

I closed my eyes. I had hoped Samuel was wrong. "Where?"

"Tulum ruins, Playa del Carmen."

"How long will it take you to get here?" I asked. I was already standing. I had gone to bed with the lights on but still squinted. Each blink felt like dragging sand across my eyeballs.

"I'm already in the lobby."

"I'll be down in a few." I hung up without saying more. I wondered, for the briefest moment, why he didn't just knock on my door. *Right...that's why.* The last time he did, we crawled into bed. Crimes needed solving, and the clues weren't on my body or his...although I was willing to take a closer look.

I looked at my watch. I had only been asleep for just over two hours. I grumbled to myself as I washed up and dressed. It was only midnight at home, which made it the middle of the night in Mexico, four hours until sunrise. Nothing good ever came from being awake at the witching hours. The jet lag sucked at me like a leech. Each time I sat to dress, I wanted to crawl back into bed. I had the endurance of a frat boy at a party, but even a frat boy knew when to call it a night and go to sleep. I could only burn this candle at both ends for so long. Eventually, whether I wanted to or not, my body would start shutting itself down. I'd start having problems with memory. My ability to carry a conversation would go next. I'd begin stumbling around and would get hurt. I knew my body well enough to know I needed a solid eight hours or I'd be in for some real pain. When I went too hard for too long, it made the nightmares worse. I wouldn't be able to focus or ground myself. It was then that I would have full-blown night terrors.

When I hit the lobby, my libido twitched at the sight of Miguel, and my face flushed. If he noticed, he didn't mention it. He passed me a coffee as he stood from one of the plush leather club chairs. I hadn't noticed them on my way in or the massive fountain in the middle of the room. "You look like hell, Ailis."

"I feel like it. Have you been to bed yet?" I asked. We both ignored the awkwardness between us now. I took a sip of coffee and instantly felt like life was somehow better. Coffee healed all wounds — or so that's what the sign over my coffeepot said. "Oh, this is good."

"Mexican coffee, it's the stuff made for gods. Cheers to a new day." He tapped his cup against mine. "Do I look like I've had any sleep?"

"No, but you've never needed much. Unlike you, I need more than a couple of hours a night."

"And miss all this?" He grinned. "Who needs sleep when we can stay awake and get front-row tickets to shiny new nightmares?"

I followed him to his Jeep. There was still a chill in the air, but I could feel the heat creeping in like a lover in the night. I hadn't bothered to check the weather app on my phone like I did every morning at home. It was going to be hot. Even if it rained, it would still be too hot for me. Why, you ask, did I choose the Riviera Maya for a vacation if I wasn't a fan of intense heat? All-inclusive, air conditioning, room service, no children, pools, spas, private six-foot soaker tubs on each balcony, a free minibar and buffets as far as the eye could see. I had initially planned on eating my weight in ice cream, not stomping through the jungle, mutilated bodies and brand-new bad dreams.

"You had asked me to speak to a few of the local professors, see if they knew anything about the significance of the sites or how the victim was killed." Miguel pulled onto the main road from the resort. The resort had stopped him on his way in and grilled him —

and did the same thing on the way out. They were armed and not concealed. It didn't make me feel safer. If something came after me or anyone else, the guns wouldn't even slow the monster down. If anything, what the guns did to the bystanders would be the garnish.

"Did they have anything we can use?" I asked. I was hopeful.

"Yes and no. They said pretty much the same thing as you did. The sites would be religious and ancient. They think whoever is doing this is tapping into the old energies stored in the land. No one knows what demon the sacrifice is being made to. There are just too many to name." Miguel had wasted his day on this pursuit. He dug around for information we already had. But it was better than not asking. I would have always wondered if we didn't check. "They said 'good luck', and most are now going on a holiday out of the country."

"Not very encouraging," I muttered.

"What about Mexican lore?" Miguel asked. "They said whatever boogey was out there could be connected to the land."

"I went through everything on my way here, Miguel. Sure, it could be something attached to the land, but it could also be something from the Arctic Circle, out on vacation." I answered back. I was tired and felt my words were snappier than usual. "Sorry. I didn't mean to be rude."

"You looked up Mexican lore?" he asked. He sounded surprised.

"Of course. Not just because you called me in but because I was coming here to vacation. I didn't want to holiday someplace where the risk to my life was higher than usual. I didn't want to pick a place that had a reoccurring demon problem. There aren't many places left on the map that are safe for me. It was here or someplace rainy, snowing or had a zero population. I won't lie, the zero population was very tempting, but then I'd have missed out on all this excitement. Nothing says vacation like fearing today will be my last day."

"Ailis, I wouldn't have called you in if I thought you'd be a target." It was his turn to sound snappy. Two tired, very stubborn people with an already strained history, locked in a fast-moving vehicle... Not a good recipe for healthy dialogue.

"Let's start over. I'll try to be nicer if you try," I suggested, and he nodded. "I looked at the lore before I came and again on the plane. I always do this before I leave home. I'm a target wherever I step out of my front door. It's no one's fault. For lack of a better term, I have a bounty on my head that'll never expire. That's just fact because of who I am. Maybe it's being a witch, or maybe it's because I'm dragging hell around in my aura. Whatever the case, I was either born with it, or I created it by making choices I shouldn't have made. That makes for an interesting life. Wherever I go, I'll have a price on my head. In some places, the trouble is bigger than it's worth...hence the research."

"I'm sorry you're hauling around hell with you." Miguel gave my hand a brief squeeze. He didn't linger. It was already awkward as all hell between us. "Did you come up with anything that could help us?"

I fought the urge to tell him I'd have brought that up already if I had something. I wasn't sitting on clues because he irritated me. I bit my tongue. I was, after all, trying to be nicer. "No, I didn't. There are a few ghosts and spirits that have lingered, but they can't do any harm. And even if they could somehow hurt a person, it doesn't fit the bill," I explained. "There's plenty of myths about ghosts harming people, but for the most part, they're only stories told to children, like your story of La Llorona. It's said she is a beautiful woman, scorned by her husband, and she drowned her two children. There are a few variations of the story, but it ends the same. By the time she realizes what she's done to her kids, it's too late. She's found, the next day, dead by the river. After that, her ghost can be seen crying as it roams the river in search of her children. But she apparently targets men and not young female women, and she doesn't gut any of them."

"I was told that story as a child. I've never seen her, and I even went looking for her. A lot of us kids did. It was sort of a thing we dared each other to do—camp by the river and call out her name...Maria." Miguel softly chuckled to himself, lost in fond memory.

"There's another story about Luz Mala. It's more a beam of light than anything else. It's said to show where the conquistadores buried the treasure of Atahualpa. Those who found the treasures died from poison. Whether it's true or not, this victim didn't die of poison, and there are no reports of weird lights. The victim was found by fluke, someone coming to check on the site before opening for the day. And she was mutilated, not poisoned." I shivered at my own memory. "There are literally thousands of stories, myths, demons and creatures connected to Mexico, but none of them match what happened in any way."

"So, we're back to square one?" Miguel asked, his face scrunched up in disappointment.

"Not square one, but we're not very much further," I replied. "Though, I did have an interesting dream that may provide a few more clues."

I told him about my dream, leaving out the parts of him being naked in his bed. Whether my dream held truth or not, it wouldn't hurt to share it. They weren't often wrong, but Miguel had no more answers than I did after hearing it. We already knew witches played a starring role in the show, and the wolf could simply represent a demon or another boogeyman. The bits of information from Samuel weren't a surprise to either of us, but I hadn't really called Samuel for information. I needed to touch home, even if it was through the phone.

I yawned a few times. My eyes were droopy. I was too exhausted to follow what Miguel was saying about the meaning of dreams in various religions. Jeeps are comfortable — the newer models, that is. The older ones felt like riding on the back of a four-wheeler on rough terrain. This morning, my seat felt as snug as my bed. I tried to keep my eyes open. I really did. I was just so relaxed that keeping my focus was bloody hard. Not but fifteen minutes into the drive, I didn't remember a word Miguel said. I was lost to fatigue. Soon, all I was aware of was the fuzziness of the trees along the roadside, passing too fast for me to see clearly. It reminded me of a painting caught in the rain, the colors melting off. The world was a blur, and I melted into my seat without a care and drifted in and out of consciousness.

Random images floated aimlessly around in the pool of my thoughts. Each time my thoughts became too dark, I'd jerk awake, bringing me momentarily back to the outside world. Seconds would pass, my pulse would slow back down, and I'd be out again. I could feel Miguel each time he looked at me. His eyes were heavy on my soul. Even with all the hurt inside me, I trusted him to keep me safe while I slept. He was one of the few I felt safe enough to close my eyes around while in a vehicle. It wasn't my job that put me in danger. It was that I was marked, for all times, as a VIP member of hell, because of a car wreck. That alone attracted a lot of evil, whether I went looking for it or not. But I trusted Miguel to keep the evil at bay long enough for me to wake up. To be honest, no matter how much we cut each other up, he'd never let anyone else cut me. I'd be lying if I didn't say the same for him. I'd never stand by and let someone hurt him. Only I got to make him bleed.

I woke from a dead sleep. My stomach was cramped from my ribs to my pelvis. It felt like a mix of an empty stomach, gut rot from too much coffee, seasickness and the worst period of my life. My last trip out of the country had resulted in an intestinal infection that knocked me on my back for over a week. *I have a soft spot for street food. What can I say?* But today, I couldn't afford traveler's diarrhea. It would put a crimp into my crime-solving schedule. Miguel chuckled to himself as I squirmed. I glanced at the clock. *One extra hour of sleep, hurray for me.* But I'd kill for eight. Since I wasn't about to stab Miguel for a nap, I watched the scenery breeze past us and came to terms with my sleep deprivation. I ate some Tums, and I held my stomach, praying it wouldn't get worse. I sent up a silent prayer that where we were going had a bathroom, just in case.

"I don't know how many times you need to get sick for you to stop drinking puddle water," Miguel teased. I let him. Laughter was the only thing that chased away the boogeyman. That, and a gun.

"I was smarter this time. Only bottled water and haven't really eaten a damn thing, let alone street meat," I replied. I tuned out his laughing and stared out of the window.

I had expected to see life outside or some sign of it. There were no vehicles on the road. No one biking to work. No one waiting for a bus. I didn't notice a single cow in the field beside us. No wildlife was sneaking around before the sun was fully lit in the sky. Not even the scavengers, who could be found everywhere, waiting on death, its greatest desire. Nothing was out here but us. I instantly wanted to turn around. If death wasn't there for the show, I damn well shouldn't be. It felt too dark, as if the sun had a choice and decided to snag the sleep I was missing out on. Perhaps it was my mood, my fatigue, but I didn't want to sit in darkness any longer. It didn't feel right. It was as if the cramping in my stomach didn't belong to me. It wasn't a sign I drank the wrong water. Something was out there in the abandoned hills surrounding us. Something was waiting. I was either too damn tired to be out here, or I was right. That was the most challenging part of my abilities. Sometimes I was right, and sometimes I was wrong. But I would bet the farm on me being right more times than not. The odd time I turned up craps, it was my own fear and anxiety that had been at fault, and I saw demons where there were ghosts. A demon could kill you. A ghost would just make you uncomfortable until they passed.

I was about to find out if I had a flush hand or not. "Can you pull over?"

Miguel looked at me and almost asked why. He thought better of it. I think he just didn't want me to puke all over his Jeep.

"I'm not feeling well, Miguel. I want to see if I'm going to have diarrhea all day or if there's a boogeyman out there." I groaned at the thought of either.

"I don't know which one you're hoping more for." He grinned but didn't argue.

"It feels almost like the first crime scene, only worse — stickier, like fresh cobwebs," I replied. "Can't you feel that?"

Miguel nodded. "Do you think there's another body out here?"

"Only one way to find out," I answered.

Miguel pulled over at the next exit. The road was bumpier than the last one we had been on. It reminded me of the road to the cenotes. He parked the Jeep next to a clearing, kicking up dust. I imagine the field was used for farming, but I didn't see any signs of cattle. I hadn't heard of any mass cattle deaths in Mexico, so they were either as uncomfortable as I was and stayed in for the night, or we were about to find a few toasted cows. In the distance, I could make out a smattering of houses, too far to see if anyone was awake. The land looked like it had seen better days, as if its luck had run out and the money dried up. It was the same story in many places around the world, including neighborhoods back home.

"It doesn't look like it's rained in years," I said. He followed me when I got out of the Jeep.

"It just rained, Ailis. Rain season for this past year started in May and didn't let up until November. The ground should be lush. Although we're in the peak of the dry season, we're standing in the middle of a rainforest. We still get a lot of tropical showers in this region that last for hours." Miguel explained. He crouched down and rubbed the dry husks of grass between his fingers. "It's like the life was drained out of it."

"My thoughts exactly. I'll track whatever power gobbled up acres of farmland. I'm sure we'll find a body at the end of the line," I replied. "Just give me a couple of minutes to find where it's coming from."

I walked a few feet up the road feeling anxious. I opened a hex bag and held it in the palm of my hand. If something came out of the shadows, my bag would either kill them or save me from that same fate. The dry grass grabbed at my legs like a dog begging for water. Once I couldn't feel Miguel or hear the ticking of a cooling vehicle engine, I stopped. I glanced back to Miguel. He was standing in front of the Jeep with his gun out. His Jericho 941, a semi-automatic pistol, was jet black, but I could still see it in the darkness. It glinted like the threat it was meant to be. My eyes were trained to look for weapons. Not every bad guy was a demon. Most of the bad guys I had run into were nutjob humans, and all of them had weapons. Call it paranoia or call it survival, but in my line of work, everyone was armed.

Miguel stood waiting for anything other than me to move. He didn't ask questions. He didn't interrupt. He knew what I was going to do better than anyone else would. He'd save the questions for later when we were safely tucked back inside his Jeep. It was a false safety. The vehicle wouldn't have stopped whatever I was feeling. We'd be nothing more than a tin of snacks waiting to be peeled open like a can of tuna.

I centered my thoughts and took in my surroundings. The sky was clear, and if it were any other day, I'd say the coming morning was beautiful. The stars were fading until they lived for another night.

The darkness fought to keep the day, but at the edge of the earth, the sun was fighting back. A shade lighter painted the edges of the hills. As much as I hated the night, it was comfortable knowing it was coming to an end and equally beautiful watching it lose its grip to the sun. I closed my eyes and breathed in the fresh warm air. My nerves settled, and all was well. Had it been all in my head? Had the body of the victim gotten to me? Was my dream still following me, haunting me? I almost turned and waved Miguel into the Jeep but stopped in my tracks. My nightmares didn't follow me around during my waking hours. My imagination doesn't make my stomach cramp or make me feel like I am going to vomit. Fear was a fickle thing, but it didn't make me feel something that wasn't already there, only exacerbated it. Sure, I had been wrong in the past about the evil being a demon, but I had always found something much worse at the end of the rope—a person as evil as a devil, a soul worth banishing to hell, a creature I've run from.

I turned back to what had been tugging at my core, making my stomach twist into pain that stole my breath. The vast emptiness of the road wasn't truly empty. There wasn't such a thing as complete emptiness, because there was darkness. Trust me when I tell you, the dark is filled with things you'd sooner not meet and only felt once it whispered in your ear. I breathed in again, cleansing my body and mind. I let go of my doubts and grounded myself. I lowered the shields I had built inside my mind, the defenses that held back who I was—a witch. I opened my arms and felt the night against my soul. I searched for whatever was hiding in the shadows. In my mind, I reached out with the power that my line was cursed with, the same power that kept me alive time and time again.

There, in the distance, I felt it like the tiniest sliver of glass in a sock. The more I focused on it, the bigger the shard became, until it rubbed up against me like a hungry cat. I turned to face it but ended up rotating in a circle. It was everywhere and nowhere. It was in the dry wind and sun-baked crops. It had an eagerness to it, similar to asking a dog if he wanted to go for a walk. It felt evil, yet not quite like hell. But just because it didn't feel like the evil, I knew didn't mean it wasn't an evil I'd learn to fear. I smelled matchsticks, sulfur, volcanic earth and the sickly-sweet smell of new blood. Unlike other demons I had the pleasure of meeting, it felt nothing like what I was familiar with. It was malevolent. There was no doubt about it. But it didn't care. Demons boast about their power. They showed it off like a new fur coat. This, whatever it was, didn't. I pushed harder and could hear screaming. I could feel souls and the horror of where they were. The souls were dead but still alive. They were nothing more than meat to be consumed. There was an active circle somewhere, with another soul trapped, being eaten at the slow and painful whim of this new monster.

When I had pushed to find it, it shoved back. I had felt it, and it had felt me. I wasn't fast enough with my shields, and its power pushed me away, slicing down my mind with blistering heat. I slammed my hex bag against my thigh and spilled thunder-stuck wood shavings down my leg. The air filled with the smell of herbs and garlic. My shields slammed shut faster than I had done before, and I staggered, my balance thrown for a loop. I heard Miguel running toward me, his feet crushing the dust and stones. I opened my eyes on the ground. One hand held on to my charm, and the other reached for a gun I didn't have. I had a momentary lapse of memory. I wasn't home. I didn't have my gun. I was unarmed. I was struggling to breathe, and my vision sparkled. But once I felt Miguel, I calmed enough to know that he'd have my back until my brain stopped sloshing around.

Miguel knelt beside me. "Be still, Ailis. Calm yourself, or you're going to pass out."

I nodded and stopped fighting to breathe. I closed my eyes and relaxed my body. I unclenched my fists from his shirt and willed my body to calm. Air came in shallow breaths, but the burn still remained. The dizziness passed, and I could stand, albeit shaking and dizzy.

"What the hell was that? I felt it crawl all over me," Miguel asked.

I gripped his arm twice and shook my head back and forth. I still couldn't talk. When I finally had enough air to keep my heart beating and speak at the same time, I broke out into cursing. I was well and truly afraid. I started to shiver. Not much scared me to my core. Sure, I get scared, but not like this. I fear a lot of things — swimming with tropical fish, heights, small spaces, big dogs and changing a light bulb without flipping the breaker for my entire house. Fear is healthy. It keeps you alive and aware. But I'd rather swim with sharks, with a stomach wound and a dead seal tied to my back, before feeling what I had just touched in the darkness, again. Something in the back of my mind told me I might not have a choice in the end.

Whatever I had touched had touched me right back. I pulled my shields chokingly tight. It could have killed me easily but hadn't. I was happy about my survival but cautious. I felt it call out to me — not by name, but by power. It knew what I was and what I could do, and it wanted me to come for a visit…willingly or not.

"What was that?" Miguel asked once I was seated back in the Jeep and after I had chugged down a bottle of water to clean the taste of hell off my tongue. The heat in the Jeep was on full blast, but it did little for my chill, and my teeth continued to chatter. Miguel was sweating but didn't dare touch the temperature controls.

"You can put your gun away, Miguel. There's nothing to shoot. Whatever that was, your gun isn't going to do a bloody thing to stop it. It's not a body. It's power." I said, and he tucked his gun under his seat. I didn't think carrying a concealed weapon was legal in Mexico for those outside the law, but I wasn't going to suggest he leave it at home, and I felt better with the gun within reach. "I don't know what it was. Remember that time, years ago, when I ran into a devil, and it shoved me out of his way and kept moving? That's what this felt like — a power so great I wasn't threat enough to kill me," I explained and groaned. "Now that I've felt it, I'd have to agree. None of us are a big enough threat to it. I've never felt power like that before, and I've sat in hell."

"That's not exactly encouraging," he replied.

"It wasn't meant to be. Get us the hell out of here. If I ask you to stop at another random place again, don't. I think I've used up all my luck for one day. I don't want to tempt fate with another stab at it." I buckled my seatbelt and ran my hands up and down my arms. The night seemed worse now. Being afraid made the sky feel like it was inches above my head and reaching out to smother me. Miguel turned us around and started back toward the scene. "It was old, Miguel. Powerful. It's feeding on souls. I could hear them screaming. Jesus, have mercy. It was eating them alive. Their souls are alive until the last drop."

"Do you think it is involved with the murders? Or are we dealing with a whole new problem we didn't know about until now?"

"Yes, it's involved. When the circle fell at the last crime scene, there was too much pain for me to focus on the evil of it all at that moment. I couldn't sense much more than the soul, but what I just felt now was the same horror I felt at the first scene. Tonight, I felt the other soul it was eating, and it felt the same. I think, whatever it is, went looking for those responsible for the murders and not the other way around. It wasn't summoned as I had thought. It called out for room service," I answered. "When I reached out to it, it recognized me for what I am—a witch. Witches, whether they're light or dark, are a sounding rod for everything that goes bump in the night. They hound us relentlessly. There isn't a day that goes by where I don't feel a ghost, hear a voice or see a monster. The dead think we can deliver messages, find their bodies or bring them peace. And the really annoying ones, demons, think we can open a door for them and let them out of hell. Most witches aren't powerful enough to bother trying to release them, but this time, the demon found several folks waiting to answer a call. Summoning is easier when the demon in question doesn't see it as a bother, when it is asking to come out to play."

Miguel looked surprised. "You've never told me that. I had no idea you were plagued by the dead and damned."

I shrugged. "We don't advertise that fact. Do you know how many bad guys would kidnap us if they knew what we could really do? It wouldn't just be the bad guys, either. Good people looking for their missing loved ones would come knocking. Even good people get desperate. And now, because I was curious, the damn thing knows another witch is in town. I'm not just any witch, Miguel. I'm a licensed, full-blooded witch. I'm damn powerful, and I've taped a welcome sign to my forehead."

"When did you start doing what you just did? You dropped your shields, and I could feel it. One minute nothing, the next, I could feel you like you were beside me. I could smell your shampoo as if you were under my nose. I didn't teach you that," he asked. "You shouldn't mess with the shields I helped you build. They protect your soul, Ailis."

"Samuel helped me. I have been learning how to strengthen my aura, how to open and close my shields. I can't just keep myself locked up. I need to draw on my abilities, or I'll die out there. I'm a full-blooded witch, Miguel. I can't just decide not to be. It's in my actual genes. And the more I ignore it, the less likely I'll be strong enough to defend myself against the real evils. What good is my aura protecting my soul if I'm dead?" I asked. I knew he was scared for me, but I also knew I was right. "I'm going to hell, Miguel, whether my soul is protected or not. Plus, the training helps me when I'm dreaming as much as it helps me when a demon knocks on my door."

"A demon knocked on your door?" He was surprised.

"Like I said, we're beacons for monsters," I answered, and Miguel stared in disbelief. "Twice.

Once, he had no idea I would be on the other side of the door. He was very apologetic. He was looking for the previous homeowners to call in his deal. He had lost track of them. I'm guessing they had been hiding out with the help of a strong spell. That explains why they took my first offer on the house, which was well below market value. Their loss, my gain. I wasn't counting on the demon perks, though. The second time, the demon tried to reach in and grab me. My entire house is one big ward. He burned his hands, and it stunk for days. He was just a wee demon, fresh off the demon line and not the smartest tool in the shed. He made a fairly good argument on why I should allow him inside. Sadly for him, I wasn't drinking his juice and sent him on his way. Maybe it was his name, Mr. Jones, that made me hesitate at first to open my door. I don't know. I told him to pick a better name. Too much baggage was attached to his name, and he'd find himself hard-pressed, in the future, for new and unsuspecting souls."

"Why Mr. Jones?" Miguel asked.

"You know, Jonestown? Jim Jones and the Peoples Temple cult? The poisonous juice?" I asked, and he shrugged. "Do you not read?"

"You lead the oddest life."

I shrugged. "But I'm alive. That's all that matters. Well, for now... We'll see how this vacation pans out."

"I didn't know the demons and spookeries were attacking you like that." Miguel's voice softened. "I didn't call you in to be a beacon for the devils. You shouldn't play with your shields here, not this close to a crime scene like this."

"I doubt a devil would even bother me. There's much more power to be found elsewhere. Most devils and demons wouldn't meddle around energy like this.

Even devils are scared of something bigger and badder than they are," I answered. "Honestly, Miguel, what did you think was happening to me back home? My life isn't exactly a picnic. It never has been and never will be. If I don't learn how to protect myself, I'm going to die." The chill was replaced by a hint of my temper, and I welcomed it. "You're the one who called me into this. You don't get to bitch about how I help you. You knew damn well who I was, that I had abilities. You have been counting on those skills to help you, so don't play the sorry card now. You may not have known the severity of the monsters on my doorstep, but you knew I'd attract every critter for miles. I always have and always will. Just because you refuse to admit it doesn't make it any less true."

"But I didn't know you were foolish enough to mess with your shields," he countered. "I didn't think you'd be crazy enough to open yourself up to demonic attacks like that. You're gambling with a deck of cards stacked against you."

"Whatever you believe is your problem, not mine. You're not upset that I'm using my aura as another tool in my arsenal. You're upset because you now understand the danger you've put me in. But you don't feel guilty, do you, Miguel? Because you're counting on me to do whatever I need to do to stop this shit from happening again. Whatever the cost, isn't that right? Isn't that what you taught me?"

"I wouldn't willingly put you..." he started and didn't finish.

"Don't lie to me. Have more respect for me than that. You not only would put me in danger, you have, many times," I countered. "If I wasn't here, you wouldn't have known there was a soul being eaten in that circle.

You wouldn't know any more now than you did before I got here. So yeah, you're banking on me to solve this, even if it kills me. If you're going to sit on your high horse, at least admit who you had to step on to climb up there."

"That's not fair, Ailis," he replied.

"Nothing in life or death is fair. You taught me that," I answered. "But on this, I've hit the nail on the head. You've lied to me from the moment you first called me. You've held out information from the start. I can feel it in my bones. You've used me, and now the damn demon knows I'm in town. So, Miguel, do you want to claim again that you wouldn't put me in danger, or shall we just acknowledge the truth and move on. I see no point in arguing the obvious just to make you feel better about your choices. I'm not here to help you sleep better at night. I'm here so we all don't die in our sleep."

He didn't say another word about it. It was either too close to the truth, or he had riled me up on purpose to push out the cold and refocus my attention. I knew him well enough to know he painted a target on his back to help me refocus. Miguel, always the martyr. Either way, I let the silence fill the Jeep until he opened a window. It made me smile. It was a small victory for my ego. I closed my eyes and let the rocking of the Jeep bring me back into a soft slumber. It wasn't a deep sleep. I could still hear everything around me. I wasn't physically tired anymore, but emotionally, psychologically, I was a zombie. I didn't often sleep in vehicles, but I did when Miguel was behind the wheel. Dying in a car crash sort of wrecks it for future road naps. I trusted the vehicle, even the biggest death trap on four wheels. It was always the driver I didn't count on. I settled into my seat. I needed to rest my psyche or I'd be useless at the next crime scene. If I wasn't of any use, I should have stayed in bed. Come to think of it, I should have stayed home, regardless of how useful I am. At home, I'd have one less demon to worry about.

Chapter Seven

"Where's here." Miguel's voice brought me out of my power nap.

The sun was still down, and I cursed out loud. "How long until the sun comes up? It feels like it's been dark since I got here."

"Less than two hours," he replied. "Welcome to the Tulum ruins."

I sat up straighter and looked around. We were in a large parking lot. Ahead of us stood a stone wall, ancient and worn. Really old places like this, inhabited as early as 564 AD, made me feel antsy. My skin itched with possibilities, none of which were desirable. I never was one to enjoy a haunted house. One never knows what they're going to find in places occupied by a past older than found in texts. These places were a coin toss. It would either make me want to turn and go the other direction, or the history would have been worn away by tourism, and there would be nothing left to spook me.

Like the previous site, when I opened the door, dread washed over me and kept me seated for a few minutes. It being dark didn't help calm the butterflies in my stomach. I climbed out of the Jeep by force of will alone. Had there not been a body on the ground, I'd have never volunteered, otherwise. Miguel and I didn't bother with the small talk with the others. Instead, I grabbed my backpack and followed him. It was my first time seeing the ruins. I had it on my list of sites to visit during my vacation and made a mental note to cross it off. One, I wouldn't want to ever come back. Two, why bother? I was seeing it now. I was a little irritated that my memories of the place would include a dead body, but at least I didn't have to deal with hundreds of tourists. *Silver lining.*

I shone my flashlight on the stone steps leading from the parking lot to the ruins and climbed one at a time. They were spaced out in a way that my legs couldn't climb up like standard stairs. Each step brought my mind to what we were going to find. I knew it would be as bad or worse as the last one. I felt sick to my stomach. Anxiety, anticipation, waiting for the bad things to show their ugly heads always made me feel like crap. Trees and shrubs lined each side of the rock path. In some places, I had to duck under branches or I'd have brained myself. If I knocked myself out because I wasn't paying attention, I was sure the others would laugh at me. The big bad demon expert taken out by a lowly tree.

A tunnel through the rocks stood to our right. We walked past it and kept climbing the stairs. I looked back once. Police were muddled there, whispering, and didn't follow us. I trusted Miguel to lead the way. This wasn't my backyard. It was his. We came around a bend that overlooked the Caribbean Sea with the setting moon on the horizon. The ruins of Tulum are walled on the east side and faced the Caribbean on the west. It was beautiful. Miguel stopped just long enough for me to take it in. If this had been a real vacation, I'd have started taking selfies with the hashtag 'blessed'. I was still tempted. No one had to know a dead body was minutes away.

"Hashtag, get me the hell out of here," I whispered to myself and laughed under my breath. Miguel turned and stared at me. I couldn't help it. I was tired, and everything was hilarious when you're worn out. Everything is worth laughing at when you're scared. "Sorry."

He turned without saying a word. With me at his back, we entered the ruins — stone buildings and worn dirt pathways. Although the site overlooked the water and was in immaculate condition, once I stood there, I was underwhelmed. Social media had taken away all the surprise and shiny newness of the place and given me the sense that I had already seen it all. But I was betting the 'meh' feeling had more to do with why I was there and less about the grounds themselves. Although I was there for death, I'd steal this moment for myself. I'd take five minutes to build a memory worth having since I'd likely leave Mexico with only nightmares.

During the thirteenth and fourteenth centuries, Tulum was one of the most powerful city-states after the fall of a rival city of Mayapan. When the Spanish began their occupation of Mexico, the ancient Maya abandoned their city. The Spanish didn't bring only conquest. They brought disease and death. Whoever didn't die had left. There are stories that they cursed the land before they checked out. Others say their coming is what cursed the land, angered the spirits and destroyed the wards that held back the demons. Some go as far as to say the site is haunted. I couldn't feel any ghosts or hauntings, but I wasn't about to drop my shields again to double-check. I didn't care enough to risk it. If they wanted to haunt this place until the last stone building fell, more power to them. It's not like they didn't have a damn good reason to be pissed off.

The buildings were stone, worn and crumbling, their decay the only marker left of a land once brimming with life. We were in a place of in-between, beauty and death. I stood at the entrance of the first building—a small one-room stone house with a missing roof. The stones were disintegrating. In the front stood a rock altar. I reached toward the slab and pulled back, shaking out the tingles in my hand. Many had died to serve that altar. It is said that it was an honor to be selected to be a sacrifice to the gods. For me, it didn't strike me as a privilege. Having your heart cut out while you were still alive sounded more like a punishment. But that's just selfish ole' me and my wish to keep all my organs inside my body. My God didn't ask for such things. Nope. Just everyday pain and suffering like everyone else in this world.

I opened my shields just enough to feel the energy. In the back of my mind, like a video on replay, I could hear the panic, death, screaming and so much horror. It was more than just noise. I could feel the emotions along my aura. I staggered and grabbed onto a tree. My hand burned with power. My eyes darted around the grounds. Something evil had been here many times over. This demon wasn't the first to swallow down souls. From the first stone placed to the last one that fell, death had been a friend to all who tried to force their occupation on this land.

"Miguel," I called him over. "There's too much death here. I can't breathe."

Miguel stood in front of me. He stroked up and down my arms, calming my nerves. The heat from his hands chased away the awfulness I felt in my gut. "I feel it. Not quite like you, but it runs down my spine like sweat."

"Has it always felt like this here?" I asked.

"Not this bad, no. But it's always had a history that could be felt. Like whatever happened here hasn't let go. It's a constant shadow, a light breeze, but tonight it has weight to it."

"It feels like the cenotes. There's a new history being made here." I shivered. "This isn't the first body to be sacrificed on these grounds. It's just the first one we've found. I'm not talking about the sacrifices of old. I mean, within the last couple of weeks. When I opened my shields enough to get a sense of what I was feeling, I could hear their screams. They were far too new for me to hear them that loud. Usually, when I go to a place that's haunted or where there are souls that haven't found a good enough reason to leave, it's faint, like someone whispering from the other side of a room. I can hear it, but I don't know what they're saying. Moments ago, I could hear them as though they were standing where you are right now."

"What did they say?" Miguel asked.

"Run," I answered.

"Do we run?" Miguel asked. I watched his body posture change. One word, and I knew he'd book it without hesitation. It was one of the reasons I once liked working with Miguel. He didn't eat up time with questions. He would run and ask once we were far enough away that the Q&A wasn't going to get us killed.

I shrugged. Wasn't that the burning question of the day? "If you see me running, you may want to follow."

"If the others see the witch and the ex-priest running, they'll follow, too." Miguel smiled. "They're as scared as we are."

"Me? Scared? Never," I joked. Although terrified comes closer to the truth. The butterflies in my stomach were drunk on it.

"Me neither." He was still smiling. "You don't always have to be the tough girl, Ailis."

"Yes, I do," I answered. "Or the bad guys win."

"Fear doesn't mean the bad guys win," he countered.

"I didn't say I wasn't scared. I am. I'm about to vomit on my shoes. My anxiety is through the roof. But I won't not show up to the party because I'm scared. When I stay home because I'm afraid, I lose," I replied and straightened my shoulders. "I won't let the monsters tell me how tough I am."

Miguel kissed my forehead. "You're a stubborn little witch."

It was my turn to smile. "It's all part of my charm."

"Take your time. Don't push yourself. I don't need you puking on the body." He left me to ground myself. If I vomited, I'd rather do it in the grass where no one could see me.

When my legs no longer felt like they'd betray me, I pressed on. Miguel nailed it. I was stubborn, but I like to refer to myself as tenacious. It sounded more refined. Whatever label we decided on, it was true. I was too bullheaded to pack my stuff and go home, even when I knew I should. But after the first night here, I didn't even unpack. I was one rabbit's foot away from bailing. Another inch, and I was out of luck and out of here. I didn't see it as bailing. I saw it as being smart. I saw it as keeping myself out of a hole in the ground.

My nerves weren't infinite. This world, hunting the bad guys, wasn't mine. I'm a consultant. I didn't work in the field when the field was still active. That I was out here, blood still wet, monsters in the shadows, made me question my life choices up to this point. I swear, the next time I needed saving, if I had to owe someone for it, I'd ask them to just let me die. I wasn't doing this again.

I knew where the body was without having to ask. The tallest building, the Temple of the Wind God, also called the God of the Winds Temple. This was the strongest point of power in the entire ancient city. I could feel it. It had been used for religious purposes up until the early nineteen hundreds. Along with the rolling energy, I could feel death, like standing in a fresh graveyard. The temple stood alone on the northwest side, on the edge of a cliff. It's said that when hurricanes approached, a whistling sound was created from a hole at the top. When citizens heard the whistle, they knew they had to leave the city or seek shelter from the storm. At the top of the stairs stood three openings in the rock. I could see, even from the bottom, that was where the body was. I didn't want to go up, but I did. The climb burned my thighs. The stairs were too high apart for the length of my legs, and I had to work for each step. That I had to exhaust myself physically to see something that would exhaust my mind emotionally didn't seem fair.

I didn't miss the body this time on first glance. I couldn't have. She was at the very top of the stairs, spread-eagled, gutted, for all the world to see. If I wasn't looking for her, I'd have stepped up and into the circle. And I didn't want anything to do with this circle. It felt the same as the last one. If I looked at it from the right angle, I could see the wall of the circle shimmer in the night, like oil on water. I built up an extra layer around my shields. Another run-in with a tortured soul would be more than I could bear, and being tossed back would send my head cracking every step on the way down. The sight, on its own, was more than enough to scar me. I didn't need to feel it as well.

I made eye contact with Miguel, who had paled since the bottom. He shook his head and made the sign of the cross. He lifted the silver cross I had gifted him and kissed it. He may have left the church, but his belief never died. I waited for him to finish his prayer before I began the reason why we were here.

The same officer who had stepped into the first circle was there, making sure no one else stepped across this one by mistake. It made those wanting to collect evidence impatient. He smiled, and I mouthed, 'thank you'. His shoulders straightened. He seemed to grow an inch. Pride does that. It wasn't the kind of pride that sent you downstairs into a cage. It was the kind that said he knew he did something right, and it felt good after his last mistake.

I stared at the victim's hair for too long. Was it red or stained from the blood? Her face was blue-gray. She had been dead awhile, long enough for most of the smell to be carried away by the ocean's wind. From her stretched mouth, blood had oozed and left a trail of stain. I wondered how long she screamed while her lungs were being removed or if that was even possible. Would she have drowned before they could be taken? Was the blood from previous wounds, or did it come up as they took away her ability to breathe? I allowed my mind to wander away from the person she was. She couldn't be real while I looked for clues. I kept my eyes from hers. I didn't want to see the lifeless stare. I knew I'd dream about this, and I didn't want those bloody eyes to haunt my dreams. Seeing a body in my dreams isn't the same as seeing a dead person. People have weight, but bodies are just bodies. Unless you've had night terrors, I can't explain it any better than that.

Aside from the injuries from being gutted, she didn't have any other marks on her now-graying skin. Her face was unharmed, with no indication of head trauma. How did they take her without a fight? I tried to imagine a situation where I'd be taken and not fight the attacker and couldn't think of any, outside of knowing and trusting my assailant. Tulum was still small enough to know your neighbors and say hello to those you passed in the streets. It was a tourist hotspot, but that tended to bring more of the locals together for work and celebration rather than drive them apart. This either meant everything or nothing at all. I made a mental note to look over the last file once again and check for defensive wounds and went back to the victim, who now had our full attention.

Where there had once been smooth skin was torn meat and a broken rib cage, as raw as any carcass at the butcher shop. The wound was heinous and rushed until the internal parts were removed. The harvest was done slowly, deliberately and carefully—unhurried, like the finest artist. Her wrists and ankles were tied down with very few ligature marks. She was stiller than the last victim. Was she dead when they tied her down? Or was she just too weak to fight a losing battle? Everything about the scene was a mirror to the last, right down to the positions of the candles, stones and burned sticks of incense. I didn't have a measuring tape, but I knew the circle would be the same size, as would the symbols. This was planned to the finest detail. This took time. The victim wasn't picked at random. She had to be a specific size to fit the circle perfectly and in good health, or the organs were useless. She had to be the perfect sacrifice. That would take weeks to find. How could they know her health unless they knew her? I've known a lot of people that look like they're in tip-top shape up until they keeled over and died from cancer. Only their nearest and dearest knew they were sick. There was no more doubt in my mind. Someone who knew the victim had stood outside the circle and watched her die.

"Some honor," I whispered. There was no honor in what lay at my feet. The officer who had held everyone back from the circle was to my left. "Officer, the last victim? Was she a virgin?"

He stared at me for a moment, frozen. I snapped my fingers, and he blinked. "Sorry. This is... I'm just...I've never seen this stuff before. How do you stomach it?"

I swallowed hard and breathed out of my mouth. "I don't. I can't. But sometimes, we have no choice but to gulp it down and force ourselves not to flee."

"My wife works in the coroner's office. Let me make a quick call," he answered, averting his eyes from the body. His wife, I assume, answered the phone. He asked my question and had to explain who wanted to know. He mumbled a few times and finally hung up. "Yeah, a virgin. She was twenty-one. My wife says they found the victim's necklace in her chest cavity. It must have broken during the...incident. It was a small cross and a St. Christopher. My wife told me that might help you. Does it?"

"Twenty-one and a virgin. That's not exactly common nowadays," I answered, more for myself. "What better sacrifice than a young, religious virginal girl? It helps. Thank your wife for me, please."

"Are you almost done up here? The others want to finish up and get the hell out of here," he asked.

"One more thing... Aren't these ruins closed at night?" I asked. "How does this happen?"

"The site security found the body," the officer answered. "They do sweeps of the area, but there's a lot of ground to cover. They come through here every two or three hours."

"More than enough time if the killers knew what they were doing and the schedule of the security," I replied. "I'm done here. Thank you for keeping watch. Give me time to clear out of here before you break that circle, please."

He looked at his watch. "I'll hold them off for a half hour. But even I want out of here. I want to go home and hug my wife and sons."

"I'll get out of here as fast as I can." I understood his desire to leave and touch love after this. Hell, I wanted out of here just as bad.

I turned and headed down the stairs to let Miguel know we needed to clear out. I wanted nothing to do with whatever was trapped inside the circle. My mind and heart couldn't take another touch like that. The officers cleared away as I got closer to Miguel. It was safe to say I wasn't very popular. I didn't really care, but I still gave them space. I resisted the urge to yell 'boo'. I wouldn't risk one of them shooting me. There were a few sensitives in the group, officers who could feel supernatural forces around them. I probably made their flight or fight responses go bonkers. Witches have a hard time forming relationships outside of other magics. We tend to make the skin crawl on mankind. As a solitary witch, I didn't have a coven to fill my dance card with, which left me with poor social skills and no friends.

"The men are calling this the apocalypse," Miguel muttered. He pulled out a white and blue handkerchief and wiped the sweat off his brown. He had a sheen over his skin. He looked pasty, paler than at the top of the stairs, which was hard for a tanned boy like him to pull off. "Could this really be it? The four horsemen and all fire and brimstone around the corner?"

"There are no four horsemen of the apocalypse, Miguel. It was a euphemism for what will bring about the end of the world. Mankind is the horsemen. We cause the wars, the death, the famine, and look around. We conquer everything we want to have as our own and kill everyone to get it. It'll be us, humanity and our lack thereof, who bring upon the end of the world, if we don't summon a demon to do it first."

He nodded. My words didn't seem to settle him. He flexed and released his hands. He blinked like there was dust in his eyes. There were so many tells with Miguel, when he was going to lose his temper or was nervous. But this, what I could see, was different and nothing like I had seen before. He was pent-up and ready to blow. I'd caught a glimpse of it at the cenotes and had blown it off. I'd chalked it up to a gruesome crime scene. We were all on edge, and I'd paid no mind to it. Tonight, though, I could feel the difference. It crackled in the air. Energy pulsed between us like static. My fingers tingled with it. I paused, my pulse in my throat. Miguel shouldn't be charging the air. I shook my head. It had to be the residual energy, my own power lending a hand to whatever was still lingering.

"It's not just the scene, is it?" I asked.

I knew Miguel. I've watched him in action against the biggest and baddest, and he never once flinched. Standing here now, he was flinching. If I stared long enough, I'd probably see his skin crawl. But it crawled for all the wrong reasons. He was hiding something. Call it intuition, call it gut instinct or call it me being used to him lying to me, but the little hairs on the back of my neck stood at attention. I could feel a lie coming a mile away. Secrets were no different. They took lives just as fast. Withholding the truth is the same as a lie, and I was watching him burn up because of it.

"You knew her, didn't you?" I asked. It really wasn't a question, more an accusation.

"Leave it alone, *amiga. Por favor.*" He backed away.

He was mumbling in Spanish. I knew his stress level was climbing. He mixed English and Spanish whenever his mind was somewhere else. I could hear him pray, the Last Rites. I didn't bother to mention how pointless it was. The Last Rites were a final purification for those who were dying, preparing their soul for their final journey. Her soul was gone, as was she. If her soul was still in that circle and not already eaten, there was no god out there who would shut the door just because some man didn't utter a few words. Hell wasn't all that picky, either.

"Miguel...stop." I didn't leave it alone. I followed behind him. I grabbed his arm. "Stop. If you knew her..."

When he turned, I stopped dead in my tracks and took my hand off his arm. Tears coated his face. His eyes were orange and wide. I could see them through the darkness. His eyes had moved from human to something closer to animal. My heart pounded. I backed up, putting space between us. I put my hands up in a show that I wouldn't keep pressing him, nor would I touch him. After that one touch, his energy rolling up my arm, I didn't want to touch him again. Whatever that was, the power rolling from him was unlike anything I had felt before.

Although it was still silent like the pre-dawn always is, in that darkness devoid of birdsong and life, I heard everything as I shuffled back — the beat of my heart, the rush of blood in my ears and the gravel under my feet. The air around me filled with a musky scent tinctured with fear. The fear belonged to me. Miguel, the man I thought I had known, was not human. I shook my head over and over. Words had escaped me. How could he hide that kind of lie from me, the monster expert? What the ever-loving hell was he? How could this be the first time I had seen the eyes of a beast on the man I had loved so fully? More importantly, how the hell did he not sound every alarm I had?

"Jesus Christ." I barely managed enough air to get the words out.

"Ailis, wait." His voice was deeper. I did not want to hear my name from his mouth, not like this.

I flinched when he reached for me. "What are you?" I held up my hand to stop him and shook my head. "Never mind. I don't want to know. I never want to know. Knowledge isn't always power. Some things I don't need to know. I don't want to hear another word."

I turned on the heel of my shoe and walked away. It would be the first time I gave my back to one of the bad guys. Part of me wished he ripped out my heart if there was any of it left. But I knew he wouldn't. I don't know how I knew, but I knew he wouldn't. My steps were too fast. I stumbled on the stone path, jerking each time to stay upright. I tried not to run. I kept my mouth closed, keeping myself from screaming for help. If I lost it, it would be chalked up to the murder scene and not the monster I had just left in the shadows.

"Everything all right, witch?" The closest officer, Martínez, approached me. I was expecting a hassle. He seemed like the kind of guy who needled a person every chance he got. But as he got closer, his face shifted to concern. "Are you okay?"

I shook my head. "Martínez, could you give me a ride back to my hotel? I'm done here," I asked. He looked from me to Miguel in the distance and finally nodded. I left Miguel at the ruins, along with his lies and whatever the hell he was.

Martínez didn't bother with conversation. He wasn't a fan of me, and I stopped caring a minute into the ride. I was grateful for his commitment to silence. It kept me from having to be rude and tell him to shut up. I sat in the hush of the truck and thought about wrapping my hands around Miguel's throat. Could I kill him? I mean, did I have the physical strength to actually strangle him? Could he die? What the hell was he? How could I miss it? It wasn't like I was the average girl next door. Monsters were my thing. It's what I did for a living. Yet, he'd snuck under the wire and into my life. I'd fallen in love with one of the bad guys. I, Ailis Kyteler, lived a life with one of the monsters.

"Thanks for the ride, Martínez." I finally spoke. "I appreciate it."

"You look like you've seen a ghost," he responded.

"A dead man. Same thing," I answered. I pursed my lips to keep my scream inside. "Good luck out there."

"You're done?" he asked.

I nodded. "I have a lecture to give in the morning. It's why I was coming here, to begin with. Other than that, there's nothing more I can do. If I think of anything else, I'll make sure you get the information."

"*Gracias.*" One quick nod, and he pulled away.

I wondered how much more my heart could take, both figuratively and literally. One day my heart is just going to stop, having reached its limit for lifetime beats. I sent Miguel a text as soon as I got to my room and locked the door. It was short and sweet.

I quit. My debt to you is paid in full.

My phone rang and buzzed, and I ignored each one. Miguel called enough times to fill my voicemail after I sent that text message. I didn't bother listening to them or reading the slew of text messages. I deleted them as they came in. I was done. He had used up his favor with his lies, at great risk to my life, with the new memories I would carry around with me for all days. I would squeak out the remaining time enjoying my vacation and hoping the next murder victim wouldn't be found floating in the pool at my resort. With my temper at peak setting, I'd have pulled her out and moved her to a different hotel, just so I wouldn't be the one having to deal with it.

Chapter Eight

Miguel wasn't at the lecture, and I couldn't have been more grateful. I spent three hours trying to convince twenty Roman Catholic cops that hell and demons were real and nothing like what the Bible said it was. They said I was going to hell for blasphemy. I told them I was going anyway. Why not go for a reason I deserved? Imagine living a life not believing in dragons or mythology, and I come in and say they are real. I have no physical proof, aside from lived experiences, and it wasn't like I could ask a demon to show up for a show and tell. That's exactly what it was like when it came to monsters. People simply didn't believe, but they believed in God and angels, even though no one had lunch with God, and angels didn't give a shit if we believed in them or not. I couldn't understand, for the life of me, how they could believe in one but not the other. People were strange in that way, having faith in only the good but not the bad, like it would keep them safer in some way. It didn't.

Unfortunately, it would be too late once the monster knocked on their door.

Aside from one person, they didn't even believe in vampires, let alone the fact that demons bought milk and eggs at the grocery store. With their little skin suits needing food or they'd wither away, some demons actually liked living a human life and took to hosting dinner parties, like that one demon who had his own housekeeping magazine and thirty-minute special on the home and garden channel. He gave Martha Stewart a run for her money. I think it reminded them of who they were before hell. Or they simply found it easier to trap unsuspecting innocents, and what better place than the local market?

The officers thought I was humanizing demons and would be smote for my demon-loving words. They couldn't wrap their heads around the fact that some monsters were once human. Humanizing what was once human wasn't sacrilege. It was merely a fact. You can't have it both ways. You either didn't believe, or you did. It was an argument that went around in circles. After an hour, I was almost willing to summon a demon out of thin air just to say, 'Ha! I told you so.' I armed them with knowledge. I gave them printouts of the symbols used at the crime scenes and the meanings behind them. Whether they used the information or not wasn't my problem. I was done. I came to do what I set out to do. I was now officially on vacation.

From arguing about souls to poolside…a perfect start to a horrific holiday so far. I sipped my frosty piña colada and leafed through my Sherlock Holmes book. It was a book of his greatest cases. I loved a good detective mystery. As long as it wasn't ripped from the current headlines or had real monsters in it, I could lose myself for hours on end. Sir Arthur Conan Doyle was at the top of my list for writings that would pull me in and push out the real world. I was in the middle of *The Adventure of the Copper Beeches*, when I started to feel antsy, like I had more important things to do. The feeling intensified to not wanting to be there at all. I ignored it for as long as I could, thinking it was residual anger from the previous night. I looked up to see if a boogeyman had taken up a post in a chair of his own. I noticed the pool and deck chairs were empty. Someone, or likely, something, had either scared the hell out of everyone, or someone damned had done it for them. I say 'damned' because idle use of power came at a high cost. Eventually, that cost was your soul. The good rarely used their abilities unless forced to.

I watched the something in question move from the edge of the property, from the stairs out to the beach. He was worth a second look, not only for his attractiveness but for the power that rolled off him like heat on cement. He worked his way past the chairs and pools to stand next to me. He was at least six feet tall, muscled, with medium-length hair pulled back into a ponytail. If he didn't make my warning bells explode, I'd have said he was good-looking. He blocked my sun with his perfectly tuned body, crossed arms and designer clothes. Sure, I wasn't tanning, not with Irish skin like mine, but I didn't like the idea of someone taking the sun I paid dearly to shade myself from.

He wasn't human. It didn't take me feeling his energy to know that. It was in the way he moved, like liquid and grace meets bare-knuckled street fighting. There was a smoothness to his movement that humans just didn't have and couldn't copy. The closest we came was a good swaggering walk. We could mimic as best we could but would never come close to monsters. But monsters couldn't perfectly copy having a soul, either. I think we got the winning hand. I'd sooner stumble around with a soul than move with elegance and not have mine, thank you very much. But his grace didn't feel right. It wasn't common, but it was deadly. The charm around my neck vibrated against my skin. *A warning*. Whatever he was, whatever flavor of creature, he was bad news for me. I didn't need the necklace to point out the obvious. All I had to do was look around at the abandoned poolside.

"Good day. My name is Caser." His Spanish accent was thick. He said his name like I should have known who he was. I didn't.

"You're blocking my sun, Mr. Caser," I responded. I turned back to my book.

"Do you mind if I take a seat, Ailis?" It was rare for someone to pronounce my name correctly when I didn't know them. People usually butchered it on their first and second attempts. It was too unique of a name to be familiar with it, which was the reason I liked it so much. Caser getting it right off the bat made me feel like he knew me more than he should have.

"Dr. Kyteler," I corrected him, "and yes, I do mind."

Caser sat anyway. Arrogance and power. A bomb waiting to go off. "Yes, Dr. Kyteler, my sincerest apologies. Named after your famed ancestor, if I'm not mistaken, Dame Alice Kyteler, the first person recorded to be condemned for witchcraft in Ireland. The stories of her escape are obviously true, given you are here. But her little servant Petronilla de Meath was not nearly as lucky. She was flogged and burned to death at the stake in the winter of 1324. Are you like your ancestor, Dr.

Kyteler? One who abandons so quickly? Do you leave others to die in your place?"

"What can I do for you, Mr. Caser?" I asked, glancing over my book. If he knew me well enough to know my name, he should know how quickly I cut people out of my life, just like Dame Kyteler. To save myself, like she did, I'd abandon who I needed to. It wasn't because I'm cruel. It was because I wanted to live that badly. I'd do just about anything, outside of tainting my soul, to keep my skin topside.

"You may call me Caser...just Caser. May I call you by your given name?"

"No. What do you want, Caser?" I asked.

Caser hadn't come with violence, but he came with something that would raise the hackles on a dog or puff the tail of a cat. He was contained violence just waiting to be unleashed. Spend enough time around the bad guys, and you could point them out in a crowd. The voice inside was screaming for me to run or find a way to kill him. My survival instincts were preparing for a run since I had nothing to kill him with. Beating someone to death with a book was a long and grueling process. I had few options available. I could feel the muscles in my thighs twitching with a warm-up before the sprint. I hated the feeling. It would take hours for my body to feel like it wasn't about to be cornered in a cave like my ancestors. Something about Caser's eyes told me he was the reason they hid in the caves.

"You're as spirited as your many generations-ago-grandfather, Dante. Much less respectful, but spirited, nonetheless," he replied.

"Your point?" I acted tough, but that was all it was — an act. I was swallowing bile. Dante Alighieri, my line's claim to fame. For those in the back, just waking up,

Dante was an author who was best known for *The Divine Comedy*, a little ditty about hell. Most, to the chagrin of the church, is more accurate than the Bible, told in a way that wouldn't have him burning at a stake. I was sure the church kept their eye on him up until malaria did the job for them.

"He is the first to walk out of hell," Caser said. "Sure, there have been others, such as yourself, but you are the only one alive currently."

I fought my face to keep it neutral. No one outside of Miguel had known about my relation to Dante. I didn't speak of it...ever. What people don't know about Dante's work is that it is a firsthand account of hell, his journey and the reason we are hereditary witches. For his freedom, he and his line would be cursed, the creation of true genetic witches — a little game the devils were playing at the time. Give mankind magic, then stand back and watch them burn the witches. I am his descendant. How is that for a front-row seat on the bus straight through the gates of hell? Dante was one of the first to have walked through hell and lived to tell the story. His story was a warning that was made into a play and movies and books. Just like every other cautionary tale out there, no one takes the serious stuff seriously enough.

"I appreciate your history lesson. Really, I do. But, please get on with your song and dance. I have plans today, and none of them include talking with whatever flavor of creature you are," I added the 'please' for my benefit. Angering the bad guys this early in the day, unarmed, wasn't always a good thing.

He winced at my comment. "You have nothing to fear from me...yet."

"Yet," I muttered. "That implies I have so much more to look forward to. Is that why you're here? To scare me? You didn't need to sit down for that to happen. I'm scared. You win. Now go away."

He smiled. "How refreshing."

"What's that?"

"Someone willing to tell the truth about their fear. Most will try to hide it." His smile said he was genuinely surprised at my truth.

I shrugged. "Doesn't do me much good to try to hide something you can probably smell or feel. Fear doesn't go away just because I will it to with my silence."

"In my line of work, silence is usually what keeps you alive," he countered.

"You must have a shitty job, then." I sipped on my melting piña colada and regretted not getting a double rum. I'm not a big drinker, but I was now wishing for the sweet slumber of intoxication. I opened my book back up as a sign I was uninterested in whatever wares he was selling. "As you can see, I'm on vacation. Let's wrap this up so I can go back to my book and drink."

"Down to business. I like that. I've come to talk to you about the murders."

"First, even if I knew what you were talking about, I'm forbidden from discussing cases with people who aren't the police." I glanced up and fought the urge to roll my eyes and shake my head. *Who does he think he is?* He must have sprinkled arrogance on his cornflakes this morning. "I'm not consulting on any cases in Mexico, currently. As I said, I'm here on vacation."

"Come now. I think you know exactly what I'm talking about." He leaned forward, close enough for me to smell his cologne. It wasn't cheap. Nothing about him said he was on a budget, from his thousand-dollar shirt and pants to his premium haircut. "You talk to Miguel. He is not police, to my knowledge."

"If you know Miguel, go talk to him." I brushed him off.

At the edge of the property, I watched people filtering through the palm and coconut trees. They didn't bring the same level of intimidation or authority as good ole' Caser, but enough for me to have gone inside if I could have. Those in the trees looked like they'd break your kneecaps for a few hundred bucks, while Cesar would do it for free just to hear you scream. "You must have known the man who created the idea of parties."

"I do not know what you mean?" Caser made it a question. He looked puzzled, and I almost laughed. All muscle and no brains. Not a good combination. I kept my laugh to myself. I didn't need to test my theory.

"Here I am, drinking alone, and you come up with a brilliant way to make things worse by inviting others," I explained. Deep down, I was a hardcore introvert. People wore me out. It took a lot of energy for me to be in a group. I didn't like gatherings of any kind, especially the menacing ones.

"Tell me, little witch. What is the first thing you noticed about me when I approached you?" he asked. It was an odd question.

"The audacity," I answered with a smile.

Energy rolled off him like a smoldering fire. I closed my eyes and breathed through it. His voice cut through my attempts to shield myself from his energy. "I can sense the fear in you. Your insides are rumbling. Your pulse is quick, like butterfly wings."

My smile was no longer a friendly one. "Do I know what you are? Nope. Am I afraid of what you could do to me if given half the chance? Of course. Being stupid isn't what's kept me alive this long." I looked him straight in the eyes and let my carefully woven humanity slip just enough to show him my skinned-alive soul. Always, underneath my control, was a person who would do anything for survival. "Truthfully, you aren't what I truly fear, Caser. I fear what I will do to you to stay alive. I fear the power inside me and its desire to peel the flesh from your bones. If hell has taught me anything, it's that I will do anything not to go back there. I will do anything to stay alive, even if that means I carry the stain of taking a life on my soul. But with you, I doubt the smut would be all that great. I'd be doing the world a favor."

"I'm happy to hear that, Ailis. So very happy we're on the same page. That's a rarity in both of our lines of work. I, too, will do anything for me and my people to stay alive. So, you will help us?"

I stopped myself from asking what kind of help he meant. I was curious, but not enough to ask, mind you. "You could have made an appointment to meet with me, and I would have met with you. You could have come to me without the show of force and power, and I would have spoken to you. You could have done this a dozen other ways. Instead, you bring the threat of violence."

He leaned close enough for me to feel the heat of his words. "You have no idea how much force or violence I can bring to the table."

I laughed. "So far, you bring nothing to the table, Caser." My charm began to heat. "You're not going to like what's going to happen if you try to bring harm to me. I promise you you'll taste regret long before I taste my death. Sure, I may die, but I'll make you wish for death first."

"As I said, I bring you no harm."

"Uh-huh, and the earth is flat, witches steal penises for pets and masturbation opens portals to hell."

Caser reached for me. His movement was smooth and as fast as any other creature I've met. I was quick on my feet but not fast enough. His hand was hot against my skin as his fingertips squeezed into my muscle. I pulled on my power, ready to kill him where he stood. He grinned, feeling the energy spoil in my soul, but didn't let go. "Enough with the jokes. I do not find the slaughtering of my brethren to be funny."

"Take your hands off of her." Miguel was at my side. I hadn't heard him coming. If I wasn't hating him more today than when I landed, I'd have been more grateful to see him. Yet, I wasn't about to kick a gifted monster in the mouth and kept mine closed. "She has my protection."

Caser let go of my arm with a huff. He snarled. It was almost animalistic. I was caught in the middle of them both. That familiar feeling of Miguel swept over me, and I stood. He and Caser felt the same. It's why I couldn't tell what Caser was. My body and mind were used to it already. The power roared between them like a ship battered by a storm. I didn't know who the ship was and who the storm was yet. Those in the trees took a step forward. One look from Miguel, and they stepped back. What a place to be in, caught between two monsters, each commanding your movements. I didn't like those in the trees, but I didn't envy their position, either.

Miguel glared at Caser. "What are you doing here?"

"I came to do what you would not," Caser replied. The energy sparked between them and made me glad I wasn't drunk. I'd have puked on them both. *Monster motion sickness.* So many regrets and so little time to pick the one that landed me between two monsters. "I came to ask for help."

I held up my hand. "Whoa, boys. Take your fight somewhere else."

"You will help us, Ailis. Mark my words. I will see you both tonight. Come willingly or not. Either way is fine for me." Caser's voice carried a demand that tugged at my belly button.

Miguel moved faster than my eyes were capable of tracking and put himself between Caser and me. Caser grabbed Miguel by the throat. His knuckles cracked and grew longer before my eyes. Claws grew from the tips, and I jumped back. My heart hammered. I covered my mouth to keep the panic in. I didn't want anyone to come and see what I was screaming about. We didn't need more hostages. That's all an unprepared human was, a hostage, a victim, just another body for me to trip on when I ran away. I grabbed onto the charm around my neck. It was almost too hot to hold. I held out my other hand, the palm toward Caser. I pulled on the roots of my power. I focused my energy on Caser and forced the harm from my presence. Whatever power that rolled off him was now being pushed back down his throat to wherever it came from. I didn't care what the cost was for my show of force. I'd carry the taint willingly. Fear does that. It clouds your mind and pushes you to survive, no matter what the payment would be. If it hadn't worked, I'd be cleaning up my blood with my beach towel. The hotel would have billed me for that. A place like this and it would have been more money than it was worth.

"You will pay for that." Caser's voice was closer to a growl than anything I had ever heard a human make.

"Get in line, Caser. It's a long one. You had better bring a book." I spoke through gritted teeth. I bet he was thinking the same thing I had thought about him. Arrogant. "You have overstayed your welcome."

He stepped around Miguel and pointed at me. "Midnight."

"And what if I don't come? How many of your people will you risk if you force my hand?" I asked.

"Only one. Miguel. He will not live to see another day. You do not live in this world, *niñita*, but he does." He called me a little child. I let it go. I'd rather them think I was childish than what I really was—a nightmare. "Do not be the fool in this. It is not a game." I saw the truth in his eyes. He meant every word. But I still had no intention of being a pawn or someone's toy, game or not.

"Don't threaten me, Caser. If you come up against me or mine, I will do everything in my power to end your life," I answered with the same truth.

"From what I understand, Miguel is not yours," he replied with a smirk.

"Then using him as a pawn is kind of pointless, isn't it?"

"We'll see how pointless it is, won't we?" Caser asked.

"Don't test me, please. I'd hate to end up in jail over your ego." I smiled like every other sociopathic monster I had ever met. "I hadn't planned on digging a shallow grave during my holidays, but I can adjust my schedule and buy a shovel."

"I feel your truth. You believe you can kill me."

"Yes. Even if it means I eat away everything that's left of who I am, I will do it. I've lived through too much to give in to a threat or bend to the will of a monster."

"Even if it means you die in the end?" he asked. He looked surprised.

"Even if that's what it means." Sure, I didn't want to die. But I couldn't really say that. It would ruin the threat.

"Then I suppose we will both be dead. Where's the victory in that?" he asked.

"I'll see you in hell. That, Caser, is victory enough for me. I don't need the parade."

It was his turn to smile. "There is no doubt we'll meet in hell, one day or the next. But I'd be more careful when talking to one of the hounds who will be guarding your cell."

I didn't let my unfriendly smile falter. But his words scared me enough not to keep pushing his buttons.

"Until we meet again." Caser bowed his head slightly and gave us his back. I wished I had a gun. I'd have shot him. There wasn't such a thing as a fair fight. I'd have shot him in the back and slept just fine for it. There were no rules that said I had to look him in the eyes as he died.

"Prick," I muttered.

He glanced back once and winked. Caser went as quickly as he'd come. His power and his people left with him like a wave being drawn back from the beach. He left behind heat in the air and fire in my bones. If there's one thing I hated more than demons, it was being lied to. It boiled my blood. Heads have landed on spikes for less. Sadly, that's considered cliché and went out of style with the fall of Vlad the Impaler. He and I had a lot in common when it came to how we wanted to deal with our tempers. If I didn't rely so heavily on the internet and indoor plumbing, I'd say I was born at the wrong point in time.

Chapter Nine

I caught Miguel before he, too, could escape. He was either a coward or too smart to stay and face the wrath that dripped off my body like flood rains. Miguel turned to walk away, and I grabbed his arm. I spun him around to face the music. He didn't look as scared as he looked horrified — a secret well kept for all these years, only to have it go up in smoke before his eyes. It was the heaviest lie between us, and it had cost him everything he said he had wanted in life, a partner, a family and a little house with a white picket fence. Sure, he wasn't going to find all that with me, but we could have haggled the difference and still come out on top.

"I don't bloody well think so. Start explaining, Miguel. If I'm going to die here, I'd like to know why I'm going to land in an unmarked grave," I demanded. "You can start by telling me what the hell Caser is."

"I don't even know where to start," Miguel said. I sat back down, and he took a seat on the lounger beside me, facing me. He ran his hands through his tousled hair. Like me, with the scar on my head, Miguel played with his hair when he was overthinking. "What do you know about Lycans?"

"Werewolves?" I asked. A small laugh escaped unintentionally. "Are we going to talk about the tooth fairy next?"

"The tooth fairy is a demon. We both know that. What do you know about Lycans or werewolves? Either is fine."

"You've got to be kidding me, Miguel." I laughed again. "This is ridiculous."

He shrugged. "Just humor me, would you? What do you know?"

"A Lycan and a werewolf are folkloric or mythological characters, Miguel. As in, not real, made-up stories to scare the village teenagers from wandering off into the woods to make out," I answered. He motioned for me to continue. "A Lycan is a folklore from the Greeks, and a werewolf is a lore from the English. There isn't much written on them based on fact. Rather, stories are handed down through generations, like with any other mythological creature. Some stories from Greek literature suggest that Lycan was a nude man running through the streets, tearing people up with his teeth. Other stories mention insanity, madness and confusion, more commonly known today as rabies. But, like with any good story, the truth washes away to make room for creative liberties. Some doctor once went on record to say the disease originated in the Far East with an estimated population of Lycans to be somewhere in the ballpark of seven hundred or so."

"I read that story, too. It was baseless." He spoke as though he kept up on the werewolf politics around the world. Then again, if I knew about it, it made sense that he read the same papers. "Keep going. It's easier for you to just tell me what you already know than have me repeat the knowledge you already have."

I paused for a moment and thought back to my mythology and religious studies classes in university. "Folklore says werewolves, which have their origin in English legends, are human beings that have been changed into humanoid wolves, whereas Lycans are humanoid wolves. Mythology says Lycans are the protectors of man."

"Lycans were the original hellhounds, Ailis. They made a deal with God that if He would allow them to live above, they would protect mankind from hell, protect the innocents from being dragged into hell. And when we die, we guard the Gates of Hell to keep out the innocent and drag in the guilty. If we break this agreement, we will be punished. This is why, when a rogue Lycan tries to build an army, they are given werewolves and not more Lycans. The weres inevitably die within the first few months. The human body was never designed to shift. And if they live, by some grace of God, Lycans hunt them down and kill them. We can't allow the virus to spread. We would damn all of humanity. We can only be born, not created. That is the deal with the man upstairs. And there can only be so many of us at once. It's why not every child born from a Lycan will become one. Some go their entire lives without shifting. Others shift at sixty years old, out of the blue, when our numbers need the boost."

I didn't miss the 'we' part. Was I actually hearing him confess to being a Lycan or a werewolf? He hesitated while I stared at him. I could have counted my heartbeats in the stagnant silence that hung between us. I shook myself back into the moment. "Sorry. Keep going."

"Are you sure?" he asked, and I nodded. "Our numbers are low because most Lycan women cannot conceive or they miscarry. It's the natural order of things. Controlling the Lycan population is the only way to ensure there would not be hell on earth. There would not be a rebellion. It is the same for Lycans as it is for Nosferatu, the vampire. Less than one percent of their offspring survive beyond their first twenty-four hours after changing. Less than half of the survivors make it to a year. If they aren't killed by their own people, they are hunted by mankind. The particularly nasty and powerful ones are hunted by Lycans. It is a natural balance found within all the cursed species."

"And you... You're one of them?" I asked. I knew the answer, but I needed to hear him say the words. He reached for my hand, and I pulled back. I was curious, not stupid and definitely not past my anger.

"Lycan. It isn't something you can contract from human-to-human touch. You are born with it. Some of us change, some don't. It depends on if the gene is active or not. But, if a Lycan attacks during Lycan form, there is a risk of contracting the virus. Their offspring, those they attack, could become werewolves. It is a curse from the demons, a parting gift for our deal with the gods. The demons are responsible for the virus, not us," he explained, as if that fact made some difference. "The risk is small, one in one hundred. Attacks are rare and carry a death sentence for the Lycan, whether they meant to do it or not. Any violence against man is against all laws. When they shift, they hunt... It is in their nature. But they don't kill indiscriminately. They don't eat people."

"How do you deliver the message of God if you're a hellhound?" I asked. "Isn't that contradictory?"

"Werewolves represent witchcraft, hell, demons. Lycans don't. Almost all of us are highly religious, and all are strong believers. You can't believe in one and not the other. Remember, Ailis, Lucifer is still an angel. Going to hell doesn't change that," he explained. "If it weren't for us at the gate, souls who did not belong would end up in cages."

"Why are you telling me this now, Miguel? Why didn't you tell me before? Before I loved you?" My voice raged at the end. "Why *now*?"

"We are forbidden to tell who we are. I couldn't tell you, Ailis," he answered. "But I wanted to. Every day, I chewed my tongue to keep you from knowing what could end your life."

I huffed a small sarcastic laugh. "What you did was lie to me. Withholding the truth is the same as flat-out lying to me."

"I did it to protect you. You would have been killed for that knowledge. The others would have hunted you down and killed you and me. It was a lie worth telling. Not everything is worth knowing."

Samuel had said the same thing to me recently. "Does Samuel know what you are?"

"He suspects what I am but has never asked. He knows about Lycans and werewolves but has never directly confronted me. He once told me, in not so many words, to keep my claws to myself, and we wouldn't have a problem. I think he was worried I'd claw you up by mistake."

No wonder Miguel didn't want to tell me the truth. "Does that happen, clawing people up by accident?"

"No. If you're infected, it was likely intentional. We have complete control of who we are—our wolves, unlike werewolves, who are governed by their beasts. If my claws come out, it is to protect you or myself, but never to harm you. I am in control of who I am." He lifted his hand and turned the palm toward me. His nails grew half an inch and back in, seemingly showing the control he spoke of. "I'm sorry I lied to you."

I knew my face betrayed my false bravery. I was surprised, and I was smart enough to be scared. "You don't get to decide my fate, Miguel."

"And you cannot decide mine, Ailis," he snapped back. That one stung. It was the truth of it that hurt. "But you have, haven't you? By branding me a monster."

"What you did was monstrous." I felt defensive. Miguel and I never fought this one out. We'd left so many things unsaid I felt it coming to a boil.

"I had no choice!" he yelled. So much rage and hurt in those words.

"We all have a choice," I countered.

"Did I? Did I really? Did you bother to ask me?" he demanded. "No. You didn't. I had no bloody choice. Do you think I wanted to do that, to take the life of someone I had prayed I could save? I knew her! I cared about her. She was mine to protect, and I failed her. And because of my failure, I had to take her life. Isabell begged me to kill her three weeks earlier, and I couldn't bring myself to do it. I tried to, but I couldn't pull the damn trigger. If I had, it would have saved lives. But I didn't until it was too late." His shoulders slumped forward. He hung his head and screamed wordlessly into the ground.

"What do you mean, she was yours to protect?" I asked.

He lifted his head. Fresh tears littered his cheeks and the ground between his feet. "Isabell was mine. She was Lycan. A demon had possessed her. When the demon left, it shattered her mind on his way out. We send people for psychological treatment, but she wasn't human. We couldn't risk her changing into a wolf in a hospital. Not only would she have killed everyone, but what if someone survived? We would have been found out."

"You killed her to keep a secret?"

"No. I didn't even care about that. I killed her because I was scared that she'd get away and slaughter innocent people. I was scared she'd attack and infect others, which would have spread the virus to countless innocent people. Fathers, mothers and children were all at risk. Those who survived her attack, I would have had to kill to protect everyone else." Miguel groaned his frustration. "When she called me weeks before that, she knew a demon was trying to get in. She could feel it. Demons love to toy with our new shifters. They think it's a game. Instead of killing her when she asked, I tried to save her soul. I ended up killing her in the end, anyway but not before she killed five people. She didn't just scratch them. She mauled them like a starved dog. I had to hunt her like I would any other demon."

"I don't know what you want me to say, Miguel. If I could change things, I would."

He shook his head. "You still don't get it. From time to time, the only choices we have are bad ones. I'm glad you've never been in the position to learn that firsthand. I forget, sometimes, how very young you are, how inexperienced you are in this world."

"I'm not naïve, if that's what you're implying. I've made tough calls, just not those ones."

"Naïve is not a word I'd use to describe you. What I mean is, you haven't lived long enough in the world of evil to have faced the level of horror I've seen. I am charged with protecting the greater good, all of mankind. And I've done everything in my power, this side of the gates, to make sure you wouldn't be touched with the life I live, that you wouldn't suffer the same choices I've made."

"What do you mean, you've done everything to make sure? It doesn't look that way from where I'm sitting. You invited me here to help you find a monster, knowing full well it would set me up to walk into the life you live. If you can't see that, you're blind," I replied and paused. "How have you helped keep me out of this?"

"I asked you to help, not roll out the damn red carpet into my Pack. Do you think my people enjoy seeing you cut me up every chance you get? Who do you think picks up the pieces after we talk or see each other? Hell, I see you on the news, and I'm a wreck. We are Pack, Ailis. How do you think they've wanted to deal with this little issue of mine? They're constantly debating on if you're human enough for our laws to apply to you," he asked. It felt more than a question.

I glared at him. "You sound like Caser. Don't threaten me, Miguel. You won't like the outcome."

"I'm not. I wouldn't. But you need to understand the risk of now knowing."

I felt my defenses rise. My eyes swept my surroundings, always on alert. "Great. I discover a new species, only to learn they want me dead for your broken heart. I didn't come here for that. I came here to pay off a debt and go home. Instead, I have a front-row seat to your inner squabbles that'll likely cause my death. Thanks for that, Miguel."

"I intend on you making it home in one piece. Don't worry about the others. It would be a direct challenge to me to defy my orders." His answer did nothing for my worry.

"That obviously doesn't matter to Caser. Why does he want my help? What does he want?" I asked, back on task. I'd deal with his bombshell later when I wasn't thinking about my pending doom. If anything, I could prioritize, deal with whatever dug my grave the fastest.

"Those who are dying, they're all Lycan. If anyone can know about us and not tell the world, it's you. We were between a rock and a hard place. If we keep our kind a secret, the weaker members of our Pack would be taking it to an early grave when they turn up dead next. There have been nine of my people who have gone missing. You've seen two of the bodies. There are three others that we've found. The first one to go missing was one of the newer Lycans. We thought, at first, it was inner squabbles or they'd run into a demon. It isn't uncommon. She wasn't powerful. We're always fighting with something monstrous or for something. When bodies started to turn up, I noticed they were missing organs. I started to think a local witch was doing it. But then the local witch turned up dead after I questioned her. Following her death, you showed up, and two more bodies have surfaced."

"It would have been easier to tell me the truth. I wouldn't have been chasing my tail. No pun intended." The lies started to make sense. How the women knew each other wasn't something Miguel could advertise, but he wasted a lot of time keeping it a secret. While I burned hours trying to figure out their connection, it was right in front of me with his mouth shut, a death grip on his truths.

"If I had told you, you wouldn't have seen the scenes with fresh eyes. I would have tainted your sight. I needed you to see it for what it was and come to your own conclusions. You saw things I missed — or at least didn't want to admit. The wounds do look like hellhound wounds, but it isn't a hellhound."

"Could it be one of your people?"

Miguel shook his head. "We would never kill each other like that. Our numbers are far too small to kill each other. Not only that, but it's a pointless death. None of the people who have gone missing are of any rank worth trying to take. They were the weakest of the Pack, Omegas. It gains us nothing."

"What is your rank?" I asked, curious. It isn't every day you learn of a new species.

"I am the Lead Warrior, sort of like a General or a Captain. I command the soldiers in our Pack."

"A Warrior of what?" I asked.

"Against everyone and everything. We protect the Pack and our secrets. More than that, we protect all of mankind who are deserving. And before you ask, it's not me who decides who is deserving. It is a drive within us, like knowing when to breathe or eat or sleep. It isn't something I can control. It's like when you know someone is lying or is a demon. It's just something within you that knows the truth."

"What if someone needed your protection? Could you still kill them?" I asked. I hoped he'd say no. Maybe if he said no, I could forgive him for what he had done.

He saw the hope in my eyes and nodded, not saving me with a lie. I appreciated the truth but still hated to hear it. "We all have it in us to do great evil, including me. For Lycan, it's difficult, but it can still be done. It would hurt our wolves to do it, and we'd carry around that sin like a dog leash too tight around our necks. It's suffocating and painful. Eventually, if we edged that line too many times, our wolves would die and take the human part with them."

"And what is Caser? Another Captain?"

"Caser is our Pack leader. We call him our Lycaon to honor the first Lycan. He has absolute control. To go against him is death. His word is law. Absolute law is the big man upstairs. That is the only law that supersedes Caser. If Caser ordered us to do something to an innocent who was of no threat to mankind or our Pack, we would simply refuse. His word would carry no force in those cases. If he ordered us to take out a monster, who deserved to taste their death, we couldn't refuse, even if we wanted to. We would be driven to follow the order and restore balance, protect mankind."

"You could kick his ass." I joked, in part. "He has way too much ego to win against you."

"In human form, I could. But in our...other form, I don't think I could. Many have challenged him over the years and lost. Regardless, I'd never challenge him. He is doing whatever he can to protect his people. I'm not happy he came to you, but he did it for the same reason I did...to save his people. If we start to die out, Ailis, we risk the bargain for the gate. You don't want to see what happens when we're not at that gate. It swings both ways, and all hell would be loosed upon mankind."

"Bargain for the gate? I thought your deal was with the powers above?"

He nodded. "It was. It still is. We bargained for our freedom, in exchange for yours, for humanity's freedom. We are everywhere, Ailis — every town, every city, every small island. There isn't a continent that we aren't protecting. We keep the innocents from being dragged to hell. We are there when a demon possesses a body and is expelled. We keep the souls from being wrongly taken. We maintain the balance between the three worlds. If we were gone, in any region, it would be pure chaos. Demons would no longer have a checkpoint. Call us customs. You can't bring in restricted items. An innocent soul is like trying to bring a machine gun onto a plane. It ain't gonna happen."

"But hell has hounds. I've heard them. I was chased by them," I answered and shuddered at the memory. "Are you saying some of you Lycans are down there?"

"We all make sacrifices, Ailis. Elders, upon their deaths, remain in hell. They are the guardians of the gate. We live two lives, one up here and one down there, before we can pass on to our final resting grounds. When we die, we change places with the Elders, allowing them to move on to their better place. We guard the gate until the next one comes to take our place. It is a cycle that has worked since the deal was struck. It is an honorable charge to have. We are born and learn to love mankind. We die and go to hell, and we guard the souls who have passed. We make sure only the deserving souls receive punishment."

"Is that why I didn't see one?" I asked. The memory of punishments washed over me.

"Yes. We do not participate in the punishments. It was a hellhound who smelled the two souls within you. If it weren't for one of my brethren, you'd still be there. Once he smelled dual souls, the punishments stopped.

They wouldn't allow another to come near you. They roamed the halls around your cage, protecting you. Your freedom was granted, and you were freed. It is what we do."

I had to put my head between my knees before I passed out. It was too much information. "Are they going to kill me after this? Because I know?"

"I don't think so." His answer was short and to the point. I'd have preferred some elaboration.

"You don't think so? How comforting." My voice was high-pitched.

"You have had my protection from the moment we met. That protection is still there. Anyone who comes for you must come for me first. But if you get word that I'm dead, run. I can't protect you if I'm dead."

I laughed. "And where the hell do I hide from Lycans, Miguel? Up until now, I thought they were a myth. You just said your people were everywhere. I can't hide from everywhere."

"You know what we feel like now. You'll be able to spot them. You'll feel their energy. Pay attention to my energy. Remember it."

"Great. Just great. Thanks for this, Miguel. This is way beyond any favor I could have ever owed you. *If*, and that is a massive if at this point, I walk away from this on this side of a body bag, I'll be hunted by fucking Lycans. You've painted the biggest target on my back."

"I know." Miguel sighed. "Ailis, if ever you meet one of us, don't let on you know. Just stay away. That's the only advice I can give you," he answered. "Now, do you understand why I kept this from you? Why I lied?"

I nodded. After a long minute of thinking, I lifted my head from my knees. "You being Lycan and me being spit out of hell… It's no coincidence that me and you met, is it?"

"No. Every Lycan felt it when you were spit from hell. It was like the world was off balance for a moment. I was the closest one to you and came to investigate. I thought maybe a devil had crawled out, wearing the suit of a witch. Instead, I found you. I knew who you were and where you had been before you told me. I could smell it on you. I could feel your pull, your need for salvation. Your soul was bleeding to death. Whether we became friends or not, I would have been in your life, one way or another. You were a bloody lighthouse for demons after that. I couldn't just let you fend for yourself."

"I love you for saving me, but I really hate you right now." My words were sharp.

"I hate myself, too. More than you know."

"This is what happens when you play with monsters. You get pulled into their crap every time." I glanced around the pool. It was still empty. "Where did everyone go?"

"Inside. Caser tends to carry around a lot of dread when he's angry. People don't like to be near him."

I frowned. "Why didn't I feel it? I mean, I felt fear but more because I could feel the energy rolling off him."

"You're used to it, in a way, because of me. Your brain was probably telling you to keep alert, but you weren't scared of him, not like the others."

"Oh, don't kid yourself, Miguel. I was well and truly scared."

"But you are brave." He smiled.

"No. I'm not that brave. I'm scared shitless. Do not confuse bravery with not having a better option." I laughed. It wasn't a happy laugh. "Now I have to go to your secret lair."

"I'm sorry, Ailis. If I didn't ask you to come to Mexico, they would have simply taken you or found some god-awful way of forcing you to come. We all do things we'd rather not admit out loud when we are desperate."

I shook my head. "Nothing could have forced me here, Miguel. I have nothing for them to take."

"Me," he muttered. "They would have used me, and we both know you would have come. You may hate me, but you still love me. That, the love, is why you hate me so much."

"No, Miguel. I hate you because you didn't love me as much as I loved you. Your lies are going to be the reason I die," I replied and picked up my pool bag and book. "I hate you because you're just another monster to me."

"I'm not a monster, Ailis. I'm a Lycan."

"You're not a monster because you are Lycan? Please. And the tooth fairy only wants teeth and not the drop of soul in the roots." I sneered at him. "Miguel, the only thing I want to talk about now is how the hell do we kill one of these monsters?"

"We're not monsters."

"Semantics. We can split hairs until another body washes up, or you can get over the fact that what I see is different than what you see. You weren't standing on the receiving end of learning about Lycans for the first time. Excuse me for being scared and pissed off. I think I have every right to wallow in it for a bit," I answered. "Just tell me how I kill a Lycan or werewolf and leave the rest for a different day. You're the one that dragged me into this. You can damn well make sure I can get myself out of it. Because if you die, I'm screwed six ways from Sunday. I won't make it out of this city, and you know it."

"Fair enough." He nodded. "For werewolves, use a silver bullet. It's the only way you could kill one without being ripped apart. As for myself, I'd tear them apart. But for you, you'd shoot one in the heart or head. Either way is a kill shot. If you had to, you could wound one and run. You'd probably get away. A werewolf would need a lot of time to heal a silver shot injury. If you manage to kill one, cut off his head and burn it. Scatter the ashes in the wind, just to be on the safe side. You don't want one waking up pissed off."

"And what about if they are in human form?" I asked, already knowing the answer.

"Same way," he answered. "Once you kill one in wolf form, Lycan or Were, they will revert back to human form anyway. That makes it easier to lop off their heads."

I nodded slowly. "Thank God, I'm a pretty good shot."

"Try doing it under pressure, running, scared, possibly injured," he replied.

I smirked. "Have you not been paying attention, Miguel? I'm usually under pressure, running for my life, scared to death and bleeding."

"What you picture in your mind? It's worse in real life. It's dangerous, Ailis. If you fail, if you're attacked, just one scratch in wolf form and you could contract the virus and die. It won't matter how good of a shooter you are if you die in the end, anyway. This isn't like the lore you've read. You're not going to banish one to hell. They don't need an exorcism. No amount of prayer is going to cure this virus any more than it'll cure the measles." Miguel looked concerned. Any time I asked how to end something, it was because I had intended on doing the job. It wasn't for curiosity's sake.

"What about Lycan? Isn't that where I've been so graciously invited to go?" I asked.

"To kill a Lycan, you have to sever the head from its body and burn all of it, scatter the ashes. A silver bullet to the brain will probably work, but I've seen my people heal some outrageous wounds. The higher up in the Pack they are, the stronger they are. Silver will slow them down, but not enough for you to get away. Don't bother trying to kill one. Just run, Ailis. It usually takes another Lycan to kill one. A human isn't strong enough. By the time you severed the head away from the body, it would have had a good fifteen minutes to kill you in fifteen different ways."

"What about my abilities?" I asked. I flexed my hand as a show of power.

He shook his head. "You can shove their power back down, but only small shows of power. Keep in mind, even in human shape, they can break your neck in a heartbeat, so wasting your energy would be pointless. Once, long ago, a dozen witches tried to flush out a Lycan Pack. They all died. They were powerful, like you, and they were all dead in under a minute. They used up all their auras but died anyway. You may be powerful, but it takes time to harness your power. It takes us no time to shift and rip you apart. We're faster than you."

"Well, that's comforting."

"It wasn't meant to be. We are charged with protecting mankind. How much protection would we be if we were easy to kill?" Miguel's answer irritated me but made perfect sense. "Will you help us end this?"

I nodded. I could do this willingly, choice intact, or Caser would force me to do it anyway. I'd sooner still have my freedom and help over the alternative. "When this is over, lose my number. My debt is paid. You will make sure no Lycan or werewolf or whatever other creatures I don't know about makes the decision that I die for this knowledge or comes after me, or I'll spend the rest of my short life finding a way to kill you all. Do we have a deal?"

"We have a deal." He sounded hurt but agreed.

We shook on it. I leaned in with a glare. "If I die, you're all coming with me. I will summon every demon under my toes with my final breath and unleash hell on your kind. I'll gladly spend eternity in hell for it. I'm going there anyway."

Before he could make his own threat, his cell phone buzzed, and he jumped. He pulled it from his pocket and read the text. There was another murder. This time, the sun was still up. Thank you for small miracles.

"What about Caser?" I asked. "Is he going to keep coming after me until I show up?"

Miguel grabbed my bag, and I followed behind him. "You will do nothing. I, on the other hand, will deal with it. Do *not* meet with him, Ailis. I will handle it."

"He'll try to kill you," I whispered.

"I didn't think you'd care. What's one more dead monster?" Miguel asked.

I shrugged. "I care that he'll kill me next without you standing between us. You had better believe I have a problem with that."

"Glad to see your priorities haven't changed. Now let's go."

They hadn't. There was no point in saying otherwise. I followed the furry monster away from the pool. This was every scary movie ever made. The stupid girl in love with the monster. How cliché. All I needed was an attic to die in, and it would be complete. I could almost hear my grandmother in the back of my mind, *"Ailis, you welcome trouble like a farmer welcomes the rain during drought season."*

Chapter Ten

The drive was bitterly silent. It wasn't the kind of silence I liked. This gnawed at my bones. It hung in the air like suspended moments, all the things that had been left unsaid. One harsh word would bring it crashing down like giant icicles waiting for someone to walk under them. The stillness that clung to us was slow-moving poison in its nothingness. It cruelly made each breath tight and shallow, a heavy reminder that I was locked in the vehicle with a Lycan, a myth, a killer, a monster. The silence was the most terrifying part. I didn't know what he was thinking. But I'd sooner drown in the silence than open my mouth. What could I say that wouldn't eat us up or throw Mr. Furry into a fit of rage? Now that I knew what he was, I didn't think he'd have to hide it from me any longer. I've never seen a Lycan in full form, only in drawings — and perhaps in my one dream of the first crime scene. I didn't want to pick now, speeding down the highway, as the exact time to experience an up close and personal viewing.

"Can a Lycan drive?" I blurted out.

He glanced at me. He could sense my fear. He grinned and looked back to the road. "I'm not going to shift if that's what you're scared of."

"Can they, though, drive? Or we would wreck?"

"I think we'd wreck long before I found out if I could drive. I've never tried it. Shifting would take my attention away from the road. We'd be in the ditch before I was done shifting. But it would be one hell of a ride until we were wrapped around a tree," he answered, and I winced at the thought. I had died once, wrapped around a pole. He noticed and had the decency of looking bad. "Poor choice of words. I'm not going to shift, no matter how angry I get."

"What if I were a threat to you?" I asked.

"Are you asking if I would shift to defend myself against you?" He squeaked out the question like he didn't want me to answer. I nodded. His shoulders were hunched with disappointment. "Anyone else, I'd shift part of my body, like my hands, and defend myself. But with you, no. I wouldn't shift to defend myself from you."

"Not even if it meant I would kill you?" I don't know why I needed to know. I just did.

"I'd rather be dead than live and know I killed you to keep my own heart beating."

I turned my eyes back to the road. "I wish I could say the same thing to you, Miguel."

"Would you kill me?" He sounded surprised. I don't know why that came as one.

"If I had to, yes," I answered. I wanted him to understand the line I drew in the sand. I would kill him to save myself. Maybe I needed to hear myself say it out loud more than I needed him to hear it.

"Good to know." His only response and the end of our conversation.

We stayed silent until we pulled into a parking spot in the middle of nowhere. The Yal-Ku Lagoon was located in the town of Akumal, about twenty minutes south of Playa del Carmen, off the 307 Highway. During my research on Mexico, I read about the Yal-Ku Lagoon. It was supposed to be a hotspot for tourists. The inlet from the ocean, where the salt water met with fresh water, was a snorkeler's haven. Today, the parking lot showed no sign of sightseers, and the only flash photography being done would not show up on Instagram. Police took up every available parking spot, and I doubted any of them had enjoyed what they had seen so far.

I jumped out of the Jeep before Miguel slid it into park. The dread slapped me across the face, along with the intense afternoon heat. I didn't complain about the blistering sun. I'd take the heat over the dark any day. Only today, the heat was accompanied by fear and the same dread we had felt at the other two locations. The air was thick enough to chew on, but it was still better than being locked in a tin can on wheels with Miguel. I didn't know which was worse, that he was my ex or that he was just another one of the monsters.

Martínez was waiting for us by his truck, his arms folded. He tried to make it look like a casual pose. I knew better. He was hugging himself. I had just gotten out of the vehicle and already wanted to hug myself. I couldn't imagine what he felt. He was in plain clothes. Most of the other officers were off-shift and dressed as if they had been called away from mowing lawns and grocery shopping. I could always tell who were civvies and who were law. It was in the way they carried themselves. For some, it was all in their eyes and the haunt they carried from too many years of working crimes that killed bits of their souls. For others, it was how they reached for their gun belt that wasn't there.

"Martínez." I nodded at him.

"I see he's brought the token witch again," he said, as he breathed in the air between us and shook his head. He looked at the Jeep, then at me. It felt like he was looking through me, like I wasn't important enough to make eye contact with. "You smell like Miguel's cologne."

What could I really say to that? I was 'the token witch', the only witch, from what I could feel, on-site, and I probably did smell like Miguel. I didn't like what he alluded to, but knew he was only picking a fight to distract himself from whatever he was feeling inside. Anger wasn't all bad. It was a mask for sadness and fear. Lashing out at the closest person helped, sometimes. I was a big girl. I could take it. Rage, on the other hand, wasn't something I'd stand around for. Plus, there wasn't anything Martínez could say that I hadn't heard hundreds of times before or hadn't had spray-painted in my living room.

"Good afternoon to you, too." I stood at his front and smiled. It was my best professional smile, the one I wore when work made me go to fundraisers I didn't want to attend, which was all of them. My smile was as empty as a demon was remorseful.

Martínez was a tall man—the kind of tall that said he hit his head on enough door jams that he ducked no matter what doorway he walked through. Tall but not lanky. He was muscular, and I bet he moved like a finely tuned machine. I guess you'd have to be when the bad guys had more firepower and a willingness to shoot you in the back or drag you into hell. I had to crane my neck to look him in the eyes or step back. I choose muscle cramps in my neck. His hair was golden brown. It was a shade I knew would change color with the amount of light that shone onto it. Women paid big money for Martínez's hair color. They also forked over their credit cards to have sun-kissed skin like his. I stared him in the eyes. His sunglasses didn't hide his squint. I didn't know if it was the sun or my presence that made his eyes scrunch. I put my money on him glaring at me over him not wanting to burn his eyes out with the sun.

"Nothing to say?" I prodded. I wanted to finish this outside and not bring the anger into the crime scene. It would be bad enough without his temper mixed in. I snapped my fingers in his face. I didn't just prod. I goaded him into releasing it. "Do you really believe your silence bothers me that much? I don't depend on your voice, but common courtesy would have been nice."

He leaned down over me. "You shouldn't be here. You shouldn't have come."

"Why, because I worship the devil and sacrifice babies?" I asked.

He let his glasses slide down his nose and peered over them. It reminded me of a professor I once had, just before he schooled me on something I didn't want to hear. "What you do in your spare time is not my concern. What you do in Mexico is. You should go home before it's your body we're fishing out of the water, Miss Kyteler."

"*Dr.* Kyteler," I corrected him. "That sounded a little too close to being a threat, officer. I came here to do a job, and I'm going to do it. Nothing you say is going to send me packing. Rest assured, though, once the job is done, I'll be gone, and you'll have Mexico back to your lonesome."

He pushed his glasses back up. "I look forward to the day you walk onto the plane, Dr. Kyteler. Anytime you want to leave, I'll drive you to the airport myself."

"How gentlemanly of you to offer. I'll be sure to call," I replied.

"I won't hold my breath," he answered, clipped and heated.

If I didn't know any better, Martínez didn't think I'd make it out alive. His fear wasn't *of* me. It was *for* me. He just didn't know how to show the new witch on the block that he feared for her safety without showing he cared. There still were people afraid of being seen consorting with witches. We were banned from churches and damned to hell. The Catholic Church had a problem with those of us who saw through their shit. They weren't in a position to judge, but they still did. Wasn't that always the case? Those who shouldn't throw stones always had a rock in each hand. I didn't bother telling the church that they didn't have the kind of juice needed to damn my soul any more than they could save it for a mere hundred bucks every Sunday. They could keep their altars, and I didn't need them to pray for me.

"You're scared." It was a statement, not a question.

"I am not scared," he countered.

I stepped back. "Yes, you are. So am I. And that's okay, Martínez. What we're dealing with *is* scary, and you'd be foolish not to fear it."

"There are scarier things out there than this," he said quietly, as if the scarier things could hear him knocking at their door.

I nodded. "You bet your sweet ass there is. But that doesn't make this any less scary."

Martínez grinned for a short moment like he had forgotten that he didn't like me before he closed his face back down. He motioned behind me. "Run along, little witch. Miguel is waiting for you." He spoke as though his opinion of me rated higher than that of a titmouse. It didn't.

"I'll see you later, Martínez." I turned and paused. I could have walked away. I could have left him in his anger. It would have served him right. I closed the distance between us. "I'm sorry my being here bothers you or makes you uncomfortable. I forgive you for your harsh words, Martínez. You're hurting, you're scared and you don't want to be here. Me coming into your space makes you have to stay here longer than you'd like to be, and I'm sorry for that. I get it. This, whatever is in the air, has made me do the same thing, bait and attack others. It feels good to let it out. Rest easy. I can take it, Martínez. I can take a lot more than what you're dishing out. And if it eats you up later tonight, you have my number. If you want to cut me up, I don't mind. I'll try to be as quick as possible so that we all can get the hell out of here and go home."

"Thank you." He nodded once. I left him to stew but gave him my forgiveness because I could. I knew it would eat at him later — that he was a prick — when he was gone from here, when the fear subsided. And lord forbid he didn't make it home. I'd have regretted not giving it to him.

I followed Miguel to a covered area, where, from the posters, they sold tickets to the Lagoon. Hanging to the left were lifejackets and snorkeling gear. A long manmade wooden counter stretched two sides of the building, connecting in the far-right corner. Miguel handed me little blue bootie covers for my shoes and pointed to a sign of rules. They didn't want your dirt mucking up their natural habitat. It also said I had to shower before trekking in. I covered my boots. I wasn't going to shower in their outdoor system. I wasn't modest or shy, but I wasn't about to strip down at a crime scene, either. They couldn't really expect us all to be walking around in little booties and underwear, could they? I didn't ask and kept my clothes on. Without the mangled body, I wouldn't have had a problem traipsing around in undies.

I walked the path, lined on either side with stones. Miguel walked ahead. He didn't slow down or wait for me. I took my time and took it all in. Call me strange, but it was beautiful, even if it was a crime scene. Every so often, I'd come across a bronze statue or bench. Hammocks and palapas were strategically placed for rest. I've been all over the world, and Mexico was one of the few countries built for people by people who loved their country. It showed in the finer details. I paused and ran my hand over the coolness of the Maya woman depicted in a statue. The artistry was enough to make me pull out my phone and take a picture. I wanted one good memory of coming here. I passed two lovers on a bench and admired the artwork and the surrounding garden. It would be the only beauty I would see. The rest would hurt my soul. I'd take in as much as I could, so I'd have something to help when my thoughts grew darker.

"The sculptures were created by a Costa Rican sculptor, Francisco Zúñiga. He was one of the most recognized and celebrated artists of the twentieth century, known for his modern and realistic style."

Martínez stood behind me. I had felt him moving down the trail before he spoke. "Some of the best ones are more hidden. That's what I think, anyway. Not many people venture out to find them. If you're diving here and go deep enough, there are some in the lagoon. If you can take your eyes off the fish, there's a lot more to see."

"Do you scuba or free dive?" I asked.

"Both. If I'm out in the blue, I scuba. I can't hold my breath long enough to see everything I want to see. I'm a novice photographer and like to take pictures below. It's my way of showing the world what we should protect. I prefer to free dive, though. I like the feeling of being one with the water, not having a tie to the world above. I like it because I feel free. There are no demands down there. There's nothing bad. There's just the natural flow of things. If something happens, it isn't because I was targeted. It happened because that's just what happens." He seemed at peace when he talked about his passions. "When I'm not knee-deep in the luxurious life of a cop, I'm in school."

"What are you studying?" I tried to find a commonality between us. Learning was my go-to. Most people liked to learn and craved knowledge. It was one of the only things I usually had in common with others. I hoped it would cut the tension.

"Marine biology. It's why I stayed in Mexico. My mother moved to New Mexico when I was four. When she got sick, she wanted to come home. I moved back in my late teens. I became a cop for the benefits and steady income. After she passed, I enrolled in university. I wanted to be more than what I am, you know? Make her proud."

I nodded. I fought the urge to hug him. "Never doubt a mother's pride. You have a lot to be proud of, and I bet she was, too."

"She loved this place. Now, it's tainted with one more horror." His voice was soft. I could hear the regret and anger. It was tangible and heavy.

We paused at a palapa. It was a small open cabin with enough shade to make it feel like a refuge from the sun. "I'm sorry this has happened in your place, Martínez. It's always worse when something you love is spoiled. We're more on edge when something we love has been threatened. It feels personal and not just another shitty thing to have happened. It feels like it was done to us, specifically."

He nodded. "How did you know?"

"A couple of years ago, some religious zealots broke into my house and spray-painted my walls with slurs. What actually bothered me wasn't the slurs. It was that it was mine, the place I loved most, the only place in the world where I didn't have to pretend that I am someone else. It was the only place in this world where being a witch was okay, a space where I didn't have to hide. They took that away from me, and now, when I look at the picture window in my living room, I remember having to clean the paint off. I still see 'burn in hell, witch' written on the glass. It doesn't matter how many times I clean the window. It's still there in the back of my mind." I squeezed my eyes shut. The memory, no matter how much time passed, still hurt. "They waited there for me to come home. I think they were going to kill me if they could have. They tried to kill my cat. Well, it's not my cat. It's a stray cat that moved into my garden shed when I bought the house. They tied it up, doused it with gas and waited for me. They tried to burn my cat alive."

"What the hell?" Martínez was disgusted. "You said tried. Does that mean it lived after that?"

"They didn't get to light the match, Martínez." I opened my eyes and smiled. "You can say what you want to me, and it rolls off. People have said a lot of mean things to me over the years. I'm used to it. They can spray it on my walls, and I'll wash it off and repaint. I learned to not care about the opinion of people who don't matter in my life. You can destroy my place of comfort, and I'll let you walk out my front door unharmed. But don't hurt my cat. Don't *ever* screw with my cat."

He leaned in quietly. Like he had a secret. "Did you kill them for it?"

And there was the secret. Murder. "No...but I wanted to. I wanted to burn them alive. I wanted to tie them up, as they had to my cat, douse them in gas and strike a match. Instead, I knocked them out with one wave of power and called the police. They weren't strong enough to fight my magic. Their souls carried so much taint that they had nothing to shield me with. The average person, without a tainted soul, and I'd have had to work for it. But them, they went down like a sack of potatoes. I untied my cat, and the police arrived while I was washing the gas off my cat. They thought I was drowning it and drew their guns. To be fair, it looked like I was holding it underwater. The damn thing screamed and clawed me all to hell. I still have scars from the homeless bastard."

Martínez laughed. "Yeah, I've tried to wash a cat. They don't compare impossible tasks to washing a cat for nothing."

"I'm sorry that this space is your stray cat, Martínez." I touched his arm, and he flinched. I didn't let my smile fall, although it bothered me to feel him pull back. I wasn't that bad of a person once you got to know me and were willing to look beyond the scent of matchsticks pouring off me. "I have a hard time, at night, in my space. I'm still angry that the bad guys invaded it. I had to work three jobs and do a lot of crap work that required me to clean goat blood out of my hair every night just to save enough for a down payment. Vancouver is near impossible to afford a house, and I had to buy one on a demon's list of collections. But I did it. Then the bad guys came into my home and tried to take away something that was mine. But what really got me was that my cat, the only thing I have that I love, was threatened. So, I get it. It sucks. It makes us angry, and we lash out. I won't hold it against you."

He looked down the trail to Miguel and stepped back from me. "Miguel is waving us over."

He didn't move because of who I am. He moved because he was scared of Miguel. "I may be his token witch, Martínez, but Miguel doesn't own me and doesn't say who I can be friends with or who I can comfort. You're hurting. Miguel doesn't get to say who can make it feel less horrible."

Martínez stepped to the side. "This isn't a fight I want, witchy woman — not for all the witches in the world. I'm not going to roast my ass over my sadness. My world just doesn't work like that. Miguel is in charge here. Making him angry isn't going to win me any points when it comes to promotions or transfers. I want out of this life more than I want a hug. I want to do something more in this world, and a hug because I'm sad isn't going to get me there anytime soon."

I walked away slowly. I was in no rush to see what I could already smell. Martínez gagged behind me. I pulled a small tube of eucalyptus from my bag and passed it back. It was the stuff the local coroner back home had given me at a particularly heinous crime scene last year. It helped cover up the smell of death in the morgue. Today, it barely covered the stench. I'd remember today every time I smelled eucalyptus.

The trees opened up to sand and smooth rock. A massive statue of a woman, nude, lounging on her back sat to my right. She looked happy. I was envious of her frozen state of joy. The lagoon was twenty feet ahead. The water was green and blue, with rocks jutting out like little towers. One look and I knew why Martínez loved this place. It was peaceful, aside from the body tied to the earth in front of the walkway to the water. It was like looking into a mirror of past crimes. She was young, petite and gutted. Incense lingered near the body. They weren't enough to cover the smell of her bowels that had spilled onto the earth in fear.

I crouched down and let my eyes wander. Unfocused, I could pretend I wasn't staring at a dead body, if only until the first tear fell. Melted blue candle wax, protection from evil spirits, pooled at each point of the circle. The candles would normally be inside the circle, but the drippings were on the outside. Whatever they were doing, they were conjuring it to the inside of the circle with the victim. I shuddered at the thought of being trapped inside a circle with a demon.

"Why are the candles on the outside of the circle? Aren't they usually on the inside?" Miguel asked. He was watching me and picking up on what I questioned about the scene.

"That's the same thing I was just thinking," I answered. I didn't look at him. I continued to scan the area. I didn't want to miss anything. "The candles are usually placed on the inside to keep out bad spirits, to protect those inside the circle — or it wouldn't be a circle of protection. Why they'd put them on the outside is beyond me. At first glance, it looks like a circle of protection, where the holder of the circle would stand inside it to keep themselves safe. But so far, that's not what they're being used for. It looks like it's being used to summon a demon and bind a soul as an offering while protecting those on the outside. Protection outside a circle is some damn strong magic."

"No one here is that powerful. The only one who we thought had the slightest chance in hell, we found dead."

"Maybe not one single person, but a group, yes," I answered and turned to face him. "Everything I've seen so far is run-of-the-mill Wiccan, but the knockoff brand. It's all stuff you can find in a book from your local library, from the incense to the stones. Real witches don't fiddle with this crap, Miguel. None of us want to pay the cost of feeding the gods. We're not that stupid."

"People show, on a daily basis, how stupid they are," he replied.

I sighed. I had to agree. Most of us would be unemployed if it were for mankind testing the limits of human stupidity. "Isn't it written somewhere that the ignorant shall inherit the earth?"

"Not the ignorant, the meek. *Blessed are the meek, for they will inherit the earth.*" Miguel corrected me. "It's a Bible verse, Matthew 5:5. But yours is probably closer to the truth than mine, in this case. Whoever did this is not meek. They're vicious. There's nothing gentle about what this woman has endured."

I stepped back and scanned the entire scene. It was too clean for a bloodbath to have happened here. Human sacrifice was a messy business. I stepped away from Miguel and motioned toward the bronze statue. A light blue towel was crumpled on the ground. Small drips of blood coated one corner of the towel. I picked it up. My hands were gloved, but it still felt odd in my hand, like I was touching something I shouldn't be. Energy ran up my arm like pins and needles. The towel had been here while the girl was killed, and magic was called on. It was fresh enough to prickle my arm. *The first clue. Finally.*

I looked over my shoulder. We were alone. "Miguel, could you track the person who used this towel?"

He laughed suddenly and stopped once he realized I wasn't joking. "What, like a bloodhound? I'm not a fucking *dog*, Ailis."

I shrugged and tried my best to smile apologetically. "So, that's a yes or a no?"

He glared at me and pulled the towel from my hand with enough force to make me stumble. "Yes, we can track, like a dog." He spat the words. "Thank you for reminding me of who I really am…a monster."

I leaned forward. "It's not *what* you are that makes you a monster, Miguel. It's *who* you are."

He paused. When he saw no remorse in me, hurt filled his eyes. "I had no choice."

"Saying the same thing over and over is for your benefit, not mine. We all have choices, and we all pay for the ones we make. It doesn't matter if we think what we are doing is for the better good. The pavement on the road to hell is there because of good intentions like yours, Miguel. But the road ends eventually, and at the end of it, there is always a bill to pay. This is just your cost for good intentions," I answered. "What's the saying you were once so fond of telling the bad guys? Oh right, '*and you will be my witnesses in Jerusalem.*' As you once told me, the fear of losing friends silences a witness. I will not be silent. I am your witness."

"Do not quote scripture to me, Ailis." Miguel turned and left me at the sculpture. I watched him make a call. When he was done, he walked from the scene.

I followed behind his quickened pace. Instead of heading back to the Jeep, he turned into the trees. I swallowed my fear and fell in line behind him until he put up his hand to stop me. He shook his head, and I stayed in place while he moved onward. I heard the faintest rustle in the trees before Miguel returned without the towel. I stumbled through the roots and branches in an effort to keep up the pace with him. He didn't slow, and he didn't keep the branches from coming back and whipping my arms and legs, either. That's what a friend would do, but we currently weren't friends. I didn't know what we were, but it was somewhere between old flames and enemies.

Miguel drove us to a coffee shop in silence. I was tempted to ask if we could stop in the souvenir shops, but I wanted a good cup of coffee more than a new tchotchke. We would wait until we got word from Caser. I didn't care that our words were clipped and short between us as we waited. I was in Coffee Heaven with a big 'C' and 'H.' I ordered a Flat White, a pump of vanilla, two cookies and a toasted bagel. I hadn't eaten much since I landed. I was starved. It tasted like home. I was homesick and hadn't noticed just how badly I craved home until I tasted my coffee, made the same way as the one on the corner by work. Miguel didn't order anything. No deer on the menu. I guess he was out of luck. As for me, I ate it all.

"Why is there no butter anywhere here?" I asked Miguel as I ate the last of my bagel from the comfort of a stuffy Jeep. "At the resort, they're frozen balls of butter, like no one uses it here. Who doesn't use butter?"

"How do you go from treating me like crap to making small talk?" Miguel asked.

"I don't know. How do you go from telling me you're one of the monsters, then become indignant when I treat you like one?" I countered. "Don't get all offended when I give you the truth. Everyone demands truth until it applies to them. Just because you don't want to hear it doesn't make it wrong."

"*Your* truth, Ailis. It is yours. Your truth isn't always right."

"But it isn't always wrong, now, is it? If it were, you wouldn't have invited me here to your little tea party," I replied. "You trust my judgment as long as it doesn't include you."

He turned his angry eyes to me, and I fought not to cower. "You do *not* have the right to judge me."

"Right, I forgot. Only you have the right to judge others—you and your holy warrior crusade bullshit. My judgment hurts your feelings. Yours takes lives. Get off your soap box."

"I understand your anger. It's always been there, just under the surface. I even understand your reaction. I'd have had the same one. But your hate? I would have thought better of you than to be so close-minded and prejudiced," Miguel said, his voice flat. "I had almost forgotten how awful your temper could be."

"You don't know me anymore. Don't pretend you do. You've been gone far too long to act like you have any idea who I am." My voice was not flat. It held heat enough for me to turn the air conditioning up a notch.

"Are you getting to know Martínez? You seemed pretty close, even just feet from a dead girl." Jealousy replaced his calm control. It wasn't a side of him I was used to. Then again, we covet the most that which we cannot have.

I shrugged. "What's it to you, Miguel? You don't own me. You don't control what I do."

He gripped the steering wheel until I heard the leather strain. "You're right. I don't control you. But I control him."

I leaned into my seat. It now made perfect sense, the fear Martínez had when it came to Miguel. The control he said Miguel had over his life and transfer. I smiled. It wasn't a happy one. I was disappointed in Miguel and his little green monster. "Are you going to hurt him for talking to me? Are you going to destroy his life simply because he was upset and needed someone to talk to? How judgmental of you, Mr. Holy Warrior."

"He's mine to protect. And I intend on protecting him from you." He turned and looked at me. His stare felt like hands pressing down on my shoulders. His eyes had a weight to them that made the air in the Jeep feel like breathing soup. "You can stomach talking to him, but not me? We're the same monster, Ailis."

"No. You're not." I replied. "I didn't even know he was a Lycan until you just told me, but that doesn't make a difference. He is not you."

"Don't kid yourself. We're cut from the same cloth."

Before we could cut each other apart with words, Miguel's phone buzzed. We both froze and stared at his phone. The fight was over. Now we were back on the clock. We'd go back to emotionally destroying each other later. I'd schedule it between monster hunting and death at the hands of a newly discovered pain in the ass.

"Caser," Miguel answered. I only caught one side of the conversation. From the anticipation in Miguel's eyes, I knew the Pack had found something. Miguel hung up and put the Jeep in gear. "They tracked the smell to a marina and into Playa. They're waiting outside a two-level apartment building. A twenty-three-year-old local woman lives inside. They're waiting for us...in case she decides to leave."

"You can smell how old people are?" I asked. It sounded like a stupid question after I said it out loud.

"No. Caser asked the neighbors," Miguel answered and shook his head. He thought it was a stupid question, too.

"Sorry, dumb question," I squeaked out, embarrassed.

"Normally, I'd say there are no stupid questions, but that one is making me rethink my opinion on the matter," he replied with a grin.

Miguel called Martínez and told him we had a lead. His lies came out like butter, smooth on a hot pan. "Tell them the witch has tracked the energy to an apartment building in Playa."

"Thanks, because they don't already want to burn me at the stake," I mumbled.

"The only fire you're going to burn in is the one your wicked tongue lights," Miguel answered. Yep, the truth sucks when it applies to you. "It's a shitty feeling, isn't it?"

"What's that?" I asked.

"To be considered a monster for who you were born to be. To be wished dead for no other reason than the prejudices of others," he answered.

"Being a witch doesn't make me a bad guy," I countered. My voice was heated. The days of burning witches weren't so long ago that my people didn't still fear the coming of The Hammer — the witch hunter of the church. The fear was so great that our own Coven had their version of The Hammer to keep little witches and magical artists in check.

"Do I point out that we're currently hunting witches? Or are we just going to ignore that fact?" Miguel asked. "Your kind has killed more innocents than mine has, a hundred times over. I can actually name the innocents around the globe who have died at a Lycan's hands. Can you do the same for witches?"

I opened my mouth once and closed it, feeling like a hypocrite. Miguel didn't keep pushing it. He made his point and left it at that. We were fifteen minutes away from the apartment and rolled up to the backside of the building to a show of force. I pulled chalk from my bag and started to hand out small hex bags of protection from my backpack. I never left home without a few dozen. When I got to Martínez, I raised my eyebrows and gave him an 'I know your secret, little pup' look. He looked at Miguel and glared. Not everyone likes when their secrets are told, but everyone should know who told them. I was a firm believer that blind trust got you killed.

I drew symbols on the shirts of each officer that I stopped in front of, wards against evil. Most of them gladly took the bags, happy I could help. But there were a few who had to be bullied into it. I listened to them whisper about my black magic and going to hell if they allowed me to help. The earlier chat with Miguel had made the comments from the peanut gallery mean a little more than they normally would have. They, like me, didn't understand what they were talking about.

"Listen… If there's a demon, a possessed or even a curse in there, do you really think your gun is going to stop an attack on your soul?" I asked. "Take it or leave it. But you're not coming up there without it. You'd be nothing more than meat for me to trip on, souls to be turned against us. The bags and symbols won't keep you from bullets, but they'll protect your soul. And trust me when I tell you, your soul is more precious than your life. Having a cut-up soul and still breathing is probably the worst pain you'll ever feel."

"Speaking from experience?" Martínez asked.

I nodded. "It's been skinned alive several times over. It isn't just painful. It hurts every day. Every breath I take, I feel it. The pain has stained me. I'll never forget it."

"Not a good way to live," he replied.

"No, it isn't," I answered and left it at that.

Maybe it was fear, or perhaps it was my personal experience. Whatever the case, it got them all into more of a cooperative mood. I wouldn't force them. I also wouldn't take them up the stairs without it. I didn't need to look over my shoulder and worry if the cop behind me was possessed and about to shank me. I had a scar on my back, just under the heart, where I had been stabbed by a little old lady who was cursed and possessed. I didn't know until I had a paring knife sticking out of me. But I knew now that an innocent was as deadly as a monster and wouldn't make that mistake again. One bad guy was enough of a nightmare. I didn't need to deal with a dozen of them.

Miguel led the team. Martínez behind him, then me. The others were at my back. If the woman focused, she'd hear us inching our way to her apartment. If not, we were background noise. I watched Miguel breathe in deeply, shake his head and stop tiptoeing to the door. I knew what it meant. There were no survivors inside that apartment. I couldn't help but sigh a breath of relief. I preferred when the bad guys were already down. But I didn't want to look so thrilled about another dead girl. People were scared enough of me. Showing my thanks for death would start them building a bonfire.

Miguel opened the door. I could smell blood and nothing more. I felt no curses, no hexes, no spells. The woman was just dead on the floor. I walked into an apartment that looked like cotton candy had thrown up everywhere. It was like every little girl's bedroom — frilly, lacey and so much pink. It was a large studio with a bathroom to the left. Books and trinkets littered every spare nook and cranny. It didn't take me more than a few seconds to know how she died, and there wasn't anything magical about it. Her throat had been slashed. She was left to die, drowning in her own blood. The police did their job with the body while I picked through her life.

"I can smell the last victim on her," Miguel whispered.

I nodded, and all my sympathy for the newest dead girl went out of the window. "She's rotting in hell."

"I hope so," Miguel replied and left me to snoop through the victim's home.

The police cleared out while we searched for clues. They didn't care much about the body. To tell the truth, neither did I. She played a part in the brutal slaying of innocents. She could rot on the floor for all I cared. I had no problem stepping around her, over her or on her. After the soul of the first victim had given me a play-by-play of her death, I would sleep perfectly fine if I had walked out of the door and locked this bitch inside. Miguel wouldn't allow it, though. I knew him too well. He'd make sure she received a proper burial. Whether she went to hell or not, he wouldn't allow her body to decay alone, unattended. *Bully for him.* I just wasn't that forgiving or kind. He had a softer spot inside than I did. But I guess monsters looked out for each other. I scolded myself for that final thought.

"She doesn't smell like a witch, not really," Miguel whispered to me. "She smells like she's been around them."

I lifted my eyebrows. "What does she smell like? Maybe if we can figure out the type of witches she was around, it could point us in their direction."

Miguel shook his head. "That's the problem. She doesn't really smell like a real witch. It's kind of like someone who has made cookies. It doesn't make them a pastry chef. She smells like a hodgepodge of witches — like she's trying everything because she doesn't know how to be a witch. She smells like someone who is hoping to be one."

"That's the same impression I get. She doesn't feel like one to me. I can pick up a little bit of residual energy but nothing more than what used to be on you years ago. Spend enough time with a witch, and you pick up their smell, like an aura that's been touched." I pointed at the bookshelves by the only window. "She has more books than I do on witchcraft. It's basically a collection of 'How to be a Witch for Dummies' and nothing a real witch would have in their kitchen."

Miguel stopped at the wall and stared at the framed photos. "She knew some of us, the lowly ones."

"She couldn't have known, could she?" I asked.

"No. Not likely and still lived. If she was anyone of importance to us, I would have known about her, and I didn't," he answered. "It could be a coincidence. Sometimes the most broken of society feel comforted around us. Those with broken souls seek us out without even knowing. Nothing more, nothing less."

"You don't sound sure."

"Nothing is for sure, Ailis. If she knew about us, the rest of us didn't know about it. If, by some fluke, she knew who we were and was sticking around, she probably has some fantasy that she could become a Lycan. If she knew the truth about us, she wouldn't have wanted the infection. No sane person would want that."

"Would you have killed her?" I asked.

His eyes darted to mine. "Yes, because that's what monsters do, Ailis. We kill people—not because she would have spread that virus and potentially killed dozens but because I love to kill people."

He was being sarcastic, but I still smiled in return. "I like to know where the line is, Miguel, or have you forgotten that my life hangs in the balance because of what you are?"

"If ever I doubt how big of a monster I am, I only need to look in your eyes for the reminder," he replied. "For the record, I'd have tried to hide her, not kill her. I don't take a life unless I absolutely have to."

Miguel left me to my thoughts, and all of them were about how I could go home with all my body parts intact. If ever there was another emergency, I was pretty sure he'd let the world burn before calling me for help again, and I was just fine with that. Miguel never again asking me to wade through murder scenes was something I could live with. As long as I was still living, I didn't care about the flames, either.

Chapter Eleven

Three in the morning was a stupid, foolish time to be awake. It was made worse by only just walking in the door at that hour. It was a cold hour to have on your heels. In January, it didn't matter what part of the world you were in. Three o'clock felt like the cold, eternal darkness slithered across your skin. They didn't refer to after midnight as *the witching hour* for nothing. Or maybe my nerves were just shot, and I needed sleep before I made my nightmares my reality. Not even the birds were happy to see me come back. They, unlike me, were tucked away in bed.

I stepped into the front lobby of my resort. Inside, it wasn't the witching hour. Too many different time zones of people kept the place lively at all hours. For that very reason, little was closed, and I could grab dinner when most ordered breakfast. Sure, I couldn't go buy a souvenir, but I could still get a banana split. I was almost certain that if I asked, they would have opened the gift shop. At the price of one night, I would expect they'd cater to whatever I wanted at any time of the day. I didn't know what a five-diamond rating would get me. I hadn't spent enough time enjoying my vacation to find out. Instead, I was eyeballing dead things and praying I'd live long enough to never talk about it. I wondered if doctors had the same problem. Wherever they went, someone was in need of a doctor? Or did they check out and let them die? I was on the verge of letting them all die just so I could see what five diamonds got me.

On the long bench to the left of the inside fountain, Martínez sat. I almost missed him. The lobby was massive, with seating and benches, a fountain and hanging lanterns. It looked like plants and flowers had been placed in every available space. It was something out of a magazine. *Home and Garden* would be proud. Beyond the lobby were two lounges, four restaurants and a club, all leading out to an acre of pools and lawns and bars. I told myself that I would see it all but doubted I would be able to keep that promise.

"Good evening—or should I say morning?" I said through a yawn. If he were here, something was up. Someone was dead, or he wanted something. Nothing good ever comes from a cop at your door at three in the morning. I knew it wasn't a poor attempt at a booty call. He wasn't that brave...or stupid. He couldn't have waited longer than thirty minutes. I'd just seen him at the last scene. "Why are you here? Miguel isn't here."

"I'm not here for Miguel," he answered like I should have known that.

"Then, pray tell, why are you here at this hour?"

"Caser asked me to come," he replied. "He was expecting you hours ago."

I raised one brow. "Are you a…member of Caser's family?"

He smiled, but it looked forced. There was no happiness in his eyes. "In a manner of speaking."

The closer I stepped to him, the more energy I could feel humming around him. Yet, my charm stayed perfectly still. He may be violence in motion, but he wasn't planning on unleashing it on me at that moment. Why could I feel him now but not before?

"You feel…different. Why?" I asked.

He rotated his neck and closed his eyes. His body shuddered. "I hold it back in public. But I'd say you've always felt me, only now you feel it a little clearer because you know what to look for. Truth be told, if you're used to Miguel, I barely hit your monster radar. He's much more than I'll ever be."

I could feel him a little better than before, but not by much. He was right. He was nothing like Miguel. He felt watered down…weaker. "What does Caser want?"

"Can we talk a little more privately?"

"Will this be a long talk?" I asked, and he shrugged. "Follow me, Martínez. I'll make us coffee that would tame any beast. I'm on the verge of falling asleep and would sooner not pass out with a monster in my room."

"I'm sure you say that to all the boys," he teased. It earned him a smile. "I'm surprised you're inviting me to your room alone."

"Are you concerned for my reputation?" I asked. "Don't worry. People already think I have sex with a devil, under the moon, covered in blood."

He leaned forward to my ear. "No. Your reputation isn't my concern. Most people are scared I'll eat them."

"Oh, please, most people don't even know what you are." I rolled my eyes. "Plus, you'd be doing me a favor, offering me mercy at this point. Eating me only screws you over. You'd be out a witch, and Miguel would skin you alive."

"Ain't that the truth." He laughed. It was a nervous laugh that held more honesty than any words could come close to.

He followed me to my room, and I let him in. Sure, he could kill me. But I could also kill him. I couldn't win a fistfight with him or any type of fair fight, but it would never be fair between us. He had brute strength, and I could squeeze the soul out of him before he could draw a claw. His aura was strong, pure, but it didn't compare to my desire to live. People underestimate their will to live. Even every day, run-of-the-mill people could move mountains to survive. I was no different. I just come to the party with a little more pizzazz at my fingertips than most people.

"Did you really threaten to kill Caser?" Martínez asked. He took a seat on the bench at the foot of my bed. He hadn't lost his smile. He looked amused as he leaned back, elbows on my bed to prop his body up.

"Threaten me and find out, Martínez," I answered.

"Francisco, but my friends call me Cisco."

"Am I your friend, Martínez?" I asked.

"Threaten me and find out."

That earned him a chuckle. "Cisco…unique. I wonder how many times you were called Sissy? I like it. Please, call me Ailis."

"Enough times for me to learn to get used to it. Like your name was any easier on you growing up?" he asked.

"I've heard them all. Kids are cruel." I stared at him and frowned. "This feels weird."

"What? Me in your bedroom?" he asked, and I nodded.

"I've never had a man who wasn't Miguel in my bedroom before," I finally admitted. "It feels awkward."

He lifted his eyebrows and sniffed the air. "Are you saying you've never?"

"Had sex?" I felt myself blush. My checks warmed instantly. "Yes, well, I have, just not a lot."

"What does 'not a lot' even mean? It's a simple yes or no answer."

"Miguel, but that's it," I answered.

"Only one partner? Were you in a nunnery your entire life?" he joked. "Your how old, mid-twenties? And you've only been with Miguel? You're missing out on one of life's only pleasures."

"I'm twenty-six. And no, I didn't grow up in a nunnery. But I met Miguel when I was sixteen. After him, it's hard to meet people when the only people who will talk to me want to kill me or want me to slaughter a goat to save them from a demon pact. Before Miguel, nothing I'd like to talk about." I trailed off, and I shook my head. I wasn't a nun, but my only other experiences came from hell. "I'm not going to talk about what happened when I was below, Martínez. I don't know you that well."

He dropped his smile and moved away from my bed. He put himself on the other side of my bedroom. "I apologize. I wasn't thinking. I didn't mean…shit. I'm sorry. We can go back downstairs if having me in here makes you uncomfortable. I was trying to use humor to put you at ease, and all I've done is make you feel like crap."

"It isn't your fault. You didn't know. No one really knows." I gave him a soft look. "You're just the first hottie I've had in my bedroom. I always stayed at Miguel's house. Before I bought my house, I had lived in some shady neighborhoods to save a few bucks. Not exactly a love nest compared to his pad."

He smiled, and his shoulders eased down. He was back to the irritating man of two minutes before. "Well, then, I'll count myself lucky."

"Don't count all your chickens before they've hatched. I may still decide to eat you," I replied. That eased the awkward moment, oddly.

"I apologize for riding you at the scene. Honestly, I wanted you to leave, not because you're a witch, but because I didn't want you involved in this. I thought if I made you unwelcome, you'd not want to come back. I didn't want you to see the horror. I don't like that the Pack has pulled you into this. I'm scared for your life," he admitted. He dipped his head. I almost missed the embarrassed flush on his checks. "And, to top it off, the scene at the lagoon, my calm space was ruined. I was itching to pick a fight, anything to take my mind off what happened there. I knew her, all the victims, and it's really getting to me. You were an easy target. None of the men feel comfortable around you, so it made you an easy mark."

"You don't need to apologize, but thank you. I get it. I was doing the same. When I realized I was picking at you, I tried to bridge the gap." I poured us each a cup of coffee. He took his same way I took mine, with a dash of sugar and a lot of cream. "I'm not the first witch to come to town. You guys had an older caplata in town. She had been here long enough that no one actually knew how old she was when I asked around."

"We had a witch, yeah."

"She was a caplata, not just a witch. She was much more powerful than that. She practiced voodoo. There is a difference. Her husband, a bokor, died years ago. No one I've spoken to knows when he died or how he died. The body never turned up. Some suspect she killed him for his wandering eyes." I corrected his witch comment. He frowned. He had the same look of confusion as other cops I've spoken to. "A caplata, female, or bokor, male, are practicing voodoo witches who serve the Loa, the dead. I don't use voodoo or serve the dead. I can't do what they did, just as they can't do what I do. We all have a specific set of skills."

"I met her a few times. She wasn't evil."

"I didn't say she was evil. I said she served the dead, the spirits. The spirits are seen as intermediaries between this life and the next — or the great creator of life. Some practicing voodoo are good, and some are bad, just like any other person. We make a choice to be a good witch or a bad one. Just because she was able to create a zombie or trap spirits in a talisman doesn't mean she did. Though, I'd bet she did. You don't survive for longer than people can remember by being a good little caplata."

"Aren't you just brimming with information?" He rifled through my minibar. The energy around him felt like he was on the verge of an anxiety attack. I watched him move around, twitchy with anxiousness. I knew he was going to either drop a bomb on me or ask me for something. If Caser sent him, either could be possible.

"It's what I do, Cisco. It pays the bills." I took a seat with my coffee and rubbed my dry eyes. I was too tired to play the good witch. "Start talking or get going."

"Have you ever seen crime scenes like this before? You must see some pretty crazy stuff. Tell me this is everyday witchcraft and not something bigger," he asked.

"I've never seen this before. Most supernatural folks wouldn't dare dabble in human sacrifice. The taint isn't worth the payoff. When you start to shave off pieces of your soul, you attract some terrifying evils. Once your soul is too weak to protect you, demons come knocking," I answered. "The weird part is that it doesn't really make sense to me. I mean, I get the monstrous acts. What I don't understand is how it's being done with the stunted level of skill I'm seeing."

"What do you mean, stunted? It looked pretty skilled from where I was standing."

"Starting from the first crime scene, they didn't need almost two dozen small bells throughout. One or two would have been fine, if at all. The perpetrator used *all* the stones of protection, not just one or two or even three. They used all the symbols for protection and to ward off harm."

"From what I've read, it sounds pretty textbook."

I nodded. "Exactly, Cisco. It's textbook. It's like they bought every book they could find on how to be a witch and used all of them at once. They're mixing every flavor of witchcraft. I don't think they know how to do this right. I'd wager any money that *if*, and that's a big if, they're witches, they're not naturally born. They're learning as they go along, and that's a scary thought."

His eyes widened. "That doesn't sound good."

"It isn't. If they don't know what they're doing, then they don't know what they're trying to summon or how to control it once it makes his grand reveal."

"But can anyone really control a demon?"

I shrugged. "Yes and no. If you know what you're doing and are powerful enough, it can be done. But you mark yourself for life. That demon will remember being summoned and cheated out of a soul. Eventually, it'll find a way to collect it. They have damn long memories. But my worry isn't for the person who can control this. I'm terrified of the person who doesn't know what the hell they're doing. Demons aren't a *live-and-learn* bunch. One mistake, one mispronounced word, one wrong stone and it all goes to hell. There will be a pretty nasty demon on the loose, all charged up and ready to go without being bound."

"Christ have mercy," Cisco whispered and motioned a cross down his body.

"He's not going to save us from this," I countered.

"You don't believe?" He looked surprised.

"Oh, on the contrary, Cisco, I believe more than most. But a holy war will not come for one demon. We'll need to be on the brink of extinction before we see an angel. Until then, we're screwed."

"I bet you're a real hoot at baptisms."

"What can I say? Most of what we believe in is bullshit and what we should believe in, the stuff that'll actually save lives is ignored. Whatever helps us sleep at night, I guess," I replied.

"Doesn't the Bible say..." he started, and I rolled my eyes. "What?"

"Let's not start quoting a book written by men in a time when you'd be put to death for planting different crops side by side or where women were stoned to death for wearing two different types of garments. Each new version of the Bible is guided by man's moral compass and his desire to own women. It's a book written by humans who were ignorant and superstitious. It teaches more hate than goodness, nothing more," I replied.

"You and Miguel must have some intense conversations," Cisco teased, but it wasn't that far off from the truth.

"You could say that." I smiled but knew it didn't reach my tired eyes. I was done with the chit-chat. "Your schooling is over. Why are you here?"

"This is good coffee, thank you." He stalled and took a seat at the table across from me.

"Did you come here for coffee, or was there a purpose? I'm sorry, Cisco, but I'm dead tired and don't have time to talk you off your anxiety ledge. Jump off or leave."

"What has Miguel told you about my…family?" He looked up from his cup.

"I don't know what you're talking about." I lied like butter off my tongue.

"You know what we are. Caser has said so much."

I shook my head. "Actually, Caser didn't say a thing about your family. He merely asked me for help…then threatened to kill me if I didn't."

"I can smell the lies on you, Ailis. They smell sickly sweet, like your words are rotting before they hit the air." Cisco held up his hand and let the claws slide out. I forced myself to stay where I was, even though my feet wanted to make the decision for me and run. I knew what he was but didn't want to see it. It scared the hell out of me. My curiosity had never included new ways to bleed. "There… Now I'd die alongside you for showing you what I am. If you didn't know before, you know now, and I was the one who broke the rules. From the lack of screaming and running, I'd say you know more than you're letting on, little witch."

"I may or may not know a thing or two. What does that have to do with why you're here? Are you here to kill me for knowing?" I asked.

"If I'd come to kill you, one of us would already be dead," he replied. "Earlier, Caser presented you with an impossible choice. In turn, you've given him the same Hobson's choice—no choice at all, take it or leave it. This puts the rest of us in a very uncomfortable position, Ailis."

"And what position is that?" I asked.

"You're human. Well, sort of."

"I *am* human, Cisco. Not 'sort of'," I corrected him.

"Uh-huh, so am I." He rolled his eyes. "You're splitting hairs. You're not fully human. Even I can smell that on you. You're more than human. A witch, a true witch, is not fully human. Under all that witchy stuff, I smell hell. I smell your soul. It smells like it's covered in bandages. So much raw meat under the dressings."

I leaned back from the table and grabbed my charm. It was cool to the touch, but I instantly didn't trust Cisco. "Raw meat, hey? Are you hungry, by chance?"

He laughed. "Yes, I'm hungry. I'm always hungry. But I don't eat people, if that's what you're asking. Lycan do not eat human flesh. It doesn't settle well."

"I take it you've tried a nibble or two?" I asked.

His face fell. It was his turn for a soft spot topic. "I knew I could become a Lycan when I was a child. It is not decided until we are almost adults whether we will become full Lycan or stay human and live a human life. The gene passes some generations. Only a few of us are selected. Why it skips some and not others, I don't know. But when I shifted the first time, it was unexpected. I had been cornered by a vampire. I had no weapons and had been shot, scared and near death. My wolf burst through me for the first time, and I killed the guy who was trying to kill me. I ate his face in the process. I puked him up and got really sick after that."

"Rough." That was the only answer I had. I smiled at my unintended joke. "No pun intended."

He smiled. "We don't bark."

"What about werewolves?" I asked. "Do they eat people?"

"You may or may not know, my ass. You're full of shit." He gave me a knowing look. He knew that I knew. "Yes, they eat people. They eat everything, up to and including food-stained trash and pets. They're nothing more than animals, only stronger."

"With people inside them," I added.

"Yeah, and I could say the same thing about demons. They were once people, according to you."

He had me there. "We could talk circles around this, Cisco, until the next sun comes up. I'm tired, you're tired and I have no intention of talking until a new day is upon us. Tell me what you came to tell me and leave."

"There is where the sticky position is. I can't harm you because you're human. But even if you weren't, you have Miguel's protection. You are his ward, so to speak. But when the boss man tells me to go fetch us a witch, I go fetch. You don't have the same protection as humans do, but you have our leader's protection. If I were to fetch you as I normally would, Miguel would rip my limbs off, garnished with my balls, and feed them to me."

"Pleasant picture," I answered. "Let me get this straight. I have to come with you or what? You suffer either Caser or Miguel's wrath, either way, but what happens to me? No offense, Cisco, but your life doesn't mean as much to me as my own does."

"Nothing will happen to you. I give my word."

"I think the reason I didn't peg you for more than a sensitive human is because you're simply not as powerful as Miguel or Caser. If you're not as powerful as they are, how the hell are you going to keep your word? How will you make sure nothing happens to me?"

"I'll try," he replied. "That's all I can promise you. I'll do my best to keep you from harm — or I'll die trying."

I nodded. It was better than most people would say. Most would lie to me and promise that I'll live. He didn't. He offered his best and his life. It didn't get much better than that.

"What happens if Miguel finds out we went without him? Shouldn't we invite him? He told me to leave it alone and not to meet with Caser. He'd deal with Caser."

"What Miguel said or didn't say to you, isn't my problem. Caser was expecting you at midnight and you didn't show." Cisco opened his arms into one big shrug. "I don't make the rules. I just follow them. He'll know, Ailis. Miguel will find out before we even get there. Secrets don't last long in the Pack, and they certainly won't last when we cross into our territory. It's Miguel's job to know who comes and goes. His troops will squeal, whether Caser tells them to be silent or not. They're more loyal to Miguel than Caser."

"That must really bite Caser's ass."

Cisco smiled a broad and happy smile. "Oh, it chews his bones to dust. If Caser does anything about it, Miguel could leave and take all the Pack's protection with him. Miguel is strong enough to start his own Pack, but he's too damn loyal to his people, to Caser."

"Can Miguel just pick up and leave?"

"He could if he killed for it. But he won't kill Caser. He's too soft to do what needs to be done. Instead, he does what he can to protect the weaker of the Pack. Caser can't really do much about it. He's not strong enough to kill Miguel to set an example."

"Miguel seems to think differently. He said he wasn't strong enough," I responded, thinking of my conversation with Miguel.

"He's not emotionally strong enough. The bloody guy could clean the floor with Caser. But he won't because he's scared of what you, little witch, would think of him if you found out," Cisco explained.

"It's a fight to the death?"

Cisco nodded. "Contrary to what I heard you call him earlier—a monster—he isn't one. He doesn't kill unless absolutely forced to do it. Every time he's been challenged, he's had the right to kill the challenger. He doesn't. He knocks them out and walks away. I'd have killed them if it were me. It would keep the others from challenging me. Kill one, and the rest are less willing to tempt their fates."

"Yet, here you are, near the bottom of the Pack." I countered. "Hard to say what you would do when you've never been in the same position."

Cisco raised his eyebrows. "I could say the same to you. But that's between you and Miguel. I'm at the bottom because I have no need to rise. I leave once I'm done with school. Why fight my way to the top when I have no intention of sticking around? Miguel has secured me permission to leave. I leave in nine months to study off the coast of Costa Rica for half a year, then to Australia for a year. Miguel has helped me gain permission to reside in those territories while I complete my studies. I'll settle down when I'm done with school."

"Why would Miguel tell me to stay away from Caser, that he'll deal with it?" I asked. "Say I go… How likely is it that I'll be killed there?"

"Miguel doesn't want you tarnished. He thinks if you see us all in our furry glory, you'll hate him even more. At this point, I don't think that's possible. He's worked so damn hard to keep us a secret from you, to protect you, only to be hated even more for it. I think he thought if he could keep it from you, you wouldn't know he was like everything else you hunted and killed."

"I don't need relationship advice, Cisco," I replied.

"Like hell you don't. You have no idea how many balls he juggles to keep you alive. His threat alone is why you've never been bothered by a Lycan back home or any other territory you've wandered into. You're too damn powerful for the rest of us not to poke around, but none are brave enough to face the wrath of an Alpha, regardless of where they are in the world. If you only knew what he's done to keep you above dirt, you'd think a little better of him."

"I'm sure I would. But now is not the time for memory lane. Right now, all I need to know is if I'll die if I come with you. Miguel mentioned the others had a real hate-on for me because his heart is broken over us."

"The chance is there. But you could take a shower and bash your brains out, too." Cisco made his point. "I wouldn't call what Miguel feels simply a broken heart. It's smashed to shit, and it's not going to heal any time soon."

"Break-ups in the Pack must be deadly." I half-joked.

"They are. We mate for life. When things come to an end, the life part still stands. Someone inevitably dies over it." There was no joke in his answer.

My coffee was as cold as I was. "When does he want to meet?"

"Now."

"Now? I'm too tired for this crap." I groaned.

"I'll give you my gun. Silver bullets. I make them myself. Would you come if you were armed and could protect yourself better?" he asked.

"But then you'd be unarmed."

"Unarmed, she says." He laughed. "I have ten-inch claws and jaws that can snap your thigh bone like it was a biscuit."

I stood and nodded. "With the gun, I'll come."

"What changed your mind?"

"Whether Miguel is working to keep me alive or not, hiding out in my room isn't going to keep me alive. All hiding will do is risk the others in the hotel when Caser comes back himself to fetch me. I doubt his next visit will be as pleasant as his last."

"I'll take it. Let's roll." He pulled his gun from under his shirt, tucked in the rear of his jeans.

"How very thug of you." I rolled my eyes. "Carry it in a holster like a big boy."

"But this way, I look cool when I draw it. Like a regular gangster." He put the gun behind his back and pulled it back out. He held it sideways, like how they do it in the movies—the wrong way. He made me smile. He was an odd man. Powerful and impressive, but had the kind of soul that could fill up a room. It said he'd die to protect me if the Pack turned on me.

"And away we go." I grabbed my bag and followed him into the mouth of a new kind of hell.

Chapter Twelve

Cisco slipped his shades on. The sun wasn't even up, but there were drivers that didn't understand the difference between high beam and low. "And on the seventh day, God said, let there be light."

"And on the ten thousandth day, God introduced a new Angel to mankind. The Angel asked, 'How do they work?' God replied, 'Not very well. They're all broken with anxiety and drink too much.' The Angel asked, 'Then why did you give them free will?' God responded, 'It worked for the bloody monkeys.' The Angel suggested God wipe the earth and start over. I hear God's still mulling it over." I didn't bother opening my eyes to the sunrise. I feared it would be the last one I'd see. I won't ruin my last good memory of the sun with this one. I was, after all, on my way to a little cabin in the woods to see the big bad wolf.

"I can smell your nervousness, Ailis. You need to calm yourself. You'll scare the younger Pack." Cisco spoke over the radio.

I huffed a surprised laugh. "Why would me being nervous scare a Lycan? Young or old."

"Because you're not nervous about coming. You're nervous about how many of us you'll have to kill to get back out. I can tell the difference. It smells like a mix of trepidation and anticipation. Like you're going to hurt someone, you just haven't decided how badly you're going to do it. You're holding that gun like you're weighing a lot of options up in that head of yours."

It was a good description of what I felt inside. I was scared. I have been in a perpetual state of fear ever since I saw the first monster under my bed and realized the damned thing was real. I moved the gun in my hands to get used to the weight of it. The 9MM Glock 26 Gen 4 was designed for concealed carry. It was considered lightweight, but it felt heavy with decisions not yet made. If disease could be formed into a shape, it would be this simple soulless chunk of metal. Only, the creation of the gun was currently killing more people than disease. Disease didn't care how rich a person was. It didn't discriminate between the young or old, color of skin, or the God someone prayed to, and it didn't take your valuables on the way out of the door. But a gun did. The welder of the gun got to pick and choose who had a future and who had a funeral. I hated guns. But I sat with one in my hand and was thankful. I would choose today, if I had to, who would live and who would die. It wasn't a choice I wanted to make. If one of them made the decision to begin my funeral before I was ready, I'd fire the diseased metal in my hand. I tucked it into my jeans, in the rear and grinned. *How very thug of me*, I thought. There was no need to go in with it clutched in my hand. If I brought the threat of violence rather than the promise of self-defense, I was picking my own funeral songs.

The Pale Horse, where we were headed, was located in the heart of Cancun. The sign was a white horse with Death riding it. Little skulls were carved around the edge for effect. Aside from the sign, the building looked like every other bar I'd seen — a black building, blacked-out windows, tropical plants to cheer it up and a lineup of tourists already drunk. It reminded me of home. Downtown Vancouver, on a Saturday night, needed the local police to close down the main drag. It always turned into a bad idea to have bars open late clustered together. Packs of people would take to the streets at two and three in the morning, turning it into a small riot of frat boys and girls who *can't even*. God, I missed home.

We were in peak tourist season, and there wasn't a single vacant spot to park. Without a doubt, after tourist season, I was sure there still wouldn't be parking. The Pale Horse didn't strike me as a pop-up bar. It had roots and a history that brought loyal customers. I pointed up the road to an empty strip mall. We would have better luck walking back. Cisco shook his head and rolled down his window. One sharp whistle and a car moved from in front of the bar. I didn't ask. I didn't really want to know what kind of clout Cisco had or how he managed to get it. For all I knew, he had rescued someone's cat, and they just really liked him now. I hoped…but doubted.

"What time do the clubs shut down here? It's almost morning," I asked.

"These doors never close, Ailis. When we get inside, it'll be dark, and no one will care if it's morning or night."

"Who the hell gets a twenty-four-hour liquor license?" I was surprised.

"For enough money, you can get whatever you want." He opened his truck door and tossed his glasses onto the dash. "But here, there is no alcohol sold after four in the morning. They'll sober up with ten-dollar bottles of water, come down from whatever they snorted or popped and go home in time for the new partiers to show up."

I followed Cisco to the front door. Those lined up had heckled us as the black velvet rope was opened, and we walked in without needing to wait like the rest. *Four doormen.* That was serious muscle for a club. When the doors opened, noise poured out of the building and into the street. It didn't sound like the kind of music a person could sober up to. Then again, I had never been so drunk that I needed to hang out somewhere to ride it out. Cisco didn't stop at the coat check, so neither did I. Through two more doors, we passed several more doormen that looked like this was their second chance on parole, and we were inside The Pale Horse. There was one room with a bar in the very middle. It served from all four sides. A massive tropical fish tank took up one wall and was the only light in the room, aside from the tiny pendant lights over the bar. Those were more for decoration than light. To my left was a two-level dance club. It was all very goth — dark, skulls, a hint of blood red, and iron fixtures. It looked like every emo's wet dream. A massive stage at the far end held cages with latex-clad dancers. The place was at capacity and beyond. A fire would have killed half the people in the building, if not more. It didn't matter how many exits there were if there were too many people all trying for the same door.

"This way." Cisco's voice cut through the noise. He motioned for me to follow him. To the right, hidden behind a tall palm tree and black gauze curtains, was a door.

Cisco punched in a code on the security pad, and the door clicked open. I leaned into the doorway, stairs up and stairs down, with no real escape. I paused and grabbed Cisco's arm. "Are we going up or down?"

"Unfortunately, all the way down."

"How many ways in and out are there?" I asked.

He grinned. "We go down two levels. There is one emergency exit on each level. Once we get into the banquet room at the bottom, there are two ways out. The way we go in and the very back of the room, to the right, behind the only off-black curtain. You won't miss it. There's a door that leads to a hall and two flights of stairs, ten steps on each staircase. There are emergency supplies fixed to the walls—two fire extinguishers and two heavy-duty axes. Your elbow is enough to break the glass for an ax if you needed one."

I nodded. He knew exactly why I'd asked. "Thank you."

He leaned in closer. "The weaker of us will be in the center of the room. No matter how big they look, they are the weakest. There are a few who you'll think you can take on, on the outer ring. You can't. Trust me. They're the strongest and most cruel. They remain on the outside for a reason, to be the first to take out the coming threats. If you step up against anyone, make sure you can kill them, or you'll regret it. I mean, if you live through it. Don't cause my death because you can't keep your shit in check."

"Fuck," I whispered back. I was, without a doubt, scared. I shook on the inside and wanted to be sick.

"Ready?" he asked, and I shook my head. I wasn't. "Good. Let's go, little red."

"Oh, Granny, what big teeth you've got," I whispered.

"All the better to eat you with, my dear," he answered back. He paused and laughed a full belly laugh. "Did you notice you have red hair and are being led by...well, a wolf?"

"Yuck it up, fur boy." I glared. It was a friendly glare if ever there was one. "If someone comes in with an ax, I'll be really impressed."

"I'm sure Miguel will when he hears of your arrival," Cisco replied.

Down the stairs, we went. Cisco paused twice to point out the red and glass cases that hung with an ax inside. He mimicked how I would smash them out of the case with my elbow. He did it all in silence. He pointed at each exit as we passed them. He motioned toward the door at the bottom of the stairs. I breathed in deeply. I couldn't ground myself. The energy in the air raised my hair like static and rode me like a wild horse. He opened the bottom door and stepped to the side. I shook my head. There was no way in Hell, with a big 'H,' that I would go in first. I wasn't that bold or that stupid. Not a drop of courage was left in my body, but I still had brains.

He walked through like he had done it a million times before, seen the show and now was bored. I did not walk in with the same level of confidence. I, unlike him, didn't even want to see the show, no matter how spectacular it would be. Imagine my disappointment to learn of a new species, only to be terrified of them. For once, I'd like a new discovery to be something closer to a ladybug—harmless, pretty, friendly...maybe granted wishes without consequence. Instead, I get saddled with a horse-sized rabies dog who could hold a gun. I hoped this was the end of my bad luck. I could almost picture the explorers who stumbled upon vampires for the first time. They must have shit their pants. But I'd still trade with them in a heartbeat.

Ahead of us sat a curtained-off room. I could feel the pressure that pushed at the curtain from the other side. Power. Raw and dangerous and everything my brain said to run away from. My charm vibrated for the tenth time this morning. It, like me, knew this was a bad idea. Cisco parted the black velvet curtains, and we stepped into a large banquette room. It wasn't like the porn set upstairs. It was brightly lit, soft colors, tasteful and dripped with money, like a high-end hall at the Four Seasons, right down to the gold silverware. I guess their aversion to silver limited their utensils. The room was set up like they had just finished high tea. Tables with linen sat in various places around the room. A large buffet of cakes and treats, coffee and tea, sat to our left. Caser was at the head of the room to the right. My eyes darted around the carpet-to-carpet room. Over forty men and women stood in little groups. It looked civil. It looked like forty different ways to die. My eyes scanned every inch of the place. To the far end, an off-colored black curtain, like it had seen more sunlight than the others, was the only other way out. As if I'd make it from one end to the next and out of the door with all my limbs. I cursed to myself. I couldn't tell who the strongest or weakest were when they were grouped together like this.

Cisco stood and smiled. The two men on either side of him didn't so much as blink. Each bodyguard, or whatever the Pack called them, was over six feet tall and built like steroids were tested on them before doctors realized it was a bad idea. The one on Caser's right had no hair at all. The only hair on his face was a light dusting of eyebrows, barely dark enough to be noticeable. The one on the left was the polar opposite. His hair was dark and to his shoulders. He didn't look like he appreciated the finer things, like a shower or a razor, and only shaved when he had to. They both stood like bodyguards in movies—legs apart, arms loose, ready to pounce. Caser stood out among them as someone who didn't belong. He was clean-cut, wore a tailored suit and I wouldn't doubt he had manicured nails. But he stood out because I was more scared of him than his guards.

"Dr. Kyteler." His voice was pleasant. He opened his arms and smiled. "Welcome."

I nodded a little too fast. It was the movement of a scared rabbit. Caser's men stepped forward, and I stepped back to hide behind Cisco. The room laughed. I didn't care. I had no ego when it came to my survival. No one laughs at the only person who lives.

"It's okay, Ailis," Cisco whispered. "They're just doing their jobs."

"I don't want to be here," I whispered back. "This was a bad idea. I can feel it in my bones."

"Do you want to leave?" Cisco asked. "Say the word."

I calmed myself the best I could. "No, I'm good. Thank you, though."

"You do not make the rules here, Francisco." Caser's voice carried through the room. It hit us like a hot slap.

Cisco turned and faced Caser. His body shook. But it wasn't fear that made him vibrate. I could feel his anger. "I brought her here as you commanded. I betrayed Miguel, as you commanded. But I gave her my word she would come to no harm, as *you* guaranteed. You know as well as I do, being here with all of us for the first time could harm her emotionally. If she's too scared to listen, it's pointless to have her here," he replied. "You do not need to browbeat me into falling in line. I'm already in line. But she's human, and her needs come before yours. It is our law."

Caser glared. "Do not quote the laws I helped write."

"I am doing what I have been charged to do. Keep her safe," Cisco countered. "Respectfully, of course."

"Of course." Caser didn't look like he enjoyed the public reminder of the rules. I was sure he'd have a more informal talk with Cisco later.

The two men stepped forward a little farther. I was thoroughly pleased with myself for not cowering again. I looked at them both and shook my head. "I'd ask, Caser, that your men stay over there, the hell away from me."

"They're going to check you for weapons," Caser answered like I should have known that.

I smirked. "You know I'm a witch, right? A gun is the least of your worries."

"We can't have you shooting up the place, now, can we?" Caser asked, but it didn't sound like a question.

"Would you rather me squeeze the souls from their bodies? I mean, that works for me, too," I asked casually. "Does it help if I tell you I have one gun?"

"Your word, one gun?" he asked. Like it mattered.

"One gun. One hex bag, which wards me from evil, nothing more. If you're going to harm me, I should be allowed to protect myself. If you're not, then it's nothing more than a bag of herbs—oh, and a small pocketknife."

"A small knife? Even I'm disappointed," Cisco interrupted. "Why not a big one that can actually help you."

"Well, I'm sorry, grannie. I didn't pack for coming to a wolf den. It's for the small cuts I make when casting circles and protecting myself from demons. Had I known I would be meeting Lycans, I'd have purchased a machete when I got to town. All I have is my ability to send them all to hell or make them feel like they were there. But yes, a bigger knife would have been more snazzy and frightening," I answered. I couldn't hide the humor in my voice. When I got really nervous, I joked. It helped me cope. Surrounded by what I had thought were mythological creatures, I struggled to manage my fear.

Cisco winked. "I'll admit, seeing you rip out a soul and send it to hell would be more entertaining. I've never actually seen it done in person."

"It's like watching someone fall asleep while they're standing and screaming in pain. Having a soul ripped from your body is hella painful. Picture being dragged behind a truck on glass. Your skin being slowly shaved off. Next, the meat goes." I smiled. I had no idea what it looked like. I had never done it before or kept my eyes open to watch a demon do it. From what it sounded like, I was probably more accurate than I wanted to be.

I knew what Cisco was doing. He'd put the fear of me into those who were tempted to try me on for size. I doubted it would work on the big bad wolves, but the weaker ones might think twice. If they had the same prejudices as everyone else, we would play into them. For the first time, I willingly made myself the whore of hell. At worst, they'd spread rumors. At best, they'd be too scared to eat me. I could live with either outcome. Until a few years ago, being a practicing witch was illegal, and rumors killed us. But after a demon killed a few politicians and their families, suddenly witches were in demand, and no one really cared about the gossip anymore. It was kind of expected that we were the whores of Babylon. Those in charge counted on it.

"This? This is what you bring into our home?" A screech of a voice took all the steam from my sails. She stepped forward.

My charm pulsed with caution. I was glad it vibrated and didn't come with a voice. I couldn't look tough with a necklace that screamed *"Run! Run!"* every time a monster was around. The thought made me want to laugh. My inner dialogue made me smile at the worst of times. I wiped it off my face with a fake cough. I didn't need her to think I thought she was funny. She wasn't. She was scary.

"Sofia." One word from Cisco made her pause. "Dr. Kyteler has safe passage here."

Sofia wasn't just attractive in the way the women in magazines made you turn your head. She was beautiful in the way men tripped over themselves to be near her. I wouldn't call it classic beauty, but it did hold the same charm of the actresses of days long gone. Think *Gone with the Wind* meets *Terminator* meets *Cujo*. Her large brown eyes held liquid gold, intelligence, confidence I envied and the very opposite of serenity. There was nothing calm or tranquil about her. Still, they had the power to hold a person prisoner. Her cheekbones weren't especially high or carved into perfection, but were something exotic. There was an undeniable symmetry to her features that would have captivated me if I weren't so unnerved by her. She wore her straight black hair back in a ponytail at the base of her skull. Her leather was tight enough that I first thought her pants were latex.

"Devil worshiper." She spat at me, quite literally.

"I can't say I am," I replied. "Have I done something to piss you off already? Or do you have a problem with me that I don't know about? I'm good enough to help you find what's killing your people but not good enough to be polite to?" I asked and cleaned her spittle from my face in a dramatic show. "It's no sweat off my ass to leave. Seriously, say the word, and I'll tap dance on out of here, and you'll never have to see my face again. You all can go down, one by one. I'm fine either way. My preference would be to leave if anyone is wondering."

"Yes, I have a problem with you, and no, you're not good enough," she answered. She was blunt. I could work with that. "Miguel marked you, and you're nothing but a human, and from the smell of you, you make a poor one at that."

"Most would argue the human part with you. But what's your point?" I kept my eyes on her but watched the rest of the room in my periphery. Everyone was at a standstill. No one moved. I didn't know if this was a play for who was a bigger monster or if this was just how things were done around here. I didn't bother asking about being marked by Miguel. I knew enough about the folklore and natural wolves to know she meant he had selected me as his mate.

"My point, witch, is because of you, Miguel won't take a mate because he won't leave your side. You are his ward, a human. He can't mate and produce offspring because he won't dare take his focus off you, a fucking human. So, yeah, I've got a problem. You're holding him back. You're holding us all back. You knowing who we are is a danger to us all." Her voice reminded me of one of those crazy women with video cameras who demanded to see the store manager. Shrill.

I frowned at first. Was she jealous? "He can do what he wants. After this case, we're out of each other's lives for good. Simmer down. I have no claim to him."

She stepped forward. Her body vibrated. "You don't get it. He can't. He gave his word to you. To break an oath is to be expelled from the Pack. He would lose everything. No matter what, he's lost it all because of you. Our people face being outed and killed because of you."

"I don't know what you want me to say. If you're waiting on an apology, I don't have anything to be sorry about. I didn't know about you all. I didn't even know you existed," I answered. It was the best one I could give. I wasn't prepared to console a wolf. I pointed at Caser. "If you want to be pissed off at someone for the knowledge I have, take it out on the man who bought me a ticket to the show."

She shook her head like a disappointed parent. "Should it matter if you knew about us or not? If Miguel was human, it would still be as bad. You're toying with people, *my* people."

"Take him. He's all yours." I took a step forward—a bad habit in the face of so much hostility. But I didn't back down, not once it was in my face. Monsters chase whoever runs away first. The weakest were the first to die, and I had no intention of digging my own grave. "Whatever the case, you don't know me well enough to throw around accusations. He's all yours if you want him. Do not stand here and presume you know me, my life or the reasons behind my actions. You don't."

She smiled. "Oh, I do. I know all too well. We've all stood here and watched you cut him down inch by inch. But if you revoke his protection, as you claim you have, you'll die where you stand."

I dropped my smile and every other emotion from my face. I pulled the gun from behind my back. I didn't raise it, but it in my hand made me feel safer. It was a false sense of security. "I may die here, but you won't be the one to kill me. You're too weak."

"I am not." Her fists clenched. I watched the muscles in her thighs tense.

"Your hate is what makes you weak. You don't even feel like Lycan, which means you're too low and too weak to fight against a power like me," I replied. "I'll warn you only once, Sofia. Do not make me defend myself. I didn't come here for violence, but if that's how I leave this place, I'll step over your body on my way out."

"Witch!" she screamed. "You will die here."

I didn't take my eyes off her. "Cisco, control her, or I will."

"Let her go to her fate since she's so determined," he answered. "The weaker must learn their place on their own. It is not for me to decide how she learns it, but I have every confidence you'll school her."

Sofia's black polished nails grew. It was a show, nothing more. She wouldn't have put her abilities on display if she intended on more. Lycans, as it seemed, were no different than any other monster I had met. The weaker went for the showoff, and the stronger simply killed you outright. I lifted my hand and squeezed it into a fist. I held the power that was raised inside her and extinguished it as I would with any other flavor of beast. I envisioned the power as rising water and pushed it back to the hellhole it came from. Had she been higher on the Lycan ladder, like Caser, it would have taken a lot more effort and ability on my part. I knew my limits, but I could also feel hers. She screamed in my face. I felt her embarrassment, her rage, and smelled wet dog. I wasn't going to mention the dog part.

"I will kill you, Sofia. Please do not make me do this," I whispered just inches from her face. "If you try to harm me, I will end your life. I am not worth your death tonight or any night."

"You forfeit his protection." Her words came out strangled, like her throat didn't have room for both air and power.

Hands rested on her shoulders and pulled her away. Cisco was there, guiding her from my front. He gave me a look, and I shrugged. "Come on, Sofia. This fight isn't worth us cleaning up a dead body. Is that what you want? To die? For Ailis to die at our hands? Do you want to curse us all?"

Sofia looked to Cisco. She shook her head but wouldn't back down. "She is going to be the death of us all."

"No, she won't. We both know that," he answered. "Don't do this, Sofia, please. I don't want to stop you." He looked sad having to tell her he'd stop her. The position he was in was worse than I thought.

"You'd protect her? You'd challenge me for that...witch?" Sofia's temper climbed higher.

Cisco nodded. "I would stop you from harming her, yes."

"Why? Did she screw you, too? Is she so fine, you'd kill me for her?" Sofia's words cut. "She's hells little whore. Is she working her way through Pack now?"

I felt her words like a punch. My eyes watered, and my face flushed with heat. I had nothing to be ashamed of, but it still stung. I wanted to turn around and leave, jump on the plane and never look back. They could fend for themselves. But my feet stayed planted. I wouldn't damn them all because of one angry woman. I wanted to, though. And it would have felt good.

Cisco squeezed her arms tighter. "That's enough, Sofia. Pick something else to yell at her for, but not that. If you want to be angry about Miguel, we get it. We *all* get it. But don't open your mouth about shit you know nothing about."

"Sofia, *enough*!" Caser yelled. I felt the base of his voice vibrate through my bones. "She has given you your life tonight. She could have ended it. We all could feel it."

"She'd bleed before I died," she snapped back.

I smiled. "I bleed every night for this crap. But that doesn't remove the fact that tomorrow your family will mourn your death."

She glared. "One day, it'll be your family mourning you, or you will mourn them. Mark my words. Don't threaten me again."

The dam that held back my rage and fear broke, and I moved forward, fast and hard. We were inches apart. "My family is already dead, Sofia. Both of my parents were killed by monsters. They died a horrific death to protect me. Their last drop of power and blood went into a circle to protect me. I couldn't get out to save them, but I got to watch it all, watch them ripped apart, slowly, before my eyes. My grandmother died alone after raising an angry girl with powers that could destroy everything you've ever thought was worth having. I have no one in this world. I have no family. I have a cat. That's it. That is all I have." My words were edged with something uncomfortably close to hate. Having me hate you was not a good position to be in. "Touch my cat, Sofia, and I'll fucking kill everyone you've ever loved. I will send the worst from hell to your bed and make sure you live for years with it. I will nurse you back to health myself just so it can start over again. Do not *ever* threaten me or mine. I will end you. I will use your own blood and dead body to curse your line. Do not test me. I promise that you will lose." My voice was almost a scream. "I'm giving you the chance to walk away. Take it now, or pay for it later."

She stumbled backward like I had slapped her. She blinked away tears. Cisco gave me wide eyes. The look asked me if I could do what I said I could do. I nodded. I could if I was willing to live without a soul. I wouldn't really kill her family. But it wasn't a good threat if I said I'd try my best to hurt her, then go home to cry. My grandmother had told me I could burn the world if I was willing to burn with it. I wasn't, but I also didn't know how I'd really feel if she touched my cat. I guess, in a way, I'd lied. But I wasn't prepared to take it back. The look on the faces of the rest told me to keep that little nugget of truth to myself. I always thought that if the bad guys could spend a year or two in hell, they'd be less likely to be bad guys. A taste of what waited for them. It had been enough to keep me from going dark but not enough to keep me from making threats that I would.

She turned in one sharp movement. She twisted her body around two small bundled-up hands that flew by her face. The fists in question were for me. To my surprise, they didn't belong to Sofia. A woman smaller than Sofia, by the height of a cookie, came at me with fists of furious rage. She didn't land a single punch. She grabbed at my hair and pulled. Her fists turned into slaps and scratches. She screamed wordlessly as she fought me like a little girl would. It was an embarrassment to my sex, to the entire population of women. I blocked her with ease. Before I could laugh at her for her failed attempt at a street fight, she lifted her arms and came back down with claws. The room erupted in screams as she dragged them down my flesh.

Sofia stepped forward, and I thought for sure I was done for it. Her arms shifted like peeling a sticky banana. One movement was all it took for her friend to be crumpled at my feet. The fit of rage had cost her a heart, which sat in Sofia's claws. Sofia turned her eyes to mine. Now I stepped back.

"I may hate you, but law is law. Be thankful for that, or you'd be just as dead." Sofia dropped the heart at my feet. She turned as she left to get one last dig in. "You may mean well, but you'll be the death of us all."

Chapter Thirteen

"Well then, that went well," I said to Cisco.

"Only one person died, and it wasn't you. It went better than I thought," he answered. "But the day is young."

I stared at the body on the floor. I didn't trust myself to look at anyone else. I blinked rapidly to keep my eyes clear. I wouldn't cry down here. I wouldn't be weak in the den of horror. Sofia had a point. Over the years, a lot of good people had died because of me. Today would be no exception. The wolf on the floor was probably a good person pushed too far with fear. My very presence hung like a hell cloud over their once-upon-a-time secrets. I shouldn't be here. I shouldn't know about them. Their desperation to save what people they had left pushed Miguel, then Caser, into asking for my help and outing their existence to get it. Desperation and fear were a deadly mix. Did I feel guilty? Not really. I didn't kill her. I didn't cause her to shift and break their number one rule. She knew the consequences long before she decided to attack me. And because of the situation we were all in, I might die because of it. My anger for Miguel dug in a little deeper. You can hate someone you love. You can't have one without the other. It's why the hate hurts the person who does the hating.

"This is on you, Caser. Control your Pack, or they'll die at your hands, my hands or those of whatever is killing your people." I pointed at Caser. I swallowed my urge to vomit. The body didn't need my stomach contents.

Cisco stepped over the body and grabbed my arm. "Did she scratch you with claws or her fingernails?"

I looked down at the skin on my arms. I had too much blood on them to tell. I was oddly calm about it all. It didn't really hurt yet. Who knew this would be the way I would die? I wouldn't have guessed it in a million years. A demon attack, yes. Hell, a fairy attack was more likely, but rare back home. They didn't like the rain, but it happened. "I don't know. Am I going to be…you know, a monster?"

"I don't know. This wasn't supposed to happen. I'm so sorry." Cisco looked like I had told him I had a terminal illness without a cure, and he was the one who gave it to me. I was damned, and he felt like it was his fault. "I shouldn't have brought you here."

"It's not your fault, Cisco. It's his." I leaned around Cisco and stared at Caser. He stood as though he was all business, and he didn't just lose one of his people. I guess you didn't stay the head honcho when blood and death made you squeamish. But the expression on his face said he was as surprised as the rest of us. "I didn't come here to be abused or threatened. If I walked into something, that's not my problem. Pack business is none of my concern. It's yours. Tell me what you want and let me leave. I need to go and clean my wounds."

Caser nodded. "You're absolutely right. It isn't your problem and has nothing to do with you. Yet here you are in the middle of it."

I looked at him like he had sprouted another head. "Really? I'm only in the middle of it because of you. First, you had Miguel call me here to help you. Then, you showed up at my hotel and demanded help, or you'd kill me. And this morning, you sent one of your wolves to fetch me. It's not like I had much of a choice."

"We all have choices. Isn't that what you say? She, Nichole at your feet, had a choice, and now she's dead." He taunted me with my own words.

I nodded. "True. Wrong choice of words. I had limited choices. Neither had a favorable outcome for me. Thus, in my opinion, I had no choice. And like Nichole, you've sentenced me to my own death — and for what? If I'm going to die for you all, I'd like to know why and I'd like to know now."

"I said you would come to no harm, yet there you are, with a gun. You came with violence and anger on the tip of your tongue and are angry when it plays out with blood on your hands. I'd say you had more choices than you want to believe. I'd even say your choices took a life."

Right or wrong, his point was made. Someone was dead. I could lie to Caser, but I couldn't lie to myself, not with her blood still wet on my face. "The gun is for my protection, and obviously, I need it. Her death is on you, not me. I didn't kill her. I didn't start a fight with her. She is yours, not mine."

"You should know by now how little that gun will help you. It didn't do you much good minutes ago." He mocked my false security. "But you're right. She was mine, and she got what the law demanded. She attacked a human in Lycan form. That is an instant death sentence. Had she stayed fully human, she'd be in pain right now for attacking one of my guests, but not dead. Her choices, her results. What choices will you make next, Dr. Kyteler?"

I smiled and glanced at my gun. It was the smile I learned in hell. The one that said I didn't care what happened, I'd make sure someone else suffered with me. "I may not be able to beat the snot out of you. But my aim is true, and I'll kill a few of you before you snatch my last breath. If you think another one of your people will get near me a second time, think again. I won't warn them. I won't make them eat their power. I'll simply kill them. Their fate is in their hands. My choice is survival. How about yours?"

"I would almost like to see that if we weren't running low on Lycan," he answered. Caser looked to Cisco. "You can leave now."

"Hell no." I stepped closer to Cisco. "Not bloody happening. I leave with him. He's the only one here that cares if I make it out of here in one piece."

Caser's eyes narrowed on me. It felt uncomfortable. I wanted to agree with him just to make him look at someone other than me. "You are not Alpha here. You do not get to decide how I do business."

I didn't disagree with what he said. I wasn't anyone special. But he wasn't my boss. "You do not get to decide how I do business, either. You aren't *my* Alpha, and I don't trust you to keep me alive. I don't trust anyone but Cisco here," I replied. "If you want him to leave, fine, great. I don't care how you run your little shop of horrors. But I am not staying here without him. That's just the price of doing business with me."

Caser laughed, fully amused. "You want one of the monsters to stay with you and protect you? That's rich."

I shrugged. "What can I say? I'm a sucker for Cisco's charm."

"Do you really wish for Cisco to remain? What an awful place you put him in. If he goes, Miguel will be angry for you being left here alone. If he stays, I will be angry that he didn't listen. He is already caught between a dilemma and discipline. How badly of a hole do you wish to dig for him?"

"He's going to get his ass chewed out by Miguel, regardless, because of you, Caser. If he leaves, I leave with him. That's on you, no one else. You're the one drawing the line in the sand. Don't blame him or me if you can't swallow your ego long enough to finish why I'm here. If he stays because I won't stay without him, he risks Miguel's temper for bringing me here to begin with. The worst of his predicaments, at this point, is whether you let him stay or not. You make the decision and live with the cost of it. How badly do you want me to be here?"

Caser nodded. It was a tired movement. If it wasn't for the shit splattered on the fan and heaped on the floor at my feet, I bet he wouldn't have given in. "Fine. You've made your point. He can stay."

"Great." I put my gun away. "Now, I'm on bloody vacation and haven't gotten more than two hours of sleep at a time. I'm tired. I'm cranky. I'm bleeding in the middle of a room full of wolves, and I don't know if you'll eat me. I'm getting hungry for breakfast, and I haven't even had yesterday's dinner. I'm testy at best, and right now, I'm downright pissed off. There are dozens of reasons on my list of why I'd like to leave. Let's wrap this up so I can pick one of them."

"Would you like something to eat? Tea? Coffee?" he asked, all of a sudden civil. It was like there wasn't a body on the floor with a vacancy for a heart. "Grab something to eat and come sit. We have much to discuss, and I don't want to stand until noon."

I grabbed onto Cisco's arm. I made it look friendly, flirty. It was neither. I was shaken to the core. The meat on my bones felt like liquid. Almost sick to my stomach, I followed Cisco to the back of the room. He loaded up a plate with one of everything. He wasn't fazed in the least. Obviously, he had seen one too many horror movies unfold and starred in a few too many of his own. I grabbed a coffee, crackers to soothe my stomach and cookies. I'm never too scared or too sick to eat a cookie. That would be deathbed, sick and tired. I was close, but not quite.

"Sweet Jesus," I whispered to Cisco. "You dragged me down here for a family feud? There's a woman dead on the floor, and you're all acting like she's not even there. Oh my God, are you going to eat her to hide the evidence? Am I going to be eaten? Don't let them eat me, please."

"Don't bother whispering. Everyone can hear you." Cisco laughed. "No one is going to eat Nichole or you, however tasty you may smell."

I felt the heat rise from my toes to the tips of my ears. "Sorry. I'm freaking out inside."

"Don't sweat it," he replied. "We've heard worse by better. Plus, you look like you'd be stringy meat, too gamey. Fear and hormones make the meat tough to chew. You'd be like eating mutton right now."

"Ouch." I smiled. He was doing his best in a bad situation. He was caught between a rock and a hard place—Miguel the rock, Caser the hard place. Me and Cisco in the middle. What a beautiful start to the day, and I haven't even ended my yesterday.

I followed Cisco to one of the tables on the inside. The body was cleaned up. I didn't see where they took her. I suppose I didn't really care. I glanced around. I could feel the energy roll off the edge of the group when I got too close to those on the inside. Those in the middle of the room stepped away from me. I wanted to smile. I liked the idea of being too scary to screw with, especially in this particular situation. It usually bothered me. I didn't like people scared of me, not really. I didn't have any friends for the same reason. People thought they'd go to hell, guilty by association.

I could feel their eyes on me. It itched between my shoulder blades from their stare. Through the distrust and fear, I could feel hate. I could have painted the walls with it. And for the first time in my life, I wasn't the one hated the most in the room. I didn't know who it was directed at, but the Pack had a bigger problem than me. I'd tell Cisco later. Now didn't seem like the perfect timing for me to start off with fingers in faces. I'd likely lose a few digits if I tried.

"Everyone else, out," Caser commanded, and the room cleared, save for me and Cisco. Caser sat at the table with us. How very civil of him. "I asked you to come for two reasons."

I looked up from my coffee and a mouthful of crackers. I covered my mouth with my hand. "I'd hate to see what would happen if you had called me for three reasons. I appreciate you cutting to the chase. I'd like to leave any time now."

He smiled. When he was calm, he looked like everyone's boy next door, the man you could bring home to meet your parents. "It appears you're not the only one who is tired tonight."

I motioned with my blood-crusted hand to keep going. I would have a breakdown later over potentially being a furry monster and being hunted down until they killed me. I've died a million deaths in hell, but death at the hands of a Lycan was a new one. Apparently, inching my way to my deathbed was my latest hobby. "I'm listening."

"Sofia is right. Well, up until the point you were attacked. We all see it. Miguel is wounded, and you're the knife that keeps cutting away at him. Before you tell me he's all ours to have and you're not holding him back, you are. He's broken, and you're the one who broke him. He won't defend our land or himself like he should. When you agreed to come here, I made the decision to talk to you about it. You're not even shocked by that statement. Cisco, I assume, has told you."

Cisco nodded. "She had the right to be prepared."

"Yes, she did." Caser didn't bully Cisco about the heads-up he gave me. "When I say he won't defend, what I mean is that Miguel won't kill when he must. We've had vampires come into our territory and drink from the unwilling, and Miguel was too scared of what you would think of him if you were to find out that he did what he is charged to do. They almost killed him. Hell, he's exorcising demons and damn near dying himself, in the process, because of what he had to do to Isabell those years ago. I don't think you truly understand what happened. Maybe if you did, you'd stop cutting him up for it."

"He told me." I swallowed my cracker. My throat was dry, making the cracker scratch all the way down.

"No, he probably told you some bullshit about having no choice. She was going to kill others, yada, yada. The thing is, I ordered him to do it. It was the first and only time he challenged me. His rage was so raw and pure. I remember it like yesterday. We fought almost to the death. He screamed your name the entire time. And at the end of it all, when he almost killed me, he gave up." Caser stared off like he was lost in the memory. "I got up and ordered him to do it again. He wasn't scared of me. He was scared of you and what you would think of him. He wanted to tell you about who he was, who we are, but I forbade him. I see now that was a mistake. I suppose, in a way, we are both to blame for who Miguel is today."

"You did your best," Cisco spoke up. "It was a bad situation Miguel was in. On one hand, he had his people, who he loves. On the other, the person he wanted to love him back."

I stayed silent. What could I say?

"He did it, eventually. I ordered him after Isabell called me and begged me to order Miguel. She didn't want just anyone to take her life. Izzy wanted it to be someone she trusted, loved, her spiritual guide. Her last wish was to die in the arms of someone who would pray for her before she killed someone. She didn't want to tarnish her soul. She wanted to go on to her next life, to serve the gates and move on to heaven. You see, Izzy had a family once. She had a husband and two young ones, Grant and Izzy. They were attacked and died a few years before. But she didn't break. She pushed on. Her belief held her together. She knew when she died, she would see them again. It is the way of Lycan. She stayed on the straight and narrow when anyone else would have gone ballistic and hunted the monsters who had killed their family. She wouldn't dare, or she'd have risked not seeing her family again. It was the reason Izzy was at the very bottom of the Pack. She refused to take a life for fear it would condemn her soul. She had the protection of me and several others for that very reason. Anyone who challenged her had to fight the rest of us. Her conviction was so pure. How could we not do that for her? How could we take away the only thing she had left?" Caser explained, his voice soft, almost kind. "I ordered Miguel to fulfill her last wish. By the time he got to her, Isabell had killed innocents because Miguel couldn't do his duty. She will not see her family again because he hesitated for you. Your moral high ground came with a cost for Isabell. When Miguel finally did it to save lives, you branded him a monster, and he believes you like you are the word of God. He'd rather die than do something that proves he is what you say he is."

Cisco squeezed my hand. "Ailis, you don't have to do anything you don't want to do. But, as his friends, his brothers, his only family, we are asking you to understand where he is emotionally and how bad it really is. His hurt is tearing him apart. It threatens the safety of us all. It threatens the safety of our community, those we're charged with protecting. If he flinches, an innocent will die."

"Did you call me here to tell me Miguel has hurt feelings?" I pulled my hand back and folded my arms. "And you want me to what? Fix him?"

"If you weren't human, I'd have dealt with this the Pack way," Caser replied.

I knew what he meant by that. "A hole in the ground about five foot, eight inches?"

"Miguel doesn't have hurt feelings. Grow the hell up." Caser snapped. "I'm too tired to pretend you don't understand what I'm saying, and you're far too old to play the game. He is broken, and you are to blame for your words. I'm not asking you to be responsible for his actions or mine. Take ownership for being cruel. There is no need for it. You have no idea what it's like to be one of us. More than that, you don't know what it's like to have someone you love call you a monster."

"I'm thankful that I'm human then, and you're limited to how you'll deal with me. Although, so far, it hasn't been pleasant." I answered. I blocked out the rest of his words. They hit too close to home, too close to the truth. I swallowed the guilt. Was I guilty of anything besides the truth? Just because the truth hurts doesn't mean I should be hauled down to the wolf den for a stern talking to. "I can't believe I've been dragged down here by bloody Lycans to talk about Miguel's feelings or heart or whatever it is."

"Stubborn to the end," Cisco grumbled. "You and Miguel are so much alike."

"Alas, my dilemma. You're not human. But you're not exactly a monster, either. Yet, I should add." Caser smiled and glanced at my arm. The reminder of my scratches made me uncomfortable.

"I'm a witch, Caser," I replied. "Until I am something else because of you, I should add, I am a witch."

"I've heard the story before. You were born this way. It's not your fault. Welcome to the club." Caser pointed out my poor defense.

"We could argue about this until it's lunchtime tomorrow. Skip to the end. What do you want from me? I'm assuming you wouldn't have wasted my time or the life of one of your people just to tell me the story of how Miguel became broken," I asked. My exhaustion made me impatient, as did the blame. The pain in my arms didn't help.

"I'm asking you to stop with the cruelty. I'm asking you to let him go."

I nodded. "Deal."

"That was quick. Do you understand what I'm asking of you? What letting him go does?" Caser asked.

"I no longer contact him, I don't have his protection, I stop saying things to him that hurts his feelings, I leave him to mend his broken heart." I started my list. To be frank, after tonight, I didn't ever want to come back or have another run-in with a Lycan. I would lose.

"Without his protection, you're anyone's meat," Cisco pointed out.

I lifted my arms. "The protection so far hasn't exactly been stellar."

Cisco leaned over and looked. "Yuck. Looks gross. Looks like you may need a stitch or two."

"Thanks, I could have told you that." I rolled my eyes.

"If Sofia hadn't stepped forward to honor the protection you have, you'd have needed more than a few stitches. You'd be dead," Cisco said. A subtle reminder that I had been protected.

Caser nodded. "While you are here, helping us solve the murders, you will come to no harm. But once you leave, you no longer have the protection of the Pack. That extends to your home. The local Pack can show up at any time and kill you for your knowledge of us. It is the law that we keep the secrets of Lycan. If they were to find out you knew, they'd come for you. It would be in your best interest to forget about all of us and never step foot back in Mexico."

I sighed. "Well, that sucks. I'm either going to die because of these scratches from one of you, or I'll die if the local Pack at home finds out that I know about you because of you. It seems, Caser, I'm dead either way because of you."

"Yes, it does. Such is life. Welcome to the world of adult decisions. I'll ask again... Are you willing to let him go, so he may heal and move on? Marry, have children, start his own Pack or take over this one when I'm gone," Caser asked point blank. The question stung. "I need to know what you choose. Either choice has consequences, and I need to prepare my Pack for the outcome. If you leave, Miguel will rage. If you don't leave, Miguel will probably die for something stupid. I'd rather not have to bury my closest friend. The man is a dreamer, but he's loyal and has given me counsel based on what is good for us as a whole and not just to better his position. He will make a good leader when I'm gone."

"You sound like you're going somewhere." I pointed out.

He nodded. "I've had one foot in the grave since day one. I'm always planning for my death. This isn't a position you hold forever. Someone bigger is always around the corner. You should know that, given your profession."

"I'm a teacher," I replied.

"In a public school. That's as dangerous as my job. But that's not what I'm referring to. You have touched hell more times in one week than I have in my entire life. That's as big and bad as they come," he countered. "What is your decision?"

I nodded. I didn't trust my voice. I said I hated Miguel. I said he was a monster. I used the words more to convince myself than for any other reason, but he believed them more than I did. Even with my anger, I always knew he was there in the background. I think I wanted to hate him. I wanted him to be a monster. It made it easier to be without him. It made me right. But now that I was pushed into a corner, having to make the decision, the thought of letting him go killed the last bit of hope I had held out for us. It took away the parts of him I loved to death. But I couldn't love him to death. I couldn't live with myself knowing he let himself die, scared to become who I had branded him.

Mornings were too early to learn new lessons and inner truths you lied to yourself about. "I'll leave and leave Miguel when I do."

"Very well," Caser said. "The other reason I called you here was to give you this."

He slid an envelope across the table. I opened it and peered inside. "What's this?"

"Information on who has been killed so far, who has gone missing and is presumed dead, all of which belong to Pack, along with every name of every…monster…in town, names of those powerful enough to take down one of the weaker Lycan. There's a list of everyone in my Pack, where they work, their schedule, their grievances, how powerful they are and any squabbles we're having with other cursed," he answered. "I expect to get the information back."

I nodded. "Why call me here to give me this? Couldn't you have gotten Miguel to give it to me?"

"Miguel has made it clear that no one is to contact you from Pack," Cisco answered.

"Why do it, then? Why risk him kicking your butt?" I asked. "After tonight, someone's ass is going to fry."

"I'd rather Miguel takes a round out of me than go to another crime scene and see a friend tied to the ground, gutted," Cisco answered for Caser. He shuddered. "I'd sooner die than see someone else go out like that. Miguel might blister my ass, but he won't kill me for it. Even if he did, it would be worth it if this stops."

"I'll do my best to find who did this and stop them," I told Cisco.

He looked over and blinked away tears. "But would you do anything to stop them, like I would?"

I didn't need to think about it. "Yes."

"Doesn't that make you a monster, too?" Caser asked.

"I guess it does, Caser. The difference between me and most people is that I'm not hiding who I am. And I won't defend what I have to do to stay alive and keep others from unmarked graves. And I sure as hell won't blame anyone later for what I choose to do," I answered. "If I break after, it won't be anyone's fault by my own."

"We'll see, won't we." It wasn't a question.

"I suppose we will," I answered anyway.

"There are a great number of things we will see about. I pray I do not see you after the next full moon. You're on your own after that, if you survive the moon." Caser noted my pending doom. I didn't like him much, but he had a point.

"If I'm... If I turn or whatever you call it, swear to me that you'll kill me. Do not let me hurt anyone." I felt my throat tighten. "Do not make Miguel do it. Do not order him to it. He won't."

"I give my word. It'll be fast, and you won't suffer. He'll never even know," Caser replied.

"I don't care if I suffer. Just kill me," I squeaked out.

"We all suffer in the end. It's what it means to have a soul," Caser answered.

I left Caser at his table, in his basement of lies and death. Cisco followed behind me. The club's bar was open. That meant it was almost lunchtime. One look at my watch made my feet heavy. My body was tired. The adrenaline was gone. I held the envelope in one hand and kept the other loose at my side, still wet with blood. Bleeding or not, I was ready to pull the gun at the first sign of danger. I saw Sofia near the door. She didn't talk to me, and I hadn't a word to say to her. My charm stayed put. Looks like I wouldn't see the inside of another Mexican prison today. But I preferred prison to what I had just seen.

Cisco pulled up to my hotel. He had spent the entire trip drowning in guilt. He apologized at the start of every sentence. He offered to help me clean my injuries, but there was no point. I wanted to be alone, and his help wouldn't take the wounds back or make me any less at risk of contracting a virus I knew nothing about. I didn't feel particularly wolfish. Would it take until the next full moon for me to feel it? Or would I wake up tomorrow with an urge to eat a deer? The thought of meat made my stomach churn. Could a werewolf be a vegetarian? If I turned, I prayed I didn't live long enough to find out.

"I'm so sorry, Ailis. Take care of yourself and call me if you need anything or get scared. No one should go through this alone. I'll be there if you need someone," he said, and I believed every word. "Don't worry about me and Miguel. It won't be that bad."

"I hope so, Cisco, I really do. You're not that bad for a mythological creature." I smiled. "You may fare well, but he's going to lose his ever-loving shit on me."

"I'll call you later to see if you need a hand with that list from Caser and make sure Miguel didn't eat you."

"Thanks. If he does, burn my body and salt my grave. I don't need to come back again for round three. Life hurts way more than hell ever did. I'd rather stay down there." I grabbed the door handle and paused. I thought about what I'd sensed at The Pale Horse. "Cisco, I think you have a traitor in the midst. Something felt off tonight. I mean, it's the first time I've been in a room filled with Lycan, and I'm not used to the energy, but that's not it. The hate was too great."

He laughed. "It's not like you made a good impression, Ailis. Maybe someone just doesn't like you? You did threaten to hunt down everyone loved by Sofia and kill them. Then Nichole dropped dead. That's bound to make a few people dislike you."

"Perish the thought, someone not liking my winning personality." I joked back. "That isn't it, Cisco. It's more than an instant hate or me rubbing someone the wrong way. It didn't grow after Nichole, either. It wasn't that. I mean, it didn't help the situation, but that wasn't the cause of it. The hate wasn't directed at me. I could feel disgust, distrust and straight-up fear, but that hate only came from Sofia, and the worst of it came only after I made her chew down her power. Nichole was scared, and that's why she did what she did. This, what I felt, has been grown and nurtured. This isn't just dislike for the wicked witch of the North. This is pure hate. Couldn't you feel it?"

He nodded. "Yes, but this is Pack. Someone always hates what they are, who they are, where they're stuck. It isn't a new flavor around here."

"Mark my words, Cisco. Someone in your Pack is helping to destroy it from the inside. I know anger so thick you can choke on it, and I know how it feels to want revenge. Find them before they find you." I opened the door and climbed out. "Also, tell Miguel and Caser what I said. Don't be a hero and look for them alone."

I walked into my room and finally let the tension out of my body. Out of the pot and into the pan. *Story of my life.* I was neck deep, and each day I sank a little more. The wolves wanted me out of Miguel's life. Was I really the problem, or was he? Maybe we just brought out the worst in each other. I tended to have that effect on people. But if I was the problem, could I love him enough to leave him to have a better life? If I truly cared, why would I stay and make him more miserable each day he heard my name or saw my face?

This was the price of playing with the monsters. Sometimes, the hurt came in a different form. No matter if I stayed in Miguel's life or not, I was in for a world of hurt. I went into a wolf den and made it out the other side, not unscathed. I was clawed up and could die because of it. If I made it and didn't contract the virus, the trouble wasn't over. I can't wait to meet the local Pack at home. I'm sure it'll go about as good as a stroll through hell.

Chapter Fourteen

It took a shower, lunch and a nap for Miguel to find out about my visit to The Pale Horse and call me. I preferred the call over his physical presence. I was braver over the phone and quite the chicken in person when I knew I had done something wrong. I ignored the first two calls until he threatened to come to my room for, as he put it, an all-out bloody chat. If his calls were about a crime scene, I'd suck it up. They weren't, so there was room for me to be petty long enough for him to blow off steam. As Timothy Spall once said, 'Never fear being a petty fool. It means you ain't dying.'

"Good evening, Miguel," I answered on the seventh ring. I picked at the bandages on my arms as a calm distraction. I didn't need stitches. Butterfly tape would work. They hurt once I cleaned them and put ointment on them. Nothing good ever came from playing with monsters — a lesson I seem to need to relearn every few years.

"Ailis, what the hell were you thinking? I told you I'd handle it. Now it's an even bigger mess." Miguel's voice was heated. It wasn't a scream, but it was close. "Who the hell do you think you are, threatening to kill Sofia's family?"

"In my defense, she was going to eat me," I replied.

"Do you really believe that? Do you really think Cisco would have stood there while she ate you? We're not animals!"

"Okay, maybe 'eat' is a bit of a stretch, but she was about to change. I could feel it. It felt like a tub filling up with blistering hot water and about to flood over."

"Sofia is not yours to abuse or threaten," he snapped. "She is mine, and now we have a problem."

"And they can abuse me and that's just fine?" I asked, but before he could answer, I launched into my defense, however weak it was. "Don't worry. We won't have a problem for long, or didn't she tell you that, too?" I asked. "I've been asked to leave you alone, cut our ties and walk away because you're too screwed up in the head and heart to do your job."

"No, I wasn't told that." His temper ended in that sentence. "I just left Cisco. He didn't mention it. He told me about Nichole. Are you okay? Did she pierce skin?"

"I hope you didn't hurt him, Miguel," I spoke through gritted teeth. "He had no choice."

"Oh, it's fine for him to have no choice but not me?"

I kind of deserved that, but I still didn't like it. "Way different, and you know it. His choice didn't result in someone dying." The moment I said the words, I wanted them back. It was a lie. I could die, hunted down and killed over the scratches. Isabell died because Miguel had been ordered to do it. At the end of the day, so few choices we had were really our own to make. "Why didn't you tell me the whole truth about Isabell?"

"You will not say her name here, Ailis. She will not be used as a part of an argument. Her memory doesn't deserve your anger. I gave you all the explanation you deserved. You are not Lycan, Ailis, so don't act like our business is yours. It will not end well for you."

"First, don't threaten me because it will not end well for you, either. Second, I agree. Lycan business isn't mine. But here we are. I was volun-told to come to The Pale Horse. Caser sent Cisco to fetch me since I didn't show up as requested. You saying you'll handle things then not handling it put Cisco between you and Caser and put my ass on the chopping block." I explained. "As soon as I got there, Sofia approached me. I didn't say a damn thing to her, and she stepped up to me. She knew what I was, and she still did it. Did she think I'd stand there while she threatened to harm my family? I don't even have one, but those I do care about are important enough for me to defend them and myself. She threatened to kill me when that didn't work. What should I have done? Run? She'd have chased me down, and we'd have been alone. She would have killed me." I groaned out my frustration and newly scabbed fear. "I did what I had to do, Miguel, nothing more. I didn't do what I could have done, just enough to get her damn claws away from me. Some good that did. Nichole, who I didn't even speak to or threaten, attacked me. She had claws and started to cut me up. And yes, so you're aware, she pierced my skin. If Sofia didn't take her heart, I would have killed her to save myself. Not that it matters. If I become a werewolf, I'm dead anyway."

"I heard the story, Ailis...all of it."

"Well then, you know I didn't have much of a choice." Even I knew it wasn't the whole truth. I could have called Miguel. I could have said no. There wasn't a soul on this side of the gates who could make me do something I didn't want to do. My curiosity led me to the wolves, and now I had hung myself for it. They say that curiosity is one of the most powerful things you own. They also say that it killed the cat. I am the cat. I huffed at my comment. Like Miguel had once said to me, about not having a choice, I had just echoed those words back.

"Is this it, then?" His voice was softer. He feared my answer.

"I told them yes, I'd leave," I replied, but it wasn't an answer, not really. "Miguel, there's still so much hurt between us. All we do is cut each other up. Yeah, me more than you. But just the same. We're both screwed up, and neither of us functions well around the other. In my world, I can take a leave from work and lie in my bed until I feel better. In your world, people will die. *You* could die. I don't want you to die because you don't know how I would react if I found out what you had to do to survive. I won't be responsible for your death or the death of one of your people. If it means the local Lycan at home come a-knockin', so be it. If I survive what Nichole did, I'm walking away. I don't want this life. I don't want this life for you, either. I want you to be happy — to live, to be who you need to be for your people and community."

I heard his work phone ring. I prayed it wasn't another murder. I couldn't be in the same room with him now — not after today, not after this talk, not after the hell this trip has been. It's too much, even for me. I needed to pull back, not because of him, but for myself.

"I told you not to worry about it. I would handle it," Miguel started to say, and I cut him off.

"Your Pack blames me for your woundedness, and they're probably right. They need you more than I do. You need them more than you need me. I can't be all you need, and they made that perfectly clear. I'm just a witch." The last words stung.

"Do not talk about Pack like you know anything about it. You don't know what they need. You have no idea what I need, don't presume to know," he replied. His phone rang again. "You went to The Pale Horse and shoved Sofia's wolf down. You played dominance games. You've involved yourself, and now you cut and run again. Nichole is dead because you played a game you don't understand."

"I don't understand because I'm in the dark. I'm in the dark because you never told me what you are. I was pulled into a game you could have trained me to play. I'm not asking you to clean up a mess that I made. That's you trying to be my hero. Once I'm done here, you won't have to worry about me anymore. You don't have to protect me anymore, Miguel." I felt a hard lump in the back of my throat. Unshed tears. Hurt. Regret. Guilt. Love. "Miguel, I love you enough to say goodbye. I love you enough to let you go."

Miguel's phone rang again. His sigh sounded closer to a growl. "This conversation isn't over, Ailis. You're not running like last time. If we're done, fine. But we end this properly. Both of us get to say goodbye this time."

"Why did you tell them about my time in hell, Miguel? Those stories weren't for you to share," I asked. "You had no right to tell them anything."

He didn't answer right away. "I didn't tell them anything. It's common knowledge to anyone with a nose that you've been to hell. We can smell it. Why, what was said?"

"Sofia called me the whore of hell. It was really great hearing it spat back in my face." His phone rang again.

"I would never have told them. You have to believe that," Miguel responded, and I believed him. I questioned his morals on many occasions, but there were some things he wouldn't do.

"You better answer your phone, Miguel. I have to go," I finally said.

"It's not a crime scene. It's Caser. He can wait," he answered like it mattered to me.

"It doesn't sound like it. Good night, Miguel." I hung up.

That went as good as could be. It could have been worse. I could have claws in my stomach, or Miguel could be dead at my feet. If the conversation would have happened face to face, it would have hurt so much more. Instead of premeditating how I'd kill one of the Pack should they come for me again, I took a seat in the Italian restaurant downstairs and ordered dinner. It was my first real meal since I got to Mexico. How could I eat when my life fell apart around me? My stomach didn't care about the goings-on of my heart. Hunger was hunger. My meatless lasagna tasted like all was well in the world. The two witches who slid into my booth across from me didn't give me the same sense of wellness.

The moment their rears were firmly in place, I felt a ward pop up around us. It wasn't anything I couldn't bring down with my finger, but I didn't bother. It was there for our conversation to stay between us and not cause harm. Kitchen witches and their little shows of power... They were obviously new to the game, or they wouldn't use their magic idly. Even the smallest of spells had a cost, and that bill added up quickly. Whispering was easier than shaving off an inch of soul.

"Good evening, ladies," I started with politeness. My gut told me not to bother. My charm told me to kill them both where they sat. *Decisions, decisions. Prison or hear them out.* "What can I do for you?"

Witch One, I'll call her, was young but haggard. She was tired — not in the way a person is weary from lack of sleep or how I was drained from a horrible holiday. It was her soul, the little she had left of it. Her aura was black with speckles of whatever remained of her soul at the edge. Her stringy hair was pulled back into a bun. It exposed her malnourished appearance. Witch Two was much the same, only a little more attractive and not as run into the ground as the first. I bet Witch One had used her powers a little more carelessly than Witch Two. It showed. It didn't matter how pretty either was. If they had a tainted soul, they weren't really all that attractive. The saying 'beauty is skin deep' is true for a reason. The urge to tell them they looked like shit raked over the hot coals of hell was almost overwhelming. I bit my tongue instead. Opening a conversation with an insult wouldn't help.

Witch One smiled. The smile was empty and didn't invite a returned smile from me. "We require your assistance, Ailis."

"First, my name is pronounced Ay-lish, not Ail-is. It's Irish. Second, if you don't know me well enough to say my name right, you certainly should not be using it. Dr. Kyteler will work," I replied.

Her smile didn't falter. Most people with any common decency would have been embarrassed by the mispronunciation of my name. "All right, Dr. Kyteler, we are in need of your assistance."

"What could you possibly want that isn't dripping in bad decisions and soul bargaining?" I asked. I motioned at the air around them both. "You smell like hell. Your souls are stained with hellfire. It's cooked off most of your aura. Tell me, how are your dreams lately? I bet they're all kinds of terrific."

"The condition of our souls, as you've pointed out, is not why we're here." Witch Two didn't bother with a smile. She stared. It wasn't heavy, like when someone powerful looks you over, but it wasn't any less uncomfortable. My charm pulsed into a low vibration that didn't stop. It clattered against my bruised and scratched chest. I almost reached for it to move it but put up with it rather than show it to them.

"I think you've wasted your time here, ladies. I have no desire to help you in anything you're doing, good or bad. The very presence of you makes me feel nauseated. Your souls are dying, and it makes me feel like vomiting." I motioned for them to leave. "If that's all, I'm trying to eat, and you're ruining my appetite. All I'm going to taste now are matchsticks and cooked soul. It's like burned hair on a dead animal coating my tongue."

Witch Two now smiled, if one could call it that. More of a sneer. "I will kill everyone in this restaurant. You can help us, or you can help bury them. It's your choice on how you want to spend the rest of your night."

I leaned forward and smiled in return. I wasn't amused. "Why make threats you cannot follow through on? It makes you look weak, just like you both are. Not even the combined power of you both could pull that off. You may be able to make someone faint, or if you were willing to sell off the rest of your charred soul, you could kill one or two of them. But what would be the point, then? No soul, no life, no collecting whatever you've been bargaining for with a demon who owns you. You'd be dead alongside whoever you managed to kill, and I'd go back up to my room with takeout and have a bath in my six-foot jacuzzi tub. You've clearly mistaken me for someone who cares enough to bury who you kill here. I don't dig holes for people I don't kill."

"Do not fool yourself. We have the power," Witch Two countered.

"Go ahead. Do it. Dazzle me with your mighty power," I answered and leaned back. I sipped my Diet Coke and waited. I motioned at the room and shook my head. I called their bluff, and they knew it. "Let's cut the crap, shall we? Not even the three of us, put together, could pull that off. Perhaps if all the people were damned, we could, but they're not. They're innocents. Their souls are far stronger than you are. If you hadn't shilled your soul, little by little, you might have been strong enough to try it."

Witch One looked to Witch Two. She looked worried. Sure, if I wanted to go straight to hell, do not pass go, do not collect two hundred dollars, I could kill a good lot of the restaurant. But that's assuming they weren't all pure, innocent people. Which, to be honest, was unlikely they were. The odds were in my favor. But even a few innocents and I'd be spent. A soul fights to the bitter end. It would clean me out of energy, and I'd pop back into hell for another round. *No thanks.* I'd sooner die at the hands of Tweedledee and Tweedledum here.

I chuckled softly, more in amusement than anything else. "Oh, no one told you, witch? The more taint you have on your soul from demons, the weaker you'll become. You may be stuffed to the brim with power right now, but it is on loan. It isn't yours, and it's tainted. When you make demon pacts, it literally kills part of your soul. You essentially give it to hell as a down payment. It's the worst mortgage in the world...only two payments. The interest rate alone will kill you. Part of your soul now, and the rest is coming. It looks like you've made a few deals and done your fair share of nefarious and utterly soulless acts. You are already in hell. You just haven't taken the grand tour yet. But worry not. Your rooms are ready and waiting."

"Enough," Witch Two snapped. I don't think she liked the truth. "You will help us, one way or another."

"No. I won't," I answered.

Witch One nodded. "Oh, yes, you will."

"Saying it twice won't make me think twice. I've said no. All you're doing now is wasting my time and my patience," I answered. "I'm on vacation, for Christ's sake. Leave me be to enjoy it."

Witch Two slid a tablet across the table. On the screen...Cisco. My heart sank into my feet. He was bloodied, swollen and cut-up. I dropped my hands to my lap and dug my nails into my thighs. I stared at the screen and tried not to vomit. I looked into the eyes of someone who had been sold out. Between my heartbeats, I counted the ways I could end them all. It kept me from screaming.

"You will come and help us, or your wolf dies," she said. "It bothers me none to kill another one of these abominations."

"I'd be careful with spilling secrets out loud, little witch," I replied. "Some truths will dig your grave."

"His grave is the only one being dug unless you help us," she corrected me.

Until now, I had wondered how Lycan had been drawn out into the hands of a bad guy. The traitor within the Pack had lured Cisco, spilled the secret of their people and now they'd use him to bait me. I wondered why they didn't just kidnap me like any other psychopath would do. *Monsters are getting lazy nowadays.* Little by little, the puzzle started to slide together. They needed the victims to come willingly, one way or another. You can't feed the gods with a murder victim. That's not a sacrifice. That's simply just death. But you can convince a reluctant victim with the threat of harm to someone else they care about.

I had thought of what Cisco had said. He'd die to stop this from happening to another person. He would get half his wish. He'd die, but this wouldn't end. Cisco's bleeding heart would be what killed him. I never thought I'd hear myself say a monster had a bleeding heart. Obviously, fear had scrambled my brain.

"Not happening. He's probably already dead," I responded.

Witch One reached her hand across the table. Call it instinct or paranoia, but I reacted. My hand came up off my lap, and I drove my steak knife into the top of her hand. She flinched and made a strangled sound of a swallowed scream. Her eyes were wide as saucers. She didn't expect the knife. No one did. They saw a witch and prepared for a show of power. I wouldn't waste my energy if I didn't have to, not when a perfectly good knife sat there.

"Do you want to talk to him or not?" Witch Two spoke up.

I pulled my knife from the hand of the freshly bloodied witch. "May you carry that scar as a reminder of what happens when you corner someone with threats."

She smiled. "It'll heal, and the scar will fade."

It was my turn to smile. "No, it won't. I'll kill you long before you can see your pretty skin whole and healthy again. But you'll live with it for all eternity in hell as a reminder of who sent you there."

She swallowed and leaned back. She tried to keep her face neutral. But through the hint of pain, I saw genuine fear. It made me smile.

"Francisco is alive." Witch Two brought my full attention back to her.

"Prove it," I replied.

"I'm going to touch the tablet, nothing more." She was cautious. She flicked the tablet screen and live-called whoever was at the other end. Cisco came onto the screen.

"Cisco?" I whispered.

He tried to smile, but his swollen lips and broken teeth made it look more like something out of a nightmare. He closed his eyes and relaxed his shoulders. A calmness came over him that made me fear for his life. "You were right all along. Don't come. These bloodsuckers…"

A hand blurred across the screen, and Cisco's head bounced back. I flinched at the sight of it. I knew he was tied down, or he'd have fallen from the blow. The blood from a freshly broken nose didn't gush or spew. It flowed in time with the beat of his heart, which pumped slower than mine would have, calmer than mine currently was. I looked up from the screen. My vision was blotchy. The room throbbed in tune with my heartbeat. My ears swooshed with the sound of my pulse. I dug my nails into the palms of my hands and focused. Cisco said I was right. He found the traitor, and now he would die for it. Bloodsuckers, why were vampires involved? I briefly felt anger toward him. Why didn't he go to Caser or Miguel? Why'd he have to play the hero? In real life, the hero always dies in the end.

"Come, or we will kill him," Witch One spoke. Her words sounded like her voice was underwater. I struggled to hear her words over my body's response to rage.

"You're dead, all of you. You may still have a pulse, but you're dead and on borrowed time." I spoke through gritted teeth. "I won't help you do a damn thing. Do what you must, but I won't be a willing contributor to your horror show."

Witch One nodded. "That's unfortunate. His death is on your hands."

She turned the tablet back to face me. Nothing I could ever see, for the rest of my life, would come close to me watching Cisco's throat being slit. He didn't scream so much as squeal as someone sawed through his flesh. That sound would haunt me. I shut my blurred eyes. I couldn't watch the rest. I thought I was strong, but once his head lulled to the side, muscles cut, I swallowed down vomit and shut my eyes. I told myself to stay calm. Don't let the bad guys see how shaken I was. *Be tough.*

"Kill me now or look over your shoulder until I take your lives one by one." It wasn't a threat. I would kill them all. I wouldn't do it now. I wouldn't risk the lives of the other diners. But one day, very soon, I'd eat the sun that rose in their skies, and I'd burn them with it. Like demons, I had a lasting memory and would wait it out until the opportunity arose.

"Next time we come, you will agree to help us or another will die in place of your lack of cooperation." Witch One drew a line in the sand. They would come back, and they would kill again. I expected nothing less.

"Are you finished with the show?" I went back to eating. It was nothing more than a show. I wasn't hungry, not after what I had just witnessed. But I wouldn't show them my pain. They would get nothing from me. "You're interrupting my dinner."

"Demon witch," Witch Two muttered.

"Walking dead," I countered. "You're dead and soon will be buried. I'll curse the ground I shove you into."

They stood in unison and left as quickly as they'd come. I waited until the fury inside my stomach didn't threaten to burn the resort to ashes. As calmly as I could, I walked back to my room. My legs were jelly. My stomach was a hard rock. One foot in front of the other, I navigated myself to safety. I hadn't seen Cisco as one of the victims, and I always saw the bigger picture. I should have known. How had I missed this? It was someone at Pack, but I didn't know who. His death was the fault of someone from the inside. The rage built like the riptides that dragged people out to their deaths. What did I miss? I did everything right. I came. I showed up. I didn't run away when I wanted to. Maybe if I had, Cisco would still be alive. Perhaps if I hadn't befriended him, he wouldn't have been used to lure me. If I had kept my temper to myself and didn't show off my power, I wouldn't have watched someone cut off his head. It didn't matter what kind of mythological being he was. He wouldn't heal from his head lopped off. No one healed without a head. I was sure that was written somewhere. *No head, no life.*

Chapter Fifteen

I sat on my bed inside a hollow void—a never-ending darkness that consumed everything. I was content in there. I felt nothing. I was numb. I was empty. The problem with emptiness is that it is filled with everything you've tried to ignore. The emotions weigh down until they silence everything else around you. You're never really empty. You're just full of the wrong things. I don't know how long I sat like that. Enough time had passed for my feet to feel cold from stillness. When I moved again, in the back of my mind, I heard Cisco die, the squeal of his scream. I shook my head as if the movement had the power to shake the noise from my mind. I paced. I screamed into a pillow. I couldn't breathe, then breathed too fast. The numbness was gone, and I was left with pain. I can't save everyone, but this time, I didn't even try. How could I not try? I had only just met him but knew, without a doubt, he'd have come for me. Cisco would go into hell for anyone who needed him. That's who he was. His soul was one of the purest I had ever seen. And mine felt pitch black at the moment.

I turned on my phone and hit Miguel. "I... Umm... Cisco is... The witches came, and they killed him." The words caught in my throat around choking sadness.

"I know," he whispered. "Two bodies were found fifteen minutes ago, dumped at a local clinic. The tags say Cisco and his patrol partner for the day, Martins."

"I'm sorry I couldn't save him. I'm so sorry, Miguel." The pain flowed from my soul to my words. They were cracked and shaken. I hung up. I felt everything at once. The anger was there but pushed down to the bottom. My sadness and guilt drowned the fire called rage.

* * * *

"Ailis, open the door." Miguel knocked.

I frowned and looked at my phone. An hour since my call to him had gone by in a frozen blink. I was sitting on the floor, my back against the door. I didn't remember sitting down. I stood and opened the door. It took me two tries. My palms were sweaty. I glanced at his face once. He was angry, but it wasn't directed at me. He looked older in his sadness. His grief aged him. It drew the lines deeper into his brow. But there was no blame for me on his face. That look was all sympathy, and that somehow hurt even more. One glance was all I could give him. I couldn't look Miguel in his eyes again. Failure sat on my chest like an elephant. Each breath was a struggle. Guilt was a familiar path for me. I walked it every day. Everyone dies around me. Everyone who mattered went away, whether they wanted to or not. Cisco was no different. The moment he'd met me, his fate had been sealed. He was a dead wolf walking.

"I'm sorry, Miguel," I whispered. My eyes and nose tingled. I knew more tears were on the way. "It's my fault...all my fault. The witches came and said if I left with them, he'd live. I said no, and they killed him. I watched them kill him. They had a tablet, and I watched it. I didn't even try to save him. I'm so sorry."

Miguel stepped into my room and shut the door. I was in his arms before the door latched. "It's not your fault, Lish."

My nickname on his lips made me cry harder. He was the only one who ever called me 'Lish', and I treasured every time I heard it. Tonight, like every other time, it made me feel loved. "I told him there was a traitor in your Pack, and I think he went out looking. I told him to tell you and Caser. Now he's dead. If I wouldn't have meddled, he'd be alive. If I had stayed away from Pack, he'd still be alive. I wanted to have a friend here, just one person who I didn't have a history with—someone who didn't already hate me, not like everyone else does. He was nice to me. He was funny. I thought maybe he was someone who understood what it felt like to have a life they didn't want, who knew why I was so angry all the time. And they used him to get to me. They cut off his head, Miguel. They cut it off when he was still alive. I can still hear it."

Miguel pulled my hands from my ears. "You didn't do that to him. This is *not* your fault."

"The witches said they'd kill him if I didn't go with them. I didn't go. I didn't want to go. I was scared, Miguel. I didn't want to die. So Cisco died in my place." I cried into his shoulder. "I wasn't brave enough to help

Cisco. I'm so sorry. I wish I was brave like you, but I'm not."

"Lish, he was brave enough for the both of you. He knew he was dead the moment they took him. If you would have gone with them, you'd both be dead. Cisco..." Miguel's voice caught in his throat. "Cisco wouldn't have wanted that for you. You didn't know him like I did, but you must know that he wouldn't have traded his life for yours, even if he was given the chance. That's not the kind of man he was. He would have died before handing over an innocent."

Miguel putting me in the same group as the innocents made me feel less like the evil witch who'd sent a man to his death. I hugged Miguel tighter for it. "Cisco told me not to come to help him. Why did he do that? He didn't have to be brave. I didn't want him to die for me." My throat was raw. "I could have helped him, but I was too scared."

"You couldn't have helped him without your own death. No one, not even Cisco, would have expected you to die for him." He ran his hand down my head, like how you would pet a dog or console a woman on the verge of insanity and shushed me. "You smell like guilt. You have no reason to feel guilty. Shh, shh, it's okay."

My throat squeezed. I couldn't breathe past the tears and rage. The harder I tried to control myself, the tears, the scream caught in my chest, the harder I cried. My legs crumbled, and Miguel caught me. He always did. Miguel moved me to my bed and sat beside me. The feel of him so close to me, on my bed, made me pull back.

"Let it out. You don't need to control your sadness. I'm right here." Miguel stroked his fingers over my bandages. He tried to draw me back into his chest. "It'll be okay, Lish."

"You should go," I whispered. Whatever he said next was lost to the rush of pulse in my ears. I didn't really want him to leave. My heart didn't want to be alone. I touched his thighs, tentative at first, as if something inside me would stop me if it were a bad idea. I looked him in the eyes and saw hesitation. I knew what I saw was something close to the same look in my eyes. "Wait. I don't want you to go."

When Miguel didn't bolt, I leaned forward. He looked uncertain, scared even. I felt the same. I kept my eyes on his face as I leaned my mouth closer to his. I grazed his lips with mine...short, sweet, cautious. His eyes shut with a sigh from deep within. I moved to my knees and pressed my body into his chest. He brushed my skin with his fingertips as he pushed my hair behind my shoulders. He had always liked my neck. For a split second, I wondered if it was related to being a wolf and the neck being the kill spot. I leaned my head to the side, a show of trust. He kissed from my jaw to my neck. A quick lick across my collarbone made me sigh in return. I climbed over him and sat on his lap. I straddled him, pressed myself into his groin and breathed him in. The moment I filled my chest, it reminded me of home, and calm washed over me.

When I pulled back, there was uncertainty on his face now. He brushed his thumb over my chin and tried for a smile. "This has to mean something, Lish. If it doesn't matter tomorrow, we need to stop. I won't leave you, but I can't do this if it's empty. I love you far too much for that."

My shoulders slumped. "It does mean something, just not what we both want it to mean."

"What does it mean, then?"

"It means that I'm hurting and want closeness. It means I want to stop the noise in my head. It means we share a moment that'll chase away the darkness for one night," I answered. "I want so much more with you, but we know we can't. There's nothing for us down the road that isn't pain and agony, and I don't want that for either of us."

He shut his eyes. He didn't need to say the words for me to know he was disappointed. We were in the same boat. "I'm sorry, but that's not enough for me. I can't feel your body again and not have you again tomorrow and the next day. You're in a bad place, we both are, and I won't take advantage of that. You'd hate me more tomorrow than you do today."

"Don't complicate this. Just let it be what it is," I replied.

As gently as he could, he took me and my freshly bruised confidence off his lap. "You mean something to me. If I can't have all of you, I can't do this again. It rips me up inside. It doesn't need to be complicated, but it needs to be something more than just for now. I'm sorry."

"You're right. I hate that you are," I finally answered. Rejection, no matter the reason, scratches the ego. "I don't think I would have stopped us, not until tomorrow when I used it as a reason to gut you again. I'm sorry."

"It's okay, I get it. Like you, I want closeness, too, but it doesn't have to be sex for us to settle our souls with each other. Love doesn't have to be physical for it to feel good." He kissed my forehead.

I smiled softly. He had the willpower of a saint, whereas I had the drive of a demon. "Thank you for coming. You smell like home."

"I'll always come," he replied.

"I shouldn't say this, but so will I. Your Pack may chase me away, but if you ever needed me, you know I'd crawl through hell to get to you. It'll take more than Caser to keep me away," I said, and I meant every word of it. The Pack could run me off, threaten me and abuse me, but no one could tell me who I could love. I did love him enough to walk away, but I also knew that I'd always love him and would always come to his call. I hadn't noticed his posture before, but once I said the words, he grew a little more, as if the threat of being alone had been a set of boots pressing down on his shoulders.

"Let's take a look at your scratches." He reached for my arm. "Are you sure Nichole clawed you?"

I peeled one of the dressings back to expose the smaller of the wounds. "Yeah, it's not as deep as I thought, but she broke the skin."

"Dammit." Miguel hissed out a sigh. "I won't let them kill you."

I pulled my arm back and resealed the dressing. "You'd let me turn into a monster and eat people? I'm sorry, Miguel, but I would rather die than be one of those things. I know I've cut you up over Isabell, but I now understand those last wishes and why she asked for you to take her life."

Miguel sighed. "It doesn't make the memory of it any less painful, but thank you for saying that."

I smiled, but it was weak and pathetic. I was guilt-ridden for how I had behaved. "I'm sorry for what I said to you. Seeing you again brought up all my old wounds and hurts. Being an asshole was easier than admitting how much it still hurt to see you."

"Thank you. I'd given anything to go back to the moment I dialed your number and not make the call. I love the time I've had with you, but I'd give it up for your safety," he said. He put lips to my forehead, the way my mother did, when she checked for a fever. "Do you feel different? Hot? Sick? Some people get sick right away, while others don't show signs until they shift."

I smiled. "Do you know how long the incubation period is? Some viruses take one or two days. Others, they can fester inside for years before they're full-blown."

"It's different with each person. There are too many variables, and it really just depends on who was attacked and how bad the injuries are. About thirty years ago, a Pack leader in El Paso tried to boost his population and protection with werewolves. They were under constant attack from vampires. The Pack leader thought if he could tame a were, he would win the war. It didn't work, but he kept a logbook of his attempts. Sadly, his experiments are how we know so much about the virus. He was able to map most of the virus before he was killed."

"Did you guys kill him?" I asked. "I'm not criticizing your people. I'm just curious what the punishment was for such horrific experiments."

"We were too late, but we would have. His creations killed the entire Pack. The local vampire nest killed the weres. When my people got there, we took all his research logs." He reached for my arms and held them. "You don't know if you have it. Don't do anything foolish. If you have it, we'll deal with it."

"I won't," I answered. I wouldn't win an argument with Miguel, not when it came to my life. But I had no plans to involve him in this if things went south. I couldn't do that to him. He wouldn't be the one to deal with it, so there'd be no argument to have.

"Grab some things. You're coming with me." Miguel started to move around my room in search of my suitcases. "If the witches come back, you're in more danger here than on the run."

"I'm safer here, in this room. Anywhere else, they can and will take me. My room is warded. They aren't strong enough to get in here. They can huff and puff all they want. Inside these four walls, they can't blow my house down. I'm as safe as I'll ever be."

He turned a heavy stare on me. "Oh? And what if they show up here and they have me? You wouldn't cave, break your wards and let them in?"

"No. I'd want to, and it would kill me inside to shut my door, but I wouldn't go with them." It was the truth. To let them in would mean I'd have to rid the room of my wards. No wards meant not only witches could come in, but they could also tow hell in behind them, and I'd be powerless to stop them. No life was worth being trapped in here with evil. I'd have no safe refuge. I wouldn't give that up for him, would I? I told myself it would never happen. My heart, on the other hand, thought a little longer on the subject than I was comfortable with.

"We can protect you, Lish." His words sounded more like a beg.

I shook my head. "I'm safer here. Plus, you're all safer without me there, Miguel. Do not risk your people for me."

"If you're not willing to risk everything for one person, what's the point of love?"

"Would you, Miguel? If they came for me and you had to choose between me or protecting your Pack, who would you save?" It was a good question and one he needed to answer, at least for himself.

"That's not fair," he replied, but I prompted him to answer. "I'd protect you, Ailis. You know I would."

"I know, Miguel. I think that's what the problem is with your Pack. You can't send your people to their deaths for me. You shouldn't. It's why they're worried about you and where your loyalties sit. They can't reside with me over them," I replied. "It's okay. You can go, Miguel. I know your people need you, and I understand why. I can protect myself. I'm safe here."

"My loyalties are with those I love. It can be no other way. Whether you're here or not, whether I knew you or not, I will always be the way I am. It's what makes me who I am." He pulled out his phone. "I'll warn Caser of witches and the traitor. I'll be back when I can. Don't do anything stupid or heroic."

"Not heroic, Miguel. I never play the hero. But I expect their deaths. They all die, Miguel. Mark my words, they are dead for what they've done, and they'll suffer for Cisco." I replaced my sadness with anger. I let it climb back up. I preferred it over grief or guilt…or embarrassment. "Someone from inside your own Pack handed him over, and I know damn well they tried to get Cisco to lure me out. It's what they did to get the other wolves. They used someone, and I was that someone today. He didn't do it. He kept his mouth shut until the end. He knew he was going to die, Miguel. He knew it and didn't try to save himself. I was nothing to him. I wasn't Pack. I wasn't anyone he was sworn to protect. I'm barely human. But he didn't hand me over to the bad guys. The least I can do is make sure those bitches get what they deserve."

"Revenge isn't going to bring him back. It isn't going to save anyone. It'll get you killed. Promise me, you won't go getting yourself killed." Miguel grabbed my hands. "Please. I can't… I can't do this without you. I won't live a day without you alive."

I glanced around my room, and although I thought I was safe within my room, I also hated the thought of going to sleep alone. I pushed the idea from my mind. He was safer without me. I was the target. I couldn't live with myself if I caused his death. Instead of packing an overnight bag, I smiled.

"I won't go looking for them," I replied. "But I will protect myself if they come for me."

"If they come for you, kill them. Do not let your conscience get in the way. If they come, their deaths are on them, not you."

"Miguel, when have I ever let my scruples get in the way of my survival? If it means me or them, they will taste hell long before I do."

"Of that, I'm sure."

I blinked away fresh tears at the thought of Cisco. "Can you feel him gone?"

"Did you watch them take his head?" Miguel asked like he had finally worked up the courage to ask me. "The bodies were recovered, but I haven't seen them yet. From what I've heard, the wounds were too clean for it to be a Lycan body. Even in human form, it takes an awful lot of force to decapitate us — or maybe I'm holding out hope and am ignoring the truth of it."

I started to nod and stopped. "I closed my eyes. I saw them cut and saw at his neck but couldn't watch the rest."

"He may not be dead, then," Miguel answered. His back straightened a little more. I felt bad for giving him hope if there wasn't any reason for it.

"And two bodies just happened to show up out of the blue, with Cisco's name pasted on the one?" I countered. I simply did not have the optimism Miguel had. I wasn't built that way. Maybe once long ago, I believed in such things, but over time optimism was rubbed off by reality and left behind a very pragmatic witch. "Did it smell like Cisco?"

"I'll know once I've smelled him. But we're not linked in the same way bloodsuckers are. I can feel if a member is in distress, but I felt nothing from Cisco tonight," he replied. "It makes sense. Cisco has total control of his wolf. He'd never call out for help if he thought it would risk one of us."

"Bloodsucker, meaning vampire, right?" I asked. Cisco had mentioned bloodsuckers.

"Yes. They're leeches, bottom feeders. You always wondered why I hated vampires so deeply. Lycan and vampires have a long and cruel history. They're cancer on mankind, a curse. We've hunted them since the dawn of time for their crimes against humanity." Miguel's face twisted into disgust. "Please, don't compare us to them, not even in the smallest of ways."

"I didn't know. I apologize," I replied. "Miguel, Cisco mentioned bloodsuckers before they... When he could still talk. It's worth checking in to. If vampires have a nickname reserved just for them, he wouldn't have used it on someone who wasn't a vampire."

"This wouldn't be the first time a vampire has been involved in attacks on us. We hate each other equally. This would be the first time one of my people is working with one of them and selling out their own people. I'll look into both angles and get back to you."

"Go find bad guys. I'm going to premeditate murder while you're gone. Got any suggestions on how to stay out of jail this time?" I smiled.

"Witnesses, Ailis. Don't kill someone and leave witnesses this time." He smiled back. "Your stone-cold level-headedness is one of the reasons I love you."

"I'm a determined killer," I laughed. Before I said good night, I passed him my spare room key. "In case you need to come back."

"Is that an invite, or are you planning on needing me to help you move a body?" he asked.

"Both," I answered. "Mostly an invite, though. I'd like you to come back. If you want to, I mean."

"I'd like that," he replied. He kissed my temple. His hot whisper sent shivers down my spine. "I love you, Lish."

His smile from the invite never left his face and was as contagious as it had always been. Before I closed my door, I was grinning in return. I wouldn't admit it out loud, but hearing him tell me he loved me made me feel a little less like a monster right now. The moment he was gone, I regretted not saying the words back to him. They'd have helped him in the same way they had helped me. I told myself that I shouldn't be thinking this way, but damn my soul, I loved him more than I could even admit to myself.

Miguel left me wrapped in my anger. His needling me didn't go unnoticed. It was better than going to bed in frustration. We both were too stubborn to see we would be the death of each other, together or apart. I should pack my bags and book the next flight out, get as far away from him as possible. But I didn't and wouldn't until the wicked witches of the South were dead. I had a barrel of guilty gasoline in my gut. I wouldn't stop until I had burned them all with it. I'd deal with the problem of Miguel if I lived through it.

Here's to hoping I'd be alive long enough to tear out my own heart to leave it in Mexico.

Before I could close my eyes, I sent Miguel a text.

I love you, too.

Within seconds, he replied.

I know.

I showered and crawled into bed with a smile. It was the first genuine smile I had since Cisco had made me laugh, the kind that reached my soul. If I were being honest with myself, it was the first time my soul had felt settled since I had packed my things and left Miguel in my past. For tonight, I wouldn't pick it apart. As my eyes grew heavier, the night pressed down on my chest. I squeezed my eyes closed and tried deep breathing. But no amount of cleansing my soul was going to remove the stain of seeing or hearing Cisco on the tablet.

I tossed and turned, pressed my face into my pillow, screamed and cried until no tears were left. I paced, then wrapped myself up as tight as I could. Nothing would shake the hurt or horror from my head. I felt utterly alone in a world of cruelty. I tried to ground myself, thinking of home and Cat and all the things that made me who I am. I thought of Miguel and how I craved the touch of someone who didn't just love me but made me feel like home was with me whenever he was near. I wasn't homesick. My soul cried for the only person who had ever brought me peace. And I knew my soul wouldn't calm until it could feel the soul of Miguel beside me.

"It's just me," Miguel's voice called from the door. He kicked off his shoes and pulled his shirt over his head. He climbed into bed and pulled me into his chest. "It's okay."

"How'd you know?" I asked.

"You're a mirror of my own soul," he answered. "If I can't stand the dark right now, neither can you. The Pack is safe for tonight. This is where I'm needed and where I want to be."

I breathed him in, and little by little, my body relaxed. "Thank you."

He kissed the top of my head. "I love you."

"I love you, too," I replied.

"We can track the monsters tomorrow. Tonight, let's remember why we hunt them," he answered and breathed me in. "I would give anything to take away the pain you feel right now. I can taste your tears."

"I used to wonder how you always knew when I had been crying," I teased. "Cheater."

He huffed a laugh. "I can smell your tears, taste them, feel the change in energy in the air. But mostly, I can feel it in my soul when you're sad."

"So can I," I replied. "I can feel your sadness. I'm so sorry, Miguel."

He lifted my lips to him for a soft kiss. "Kiss me."

"I thought you didn't want to..." I started, and he pressed his lips into mine.

"I know this will mean something tomorrow. It doesn't have to be what it was as long as it is more than what it has been. If we're not cutting each other up tomorrow, I'll be happy we've healed the little we have. Can you give me that?" he asked, and I nodded. "We can figure out what *that* is when we're not sitting in the middle of a nightmare. But for now, let's give each other what we need — love."

His lips were wet and salty from my tears. He deepened the kiss and rolled me onto my back. Slowly, like we had all the time in the world, he removed my nightgown. Positioned between my legs, he pulled off his pants. Each time I grabbed for him, he pushed my hands away. With a teasing grin, he took his time to remove the rest of his clothes, making me wait. His mouth found mine, and finally, everything went quiet once again. The chaos of my mind went silent under his touch. It always did.

"Your hunger is insatiable," he said with a laugh, pushing my hand away again. It was the kind of laughter that danced along my bones and found the places that craved his touch.

I groaned my response, and he laughed. He pressed his lips to mine while his pants found the floor. I looked down the length of both our bodies. My breath hitched in my throat at the sight of his length. I wanted all of him. I was desperate to feel him, to finish what we had started previously. And when his hand touched me, he knew just how deep that desperation went. I was ready for him the moment he had come to me. With a knowing look, I watched as his fingers danced against me. I squirmed against the heat of his graze.

"Please," I whispered.

"Please, what?" He asked, teasing. He knew what I wanted.

"I need to feel you, all of you," I answered.

He traced his tongue along my jaw, down my throat, and hovered over my pulse. With a nip, my body stilled. He ground his hips into mine, teasing, dragging the moment out until I gripped his hair and pulled his mouth to mine. The kiss was open and deep and starved.

"Condom," I moaned into his mouth.

Miguel shook his head. "I can't catch human diseases, and you're not fertile for me."

"Can you smell that?" I asked. "Nifty trick."

"Yes, if you were Lycan," he replied.

"I thought you couldn't have children, though?" I asked.

"I can't, outside of Pack," he replied.

I paused. My breath hitched in my throat. "Oh, I didn't realize..."

"No, Lish. Get out of your head." Miguel pulled my face to meet his, when I stilled. "No one gets to tell me who I love, who I will spend my life with or who I decide is my family and what that looks like. Like you, no one owns me. Pack or no Pack, you are who I love."

"What about your people, though? They're counting on you to have children."

"I'm not breeding stock. There will be more Lycan with or without me. I am not responsible for ensuring my people continue forward. I am responsible for myself only," he replied. "I choose you. I choose this. Please, don't walk away for that. Do not treat me as though I don't have a say in what happens to my body or my life."

I took a deep breath and pulled his lips back to mine. "I won't come between you and your Pack. But I won't let anyone make our choices for us."

His body relaxed against mine. "Thank you."

"Less talking, more of this," I said as I pulled his hips to mine.

"That, I can do," he answered. He moved to my side and pushed himself into me from behind.

My moan caught in my throat and came out strangled. With his arm under my head and gripping my hip, he was unrelenting, and it was exactly what my body and mind needed. With a quick jerk, he tugged my hair and tilted my head to the side. His teeth dragged across my skin, and I moaned and pushed my body to meet his hips. Just as I caught my breath, he lifted my thigh over his and pushed himself deeper. His thumb circled the apex of my thighs, and my gasp caught in my throat. He teased, brushing up against my pleasure, but not quite there. I pushed against him until I clawed at the bed, half begging, until finally his thumb found what I had been begging for. I moaned his name into the night and pleaded for more, just a little more.

Miguel flipped me onto my back, and I wrapped my legs around him, trying to pull his body to mine. I needed to feel more of him. Instead, he inched his way down my body, sparing no inch of flesh from his mouth. He licked and nibbled until he knelt between my legs. He jerked my legs over his shoulders and held my thighs open. I stared down the length of my body. His eyes were filled with lust and need. It was a look I loved. With a shuddered breath, he lifted me to his mouth, and my entire body shattered with the press of his lips. I screamed his name and reached out for something, anything, to grab on to. He found my hands with his and brought me to the highest peak of pleasure that left me empty and full all at once. When I was jelly, he crawled back up my body and covered me with the remnants of my bedding.

"What about you?" I murmured with loose and soggy words.

"That, Ailis, was for me and exactly what I wanted." He pulled me tight against his body and breathed in my scent. "I love covering you with my scent."

"That was amazing." My words came out as a mumble. I pulled his arms around me tighter. I hadn't felt this safe since I had slept beside him, two years ago. "I love you," I whispered.

"And I, you," he replied, pulling me tightly into his arms at my side.

Once my body came back down and I could string together sentences again, I worked up the courage to talk to him about my meeting with Pack. "Miguel, Sofia had said I was holding you back. What did she mean?"

"Lycan mate with Pack members only, and I won't join with any of the other women in Pack. It's seen as holding our people back," he replied. "When I refused, they suggested I take a mate within Pack, and if I wouldn't give you up, continue seeing you in the natural world. That idea I liked even less."

I paused. My breath hitched in my throat. "Does Sofia want to be that mate? Is that why she got so angry? Am I standing in the middle of a thing between you two?"

"No. She's protective of our people but has no interest in mating with anyone, let alone me. Don't worry about Pack, Lish. I can handle it."

"I told Caser I'd leave." I whispered the words, as if each one cut my soul on the way out. "Do you think he'll actually try to kill me next time, if I don't go?"

"When I say that I'll deal with him, you need to believe me. I will deal with Pack when it's needed," he answered, although it wasn't really an answer. "Some things are worth killing for, Ailis, and he knows where my line is. You have always been my line."

"Yet he was perfectly fine with having me dragged before him."

"It is within his right to call you, just as it was my right to enforce the consequences of that call. I've made it perfectly clear. The next one of my people who comes for you forfeits their life. Caser would need to come knocking, himself, and I don't think he will risk his life to have that conversation with you," he replied. It sounded extreme, but I wasn't going to point it out. I'd rather it be them to die than me. "You have my protection. I'll die before they come for you."

"We'll go down together in a ball of flames, straight to hell," I replied. "Just like old times."

"There's no one else I'd go to hell for," he replied. He pulled me tight against his body and breathed in my scent. "I love when you smell like me."

"Smells like home," I mumbled around a yawn. I pulled his arms around me tighter. I hadn't felt this safe since I had slept beside him two years before.

He kissed my shoulder. "Get some rest, Lish. Tomorrow will come fast and hard, and we will do it all over again."

"Can you stay the night, please?" I asked. "I don't want to be alone. I'm tired of being alone."

"I'll be here in the morning," he replied. "I love you."

"I love you, too," I replied.

"I'll be here always," he whispered as he pulled me closer. "I never left."

"I know. I've felt you every single day."

As I drifted to sleep, I felt like hell could open up and spit out every monster ever caged, and I'd fare just fine with Miguel beside me. Sure, we'd die, but it would be a fight to the end, and for an ending, a bitter ending was the only way I'd leave this world. That, and in the arms of someone who would fight tooth and nail to keep me here. I didn't know how many more tomorrows I had, but I had this night and couldn't think of a better way to spend it than in the arms of Miguel.

Maybe this would change everything, or perhaps it wouldn't. We hoped it would, and that was enough for now. Whatever our tomorrows brought, we would be better prepared for them together. I knew, no matter the outcome, the love we shared would never die unless we willed it so, and right now, we were both holding on. We were bound, and I'd always come to his call. There would never be a day I didn't show up, even if I complained about it the entire time. And I knew he had never stopped watching over me and never would.

Tomorrow we'd chase monsters—and tonight, I remembered exactly why I had come. For Miguel. For us. For hope and second chances. For all the moments I'd need if I ever wanted to forget the horror of hunting the monsters. I'd carve these memories into my heart, and they'd be what I'd hold on to when I sat in a cage in hell. Me, my cat and love. It would be enough. Love was always enough, even for the cursed.

**Want to see more from this author?
Here's a taster for you to enjoy!**

The Cursed: A Witch in Time
L.A. Kennedy

Excerpt

Nothing lights a fire and warms the soul quite like the need for revenge. Both bitter and sweet, it powered man and monster alike. It raised nations and crumbled entire cities in one gulp. And a witch hellbent on getting justice, no matter the cost, was something entire civilizations had feared throughout history. It was no wonder witches were hunted to the ends of the earth some three hundred years ago. An angry, vengeful witch always left a trail of dead bodies and beheaded chickens in their wake, and I was devilishly enraged, looking up bulk chicken purchases. My soul twisted with regret, retribution and reasons hell would be worth the trip, sooner than later. Cisco, my friend, dead and dumped without a head, would be worth sitting in a cage in the pits. Innocents being tied down for the slaughter would be worth flaying my soul over and over. I'd done it once already. I could do it again. What better way to slide into hell than covered in the blood of my enemies? Justice, revenge…same difference, same outcome. But this time, I wouldn't go to hell alone. I'd drag those evil and deserving bitches with me.

Shakespeare got it right. Hell was empty, and all the devils were here. I met the worst of them since stepping foot off the plane in Mexico. The lowest, most vile monsters of them all...humans. Hell—the original social experiment, the creator of Stockholm Syndrome, the maker of gambling and addiction, the reason mothers drowned their children with a smile, the patient holder of nightmares—had nothing on the dark side of humanity, and I got a front row ticket to the dark underbelly in Mexico. Every single day since leaving Van had been one ongoing nightmare that only I had the power to stop, if I were willing to pay the price of ending it. When the total at the bottom of the bill was one soul, it tended to make a witch take pause and make sure it was worth it. There were no refunds. I couldn't change my mind later. Hell didn't work that way. *Nothing* really worked that way.

My vacation had gone from painful to bad, to worse and finally turned into another trip through hell, only this one took parts of my soul that I'd never get back—pieces that kept my mind from thinking up ways to kill those responsible for the deaths of many and the torture of my friend in the worst possible of ways. But those parts were gone now, and I was an awfully creative witch when I was pissed off. At least my first stint in the pit only left me with a broken soul, not chunks pissed down the drain. Sure, it was smashed to bits, but all the pieces were still there, last I looked. They just needed to be reglued every now and again. Mexico, on the other hand, stole from me, and I'd never see those shards of my soul again. Soon, there'd be nothing left to keep me from knocking on the door of those to blame, reminding them of why they *never* should have taken someone I cared about. They *never* should have pinched from a witch. There was a reason not many sane people meddled with full-blooded witches. Our vengeance was long-lasting and cursed the line of those who scorned us. Generations would feel the mistake of one fool, long dead, in an unmarked grave. Just ask any parent of a ginger child. That curse was still alive and well, and a bright red beacon that told the rest of the world one of their ancestors had pissed off the wrong person.

After owing a favor and getting on a plane to pay it off, things went downhill faster than the fall from grace that opened the pit, and each day passing got worse and worse. My grandmother had once said I was a magnet for trouble. I couldn't argue that point, not with scabs on my arms, dried tears on my face and a death sentence with my name on it. I wasn't just a magnet. I called it from the rooftops into my waiting arms every chance I got. I danced with the devils, then cried when my feet hurt and my soul was a few ounces lighter. I learned nothing the easy way, and coming to Mexico was a lesson I'd likely die before learning.

Discovering the lie of a lifetime, being attacked by what I had once thought was folklore and signing up for the 'you-might-die-on-the-next-full-moon' club, was all just the tip of the iceberg, the start of a very deep fall into misery. Because those twenty-four hours weren't rough enough, I tempted fate by thinking it couldn't get any worse. *Foolish little witch. Things can always get worse, with or without a pulse.* I had been eating dinner in a five-diamond resort in sunny Mexico, after having been mauled by a Lycan when my point was proven. It was the first real meal since landing, and with fresh bandages covering claw marks on my arm, I watched my friend, Cisco, suffer a cruel death because I was too scared to leave with two witches. Leaving would have meant he and I would have both died together. I hadn't even tried to save his life. I didn't ask. I didn't bargain. I didn't beg. I sat back and watched his ending play over the screen of a small black tablet. A Lycan, a man, an officer of the law, a son, a soon-to-be marine biologist, was gone in an instant. His life flashed across a screen, and the fate of two witches was sealed in a five-minute live stream. They were dead witches walking. I just hadn't kicked the dirt over their bodies yet.

The two witches had taken a seat at my table and slid a tablet toward me, one witch bleeding because of it. For however short the witch's life would be, I hoped every time she flexed her hand, she remembered the moment I stabbed her. On the screen, Cisco sat tied to a chair, swollen and bloodied. His smile would stay with me forever. His cut lips and broken teeth were something made of nightmares, but somehow, it made him look braver. The stone room he was held in was built for torture and looked like it had seen the end of many lives before Cisco's came to a sudden halt.

His last words were a warning. As he looked his death in the eyes, he still tried to save me. "You were right all along. Don't come. These bloodsuckers…"

And with that final warning, his life was taken. He was calm and didn't fight the knife at his throat. I was his witness. I was the last friend to see him alive, and as awful as it was, I was thankful he had someone who cared about him with him in those final moments. I'd remember every detail with perfect clarity, whether I wanted to or not. The brain never lets go of such things. It would stain my soul until I brought those responsible to their shallow and unmarked graves. Nothing I would ever see or hear would compare to the moment Cisco died. I had closed my eyes for the finality of it. Watching someone have their head removed would have destroyed my mind and soul, and I was barely holding onto my tattered soul as it was. To have watched would have meant I'd lose my death grip on my morality. It would have been the final nail in my coffin and theirs. I'd have done things that would send me to hell faster than I was already chugging along.

I warned the witches as they sat across from me. I told them to kill me then or risk looking over their shoulders for the rest of their short lives. I would kill them both, sooner or later. My threats weren't idle. Like demons, I had a lasting memory and would wait it out until the opportunity arose. I'd do everything in my power to end them and their reign of terror. If I had to pry open hell to get my revenge, so be it. What they had done to innocents and my friend would not go unpunished. Hanging, drowning or burning, I didn't care how they chose to die, but they'd taste death before I returned home—on that I promised. I was pretty sure I'd taste my own death as well, but the price for revenge was steep, and I was prepared to pay. I might as well get something good out of this vacation.

Instead of listening to me, they threatened to take more innocents. Others would die in my place until I willingly helped them. They left me to my dinner and the misery of what I had just seen. Once the rage had settled, I had to tell Miguel about Cisco, and that hurt almost as much as why I had to make the call. Hearing the pain in Miguel's voice crushed me. Cisco had been Miguel's to protect, a member of his Pack and had been mine to befriend. The pain of it all had rolled from my heart and soul, ending with me in the arms of the only person I had ever loved…Miguel. He had come, as he always did, when my soul was torn apart. Like the first time he had shown up, he did his best to put the pieces back together and held me until I could help hold myself up on my own. He had never been my knight in shinning armor. He was my wolf with claws and teeth, and I would never doubt again what he would do to protect me.

Two bodies had been found dumped at a local clinic. Although their tags were pinned to their chests — Cisco and his patrol partner for the day, Martins — the news had reported two unnamed officers dead at the hands of the cartels. They were just another statistic in the war on drugs. They were withholding Cisco and Martin's names until notification could be given to the families. The general public would never know who killed them or why. Cisco deserved better than that. He had earned the truth with his own blood, but the truth would never be told. If I were to tell the world of his bravery, it would end my life faster than this nightmare could play out. The Lycan secret would remain as such, even if it meant Cisco would be just another dead cop.

Even though I knew some secrets were worth keeping, it still bothered me to watch the reporter talk about Cisco as though he were nothing more than a number on someone's scorecard. He was a decorated officer, a protective Lycan. He fought for the lives of those who would never know his name. He was worth more than being a pawn in the witch's game. He was supposed to spend his life in the water, saving the parts of the world he loved. Cisco was a friend, someone who protected others to his very death. He wasn't just another number. His body was found dumped on the roadside of a clinic like garbage. I didn't know what angered me more — his body thrown away, his life reduced to a five-minute news report or that no one would ever know of his sacrifices and his utter devotion to mankind.

All of it made me dig my heels in deeper. The bad guys would pay. They had to. That's how things were supposed to work. Good guys win, and bad guys get punished. If I didn't believe that, what was the point of any of this? If I didn't want justice for those who died, wouldn't I be one of the bad guys myself? Or is that what made me just another vindictive monster? Did I really care one way or the other? If my revenge killed them all and I damned myself in return, it didn't really change the outcome of my life. I was going to hell, no matter what. When I left the first time, they'd marked me with a return order. A counted soul is a counted soul, so no, I guess I didn't care. At least, not as much as I once had and not as much as I probably should. *Shoulda, coulda, woulda.* I'll save the worrying for my damned soul for when I was back home, safe and still had a life to worry about. If I didn't make it home, the worrying wasn't going to help me get out of where I was going, so why waste time on it?

Of everything Mexico has taught me, the one thing I was absolutely certain of was that I'd never be whole again, not after coming here. I'm changed, stained and tarnished by too much pain and heartache. Could a person lose their humanity in a single moment? Could you get it back once it was gone? Was my humanity, what made me the human I claimed to be, lost for good, dumped on the side of the road like trash with Cisco? I didn't feel particularly human right now. I think I craved payback far too much to feel anything else, and that included my soul, my mortality, the little voice inside of me that told me killing was bad. If I could ignore a monster in the corner of a room, I could ignore my wildly spinning moral compass for a few more days, couldn't I?

The only thing that kept me on this side of the crust for this long was my grip on my humanity. What a waste it would be if I let go. All that suffering for nothing, for it to be taken from me by second-rate kitchen witches. I had fought to be called human my entire life, that being a witch didn't make me one of the bad guys. But I couldn't fully hold onto that argument for much longer. I wouldn't be human once I lost what made me one, when I crossed the line to punish those deserving of it. It should have bothered me more. But right now, I needed to be the bigger monster — bigger and badder. I couldn't be weighed down by any emotion that could break me. Monsters didn't have room for love of anything other than wicked things, and I was about to unleash the beast within that hungered for vengeance. Revenge, something I considered to be a much-belied concept, made sense now. It felt right, and it gnawed on me like a starved rat. This time, I would feed it. I would let it gorge until it puked. It was the only way to win. I understood perfectly how an otherwise kind and loving person could become a monster and need to be hunted down. A soul could only take so much, and mine was done fucking around.

I sat on my bed in a hotel I hadn't seen much of and picked through a file from the local Pack Leader, Caser, and the police reports from Miguel with a determined eye. No detail was too small. Ordinarily, I came into the game late. The bodies were gone and picked apart for the second time by the medical examiner. This time, I was on the scene before the body grew colder than the stones they were found on. Although I wasn't a detective or a crime scene analyst, I knew evil. I knew monsters. I knew them better than most. We can't be good at everything, but the one thing I was good at made me more valuable than I wanted to be. Going to hell for two long minutes, lifetimes for a soul, had left me tainted and allowed me to see the world for what it truly was—a sunnier version of hell with parking tickets and taxes.

I flicked through the pages and photos of horror and death, last moments frozen in time. I couldn't shake the feeling in my gut that I had missed something, but I couldn't quite figure it out. But that was the thing about looking at evil. The devil was in the details. I kept going back to the same group of photos. I compared them to each other. Each victim was roughly the same height and size as the other, but they were too different in appearance to think there was a preferred brand of victim. Most serial killers had a specific type of victim — twenty-eight, blonde with blue eyes, size thirty-two hips. They were particular with who they selected, down to the details no one else would notice but them. But with these victims, aside from Lycan blood and living a somewhat humble life, they shared nothing more. Like most of their community, they went to church, were unmarried, virgins, led normal lives outside of turning furry and shopped at various local markets. Like the tune of a favorite song that I couldn't remember the lyrics to, it sat on the tip of my tongue. I just couldn't put my finger on it.

I went back to the notes I had made on my laptop, reading and rereading every detail about where they went missing, when they were last seen, who saw them last, every physical attribute, right down to the size of their shoes. I made myself another coffee and rubbed my eyes. There was something. There was *always* something. But I was missing it. I was either too tired to see it, too emotionally invested or my mind had seen enough and simply refused to help me traumatize myself more. But I wasn't a 'call-it-quits' kind of witch.

Rather than give up, I called Samuel. A live video feed on my laptop filled my screen. Sure, it was against the rules to share information, but if it got the job done, I'd break more than a few rules. I'd go for kneecaps. It wouldn't be the first time Samuel had helped me pick through a case. He'd seen worse. Even if he had virgin eyes, I'd have scarred him willingly. A few bad dreams were worth saving a life. The moment he answered, I went straight to it. Time wasn't a luxury I had. And just as he did, every other time I consulted with him, he pulled out a pad and pen to take notes while I showed him every scrap of paper in the file. I didn't hold anything back. From the lack of surprise and questions, he knew about the unmentionable Lycan. I was thankful there wasn't a need to keep Pack's secret a secret. It would have limited our conversation and the ability to find what I couldn't see or think of.

I wondered for a moment, while Samuel took notes. If he didn't know, would I have risked his life with the knowledge of Pack to save more lives? It was Samuel, the closest friend I've ever had. He was like family to me, and the only family I had left. If I were being honest, I'd have watched more die before I willingly served him up on a silver platter. But from his nods and murmurs, I wasn't telling him anything he didn't already know.

Showing Samuel each page didn't stir so much as a flinch in me. The photos and reports didn't bother me as much anymore. I had gone through the files enough times that the blood didn't look as brilliant. The bodies were just bodies. They weren't people. They were nothing more than a book read too many times. It didn't carry the same weight as the first few glances and would never be as bad as seeing it all firsthand. Samuel didn't recoil a single time. It made me sad for him to know he had seen so much over his lifetimes that horror like this didn't phase him.

"What's going on, Ailis?" Samuel stopped the show. "Something, not just this, is bothering you. Spit it out. I can't focus on your crime scene when I'm worried about you. You're off—and don't tell me it's these crimes."

I groaned. "I think you already know. It's Miguel. It's always Miguel."

"What did he do this time?" Samuel asked, making me smile at how protective he was of me. Whenever I felt completely alone in the world, one call to Samuel changed my mind. "I'm guessing it isn't as bad as what he did to drive you away, since you're still there."

"Oh, it's bad…life or death kind of bad. Miguel and I are going to have some serious words when this nightmare is over. He held back a secret that kills," I replied, and Samuel nodded, fully understanding the secret I was referring to. "But that's oddly not why I'm upset. I mean, it pisses me off, but that's not what's bugging me." I released a deep breath, knowing I had to say something or Samuel would never drop it. "Miguel was here, and things got pretty heated, as they always do between us. Not the usual hot-headed tempers flaring, but…the touchy-feely kind of heat."

"And?" He raised his one eyebrow.

"And? And, Samuel, it's complicated," I answered. I felt awkward talking to him about my love life. Another glance from Samuel and I groaned. "At first, he was a good distraction. And now it's more."

"What's wrong with more?" he asked.

"For starters, *more* comes with fur and claws and an entire group of people who are calling for me to head for the hills and not look back," I replied. "If I don't back down, I don't have a good feeling about my next little chat with them."

"You two are foolish in love. The sooner you both realize this, the easier your lives will be." Samuel smiled.

"I don't think that's an option," I replied. "They're pretty keen on him finding a nice little furry lady and settling down, spitting out a pack of pups of their own. How the hell do I go up against that? Love or no love, I don't want to die to keep sleeping with a guy."

"I doubt his people will knock on your door if you choose to be with him. They'd have come for you a decade ago if you were easy to pick off. But you're not, and neither is Miguel. Together, you are not worth the devastation you both would bring if one of you was under threat," he answered. He looked more confident than I felt. "That isn't the kind of love you just throw away."

"I never said I didn't love him. But it takes more than love for a relationship to work, Samuel." I countered.

"No, it doesn't. Sometimes love is all you have and all you need. In a world like ours, love is mighty precious."

"I don't want to die for a date," I answered and squirmed a little. Samuel was a brilliant man, but sometimes I think he forgets what dating and relationships are like. "It's complicated, and those complications aren't in this file tonight. When this is over, I'm all ears." I lied. I wouldn't be.

About the Author

L.A. Kennedy, beyond the story…

L.A. Kennedy is a Canadian born writer, living in the ever-growing city of Vancouver, Canada. Here, she spends her days getting lost in the beauty of reading and writing. L.A. Kennedy mainly writes fictional books. And can be found researching myth, folklore, and everything in between, with a special interest in edge-of-your-seat paranormal romance. L.A. Kennedy can be found behind a mountain of books, on any given Sunday.

L.A. Kennedy's writing credits include two hit series that mix mystery, horror, paranormal romance, fantasy, and intrigue.

L.A. Kennedy loves to hear from readers. You can find her contact information, website details and author profile page at https://www.firstforromance.com

Home of Erotic Romance

Sign up for our newsletter and find out about all our romance book releases, eBook sales and promotions, sneak peeks and FREE romance books!